WIZARDS AND ROBOTS

Follow the authors on Twitter
@iamwill
@BDJFuturist
#WizardsAndRobots

WIZARDS AND ROBOTS

will.i.am + Brian David Johnson

PENGUIN BOOKS

With thanks to Tom Becker

PENGUIN BOOKS

UK | USA | Canada | Ireland | Australia
India | New Zealand | South Africa

Penguin Books is part of the Penguin Random House group of companies
whose addresses can be found at global.penguinrandomhouse.com.

www.penguin.co.uk
www.puffin.co.uk
www.ladybird.co.uk

First published 2018

003

Text copyright © William Adams and Brian David Johnson, 2018
The moral right of the authors has been asserted

Cover design: Eddie Axley, Cody Achter and Monika Arechavala

Set in 12.2/18 pt Sabon LT Std
Printed in Great Britain by Clays Ltd, St Ives plc

A CIP catalogue record for this book is available from the British Library

HARDBACK
ISBN: 978–0–141–36068–3

INTERNATIONAL PAPERBACK
ISBN: 978–0–141–36596–1

All correspondence to:
Penguin Books, Penguin Random House Children's
80 Strand, London WC2R ORL

For the Next Generation –
you will build the future

Prologue: Iron Knights

1489
Predjama Castle, modern-day Slovenia

Dawn broke over Predjama Castle, the cool air tinged with smoke drifting up from the campfires in the valley below. A blacksmith's hammer rang out upon the anvil, shattering the watchful silence and startling birds into the air. Swords were being sharpened, steel polished. The army of Emperor Frederick III was preparing for battle.

High up on the battlements, Matthias stood and looked out over the enemy. The castle was built into the mouth of a cliff face, a stern fortress in a yawning natural cave. Even up here among the tower tops, pennants fluttering in the wind around him, Matthias could feel the cave's shadow settling round his shoulders like a cloak. He was fourteen years old, with a messy nest of brown hair and skinny limbs hidden beneath his robes. His master, Gauer, leaned on the gnarled staff beside him, the chief scribe's bare skull gleaming in the morning sunlight.

'The Emperor's men are ready for an attack,' Gauer declared.

'Let them,' Matthias said. 'I'm not scared.'

The Emperor had been laying siege to Predjama for over a year now, but the castle showed no sign of falling. It never would, Matthias thought proudly. Predjama's walls were sheer, its doors hewn from thick oak. Eagle-eyed archers manned the battlements, ready to unleash a hail of arrows at anyone foolish enough to try to cross the open ground to the castle gates. In desperation, the Emperor had tried to starve the defenders out, but despite the passing months Predjama's pantries still overflowed with grain, berries and meat.

Almost as if by magic.

Glancing over at the next tower, Matthias saw Lord Erazem step out on to the parapet. He was a burly man in a fur-lined cape, a broadsword strapped to his side. His advisor Cavelos accompanied him as usual. A graceful figure with a cropped beard and sallow complexion, Cavelos's soft footsteps followed Erazem's heavy tread round the castle passageways like night upon day. In the kitchens and stables of Predjama, it was whispered that the advisor was a sorcerer who drew on arcane powers to help protect the fortress from Frederick's men. Now, as Matthias stared, Cavelos turned round and gazed coolly back at him. Matthias looked away.

A discordant trumpet blast echoed round the valley: in reply, banners bearing the imperial coat of arms – a black, two-headed eagle, tasting the air with its long tongues –

were hoisted proudly into the air. With a furious cry, the Emperor's soldiers swarmed forward. Predjama's bowmen replied with a volley of arrows, felling men in their tracks. Matthias's hand closed round the hilt of the dagger in his belt.

'You should have let me stand with the archers, master,' he told Gauer. 'I have been practising with my bow, and can hit a target from twenty paces.'

'You will see more of the battle from up here,' the scribe said calmly.

'I don't want to see!' Matthias retorted. 'I want to fight!'

Gauer chuckled, a sound like rustling parchment. 'Wait until you get to my age,' he said. 'You will learn the wisdom in avoiding battles wherever possible.'

Frustrated, Matthias could only watch as the Emperor's men continued to die under the sharp-tipped rain. Screams filled the air. As the sun climbed in the sky, something glinted on the ridge to the east. Matthias frowned. Five knights arranged in the shape of a letter V were running on foot towards the castle. Their armour was tarnished with rust, and they carried neither flags nor pennants to identify themselves. As Matthias looked on in amazement, the knights drew their swords and charged into the flank of the Emperor's army. Cries of alarm went up from the horrified soldiers as they were cut down where they stood.

'Look, master!' Matthias cried, grabbing Gauer's sleeve. 'Knights have come to lift the siege! They must be allies of Lord Erazem!'

The scribe said nothing, his face grim. Matthias felt

unease slosh around inside his belly as the knights drew closer. They were a head taller than any man he had ever seen, their faces hidden behind their visors. Killing with terrifying ease, they carved a bloody path through the Emperor's men, trampling over the dead and wounded.

'Who are these knights?' Matthias asked Gauer.

'I do not know,' the scribe said quietly. 'But I have never seen men kill like this before.'

The Emperor's army was scattering in terror, but there were no cheers from the defenders on the battlements. Lord Erazem appeared to be arguing with Cavelos – pushing his advisor to one side, the gruff warrior drew his broadsword and stormed back inside the tower. For the second time that morning, Matthias's and Cavelos's eyes met. Gathering his robes about him, Cavelos followed his lord off the parapet.

Below them, the knights had butchered their way to the gates of Predjama. At an unspoken signal they stopped and sheathed their swords, craning their necks up towards the battlements. As their gaze passed over him, Matthias shivered. Suddenly the knights ran forward and began to scale the castle walls, climbing with astonishing agility, like huge metal spiders.

'Impossible!' Gauer gasped. 'What sorcery is this?'

Warning shouts went up around the towers. Archers turned their bows upon the clambering knights, only to see their arrows bounce harmlessly off rusty armour. Further along the battlements, Matthias caught sight of a mailed fist gripping the top of the wall. A knight hauled himself up on to the parapet, his shadow blotting out the sun. Drawing his sword with an icy scrape of steel, he jumped down into the terrified bowmen.

Gauer's bony hand fastened round Matthias's wrist, drawing him back from the walls.

'The castle is in danger!' Matthias protested. 'We must stand and fight!'

'With what?' Gauer said pointedly. 'Five knights have defeated an entire army – do you think they will cower at the sight of my staff and your dagger? Come, my apprentice. We have work to do.'

The scribe marched Matthias through the doorway into the tower, where they descended a set of steps into the innards of the castle. Wide-eyed servants ran by, wailing about devils in armour. Matthias could smell burning – looking out through the window, he saw smoke rising up from the keep. A fire had started somewhere within the fortress. But Gauer didn't break stride.

'Where are we going?' Matthias panted.

Gauer ducked through an archway and climbed the steps into the east tower, stopping outside an oak door with a pair of stag's antlers carved into the wood. It was Lord Erazem's private library – the most jealously guarded room in the entire castle. Gauer drew a key from within his robes and unlocked the door, gesturing at Matthias to enter. With a gulp, Matthias crept inside.

He found himself in a vast chamber, thick stone columns supporting a roof that disappeared up into shadow. Frowning portraits hung from the walls, beside tapestries telling tales of battles fought and crowns won. Bookcases crammed with volumes stretched in all directions. The air was thick with the smell of musty parchment. After the din of battle outside, the silence inside the library throbbed in Matthias's ears.

Gauer was already hurrying away down an aisle, the base of his staff rapping against the flagstones. Matthias hastened after him, following the scribe along a bewildering path through the bookcases.

'What are we doing here, master?' he called out.

'We must save what we can,' Gauer replied over his shoulder. 'Some of these manuscripts are the only ones of their kind – if the fire takes hold, they will be lost forever.'

At the end of the aisle he stopped at another door, which he unlocked with a second smaller key. The door led through into a star-shaped antechamber with no windows. Torches flickered in a mirror hanging upon the wall, outlining two figures standing before it. One was a slender, dark-haired woman whom Matthias recognized as Mara, a servant from the kitchens. She held a baby wrapped in swaddling clothes in her arms, shushing it gently. Beside her stood Cavelos. The advisor glanced round as Gauer and Matthias entered the chamber, his mouth creasing into a smile.

'Ah, scribe – I should have guessed,' he said to Gauer. 'Like a proud father, you rush to protect your precious books.'

'What are you doing here, Cavelos?' Gauer's voice was level. 'Where is Lord Erazem?'

'Lost,' Cavelos replied shortly. 'And the battle with him. I warned Erazem the knights were more powerful than he, but he was too proud to listen. He challenged their leader in battle and was cut down like a stalk in the wind. His blood now stains the cobblestones of the keep.'

Matthias gasped. 'Lord Erazem is dead? He can't be!'

'More will join him before this day is out,' Cavelos said matter-of-factly.

'And so you came here,' said Gauer.

'As did you,' the advisor replied. 'But, while you try to save your beloved library, there is only one book I care about.'

He made a gesture with his hands and the surface of the mirror on the wall shimmered, as though turning from glass to water. Now, when Matthias looked into it, he could see a bound volume resting on top of a stone pedestal on the other side. The breath caught in his throat.

'How is this possible?' he whispered.

It was Gauer who answered. 'Magic,' he said. 'Cavelos has been using his power to protect the castle since the siege began. Do you really think we could have repelled the Emperor's men for this long with swords and arrows alone?'

If anyone else had spoken, Matthias would have thought they were joking. But his master did not joke about anything. And hadn't Cavelos turned the glass mirror into water before his very eyes? Matthias peered through the shifting surface at the book. It was a heavy volume, bound in black leather. There was no title or clue as to its author, but on the cover he could make out the shadowy design of an ankh, a cross with a loop at the top.

'The Book of the Apocalypse,' Gauer said in a reverent tone. 'The secrets of magic are stored within its pages, passed down through the ages from one generation of wizards to the next.'

Cavelos raised his eyebrows. 'Will you share *all* our secrets with this boy, scribe?'

'Not all of them,' Gauer said pointedly. 'Some secrets are more shameful than others. But only by standing together can we hope to save anything.'

'And yet you stand there bickering while the castle burns!' Mara said impatiently. 'This book may be important, Cavelos, but it is not more important than your son. You promised you would take us to safety!'

'And I will,' Cavelos replied. 'No harm will come to my flesh and blood, especially not with the Book of the Apocalypse in my grasp.'

'What about the rest of us?' Matthias said. 'If you're such a great wizard, why don't you stop these knights?'

'They draw on a magic of their own that I do not understand,' Cavelos replied. 'I cannot be sure I can stop them.'

'But people are dying!'

'*Humans* are dying,' Cavelos corrected him. 'And I am not a human.'

A piercing scream came through the library walls – Mara drew her baby closer to her chest, hushing it gently as it cried. The sounds of battle were drawing closer.

'Your words shame you, Cavelos,' Gauer said.

'Careful, old man,' the wizard hissed. 'You of all people should know the extent of my power.'

'Don't threaten him!' Matthias said angrily, pushing forward and showing the dagger tucked into his belt.

Mara let out a scream – whirling round, Matthias saw a shadow loom in the doorway behind him. It was a knight, its rusted armour splattered with blood. As it strode into the antechamber, Cavelos made an intricate gesture with his fingers. A jet of fizzing light shot out from his ring, striking the knight in the breastplate and sending him flying back into the wall. Matthias's heart leaped, only to see the knight shake his head and silently pick himself up from the floor. Cavelos muttered something under his breath, pulling Mara behind him.

The knight raised his sword and charged at the wizard, the antechamber echoing to the clash of magic and steel. As Matthias looked on in amazement, Gauer reached inside the mirror and snatched the Book of the Apocalypse from its pedestal. He bundled Matthias through the door back into the library.

'What about Mara and the baby?' Matthias said.

'Cavelos can take care of them,' the scribe replied. 'Quickly, boy!'

Gauer hurried over to a portrait of Lord Erazem and reached up to take down a volume from the nearest bookshelf. There was a loud click, and a section of the wall slid back to reveal a dark portal.

'This passageway leads out to the top of the mountain,'

Gauer explained. 'It is how Erazem kept supplies coming in during the siege.' He thrust the Book of the Apocalypse into Matthias's hands. 'Take this and run as far and as fast as you can. We cannot risk it falling into the hands of these knights of Hell.'

'What about you?' Matthias asked. 'What will you do?'

The elderly scribe drew himself up proudly, gripping his staff. 'Hold them off for as long as I can,' he said.

'But, master . . .!'

'Go, boy!' urged Gauer, pushing Matthias into the passageway and pulling the lever. As the wall rumbled back into place, Matthias caught a glimpse of another knight clanking towards Gauer. He cried out, and his master raised his staff to protect himself. Then the secret door slammed shut.

Matthias ran for his life, his sandals slapping against the stony floor. The mountainside swallowed him up, the ringing steel and wounded shrieks growing fainter with every step. The Book of the Apocalypse weighed heavily in his grasp. In a handful of bloody, terrible minutes, the once-impregnable fortress of Predjama Castle had fallen. It felt to Matthias as though a part of him had crumbled with it. His master was gone, and soon everyone he knew would be dead. He was utterly alone.

The walls narrowed, the passageway closing in around him. Up ahead the way was completely black – it looked as though the roof had fallen in. Matthias skidded to a halt, breathing hard, and glanced back over his shoulder. All it needed was for one knight to find the secret passageway from the library and he would be trapped. He *had* to find a way through.

But, as Matthias took a step forward, there was a movement in the darkness, and he realized that the roof hadn't fallen in after all. A hulking shape was blocking the passageway, a dull gleam of metal in the darkness.

A knight was waiting for him.

Matthias turned to flee, but a mailed fist reached out of the darkness and seized him by his robe, lifting him into the air with contemptuous ease. The Book of the Apocalypse fell to the floor. Fumbling, Matthias pulled the dagger from his belt and drove it into the gap between the knight's rusting breastplate and arm guard. He was expecting to feel his blade sink into soft flesh, but instead he hit something hard, jarring his wrist. Matthias cried out, his dagger clattering to the floor. He stared in disbelief at his attacker.

It was impossible. The knight was not flesh and blood but fashioned from some kind of iron.

'W-what are you?' Matthias gasped.

The iron knight said nothing. It didn't even move. When Matthias reached out and pushed up its visor, he gasped in horror. The knight had neither eyes nor mouth nor ears, just a smooth steel plate and a thin bar of red light that burned brighter and colder than any fire Matthias had ever seen. The blood drained from Matthias's face, and he realized that he had failed Gauer. He would not be able to protect the Book of the Apocalypse after all. The world was doomed.

The iron knight closed its fist round his throat and began to squeeze. The last thing that Matthias saw was the red light in the iron knight's face, pulsing mercilessly.

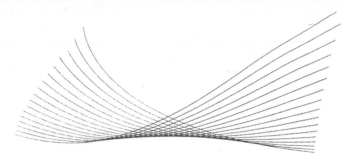

01: The Ghost

2052
Scott Memorial High School,
Gainesville, Florida, USA

The sec-drone made a choked whirring sound as it rose into the air, training its lens on the students pouring out through the gates of Scott Memorial High School. From a distance, it resembled a giant blue-and-white bumblebee with a scratched Gainesville Police Department logo on its underbelly. None of the chattering students paid it any attention.

Except one.

Ada Luring leaned against the side of the bike dock, brushing her hair out of her eyes as she watched the drone stutter through the air. The other students didn't even glance at her as they went by, laughter breaking around her like waves on an island. Ada fished her phone out of her backpack and aimed it at the sec-drone, zooming in to capture the ident number beneath the police logo and taking a photo.

An excited voice called out Ada's name. She looked up to see Pri elbowing her way through the crowd towards her.

'There you are!' Pri said breathlessly. 'I've been looking absolutely *everywhere* for you since math, but it was like I was asking about a ghost because no one had seen you, and I was about to give up when I saw you here and –' Pri stopped. Following Ada's upward gaze, she waved her hand in front of her friend's face. 'Hello? Earth to Ada?'

'Sorry,' Ada said. 'I'm listening.'

'Sure you are. What's wrong?'

'Nothing,' Ada replied slowly, her eyes still fixed on the drone. 'But someone needs to fix the engine on that thing before it falls out of the sky.'

Pri shrugged. 'So? It's only a sec-drone.'

'I know. I'm just saying.'

Pri linked her arm through Ada's, pulling her away from the bike dock.

'We've got something much more important to discuss than silly sec-drones,' she said. 'I was thinking that we should do something together tonight.'

'Like what?'

Pri glanced around conspiratorially before answering in a whisper: 'Han's parents are out of town, and he's having a party at their lake house. There's a live DJ feed from a club in New York and a light show over the lake. The guest list is *très* exclusive – anyone who even mentions it on R8 won't be allowed in, because Han doesn't want anyone lame trying to crash it. But that's OK, because your good friend Pri has been invited and she can get you in.'

14

'I don't know, Pri. I think if you asked Han he'd say I was pretty lame.'

'What is it, a year since you guys broke up?'

'Eight months,' Ada replied automatically.

'People move on! Han's not a bad guy. I'm sure he'd be cool if you came.'

'You'd be even surer if you actually asked him.'

'Ada! This isn't any old party. It's *the* party. Han's throwing it for Ben's seventeenth birthday. Remember Ben, with the strong arms and the blue eyes that make you just *melt* when he looks at you?'

'I don't have to remember him,' Ada said drily. 'He's in my poli-sci class.'

'Perfect! You can introduce me.'

'I don't know, Pri . . .'

'C'mon, you know I'm right! It'll be me and you, just like old times. Forget your computer and come hang out with some *real* people. Dance to awesome tunes and flirt with some really hot guys. Go skinny-dipping in the lake. Switch off that big old brain of yours and do something dumb for once!'

She gave Ada a winning smile.

'Me and you,' Ada repeated. 'At a party at Han's parents' lake house.'

'Me and you and Kit,' Pri corrected her. 'How else do you think I got on the guest list?'

'Did somebody say my name?'

Right on cue, Kit Somers appeared at Pri's shoulder. Dressed in a cream jumpsuit that left her slender arms bare, with matching heeled strappy sandals, she was attracting glances from every boy who walked past. Her hair was tied up in an elaborate chignon that must have taken hours to fix. Ada was suddenly conscious of her scruffy jeans and sneakers, the chipped polish on her bitten nails. Kit had a habit of doing that to her.

'I was telling Ada about the party,' Pri told her.

'You should come!' Kit said brightly, looking down to check her R8 feed on a sleek watch.

'I can't,' Ada replied. 'I haven't finished my project for the Science Fair, and it's due in by the end of the week.'

'The Science Fair?' Pri groaned. 'What about Ben with the strong arms and the melty blue eyes?'

'What kind of grade would I get for him?'

'*I'd* give you an A.'

Ada laughed. 'And, if you were grading me, I'd come to the party,' she said. 'But I think Mr Pirelli is more interested in particle physics than Ben's melty blue eyes.'

'That's his loss,' said Pri.

'I've been reading up on particle physics and it's kinda cool actually,' Ada told her.

'Really? Tell me more.'

'Well, it's –'

Pri slumped her head on Kit's shoulder and closed her eyes, snoring loudly. Kit laughed.

'Fine,' said Ada. 'Forget about it.'

'Ignore her, Ada,' Kit said airily – as though *she* was the one who had been Pri's lifelong friend. No matter that Kit had only joined Scott Memorial at the start of the semester. 'I'm sure that particle physics is cool. You know scientists, always looking for new toys to keep themselves amused. Though, if you ask me, we've got all the technology we need.'

Pri grinned. 'Ada's always been the Queen of Tech. When we were little kids, she always used to fix my holo-pet when it got sick.'

'Sorry, excuse me?' Kit raised an eyebrow into a perfect semicircle. 'Holo-pet?'

'Don't tell me you don't know what a holo-pet is! Everybody had one!'

'I didn't,' said Kit. 'I had an *actual* pet. A beautiful tortoiseshell cat called Serenity.'

Of course she did, thought Ada. And it was probably the most perfect cat in the history of pets.

'Listen, I really gotta go,' she told Pri. 'Have fun tonight.'

Pri nodded, resigned to defeat. Ada slipped her backpack over her shoulders and pulled up her hood. Immediately the soft material moulded round her skin, forming a rigid mesh that protected her head like a helmet. She deactivated the micro-computer security block on her bike and climbed on to the saddle.

'Good luck with your science project!' Kit called out.

Ada smiled half-heartedly back. Weaving a path through the other students, she cycled out of the school gates, leaving the malfunctioning sec-drone behind her. As the crowds thinned out, she picked up speed, the wind whipping past her face. Maybe Pri was right: maybe she should go to the party. A year ago, Ada wouldn't have thought twice. But that was before. Before her dad died and her world came crashing down around her. Before the bleak aftermath and her break-up with Han. Now Kit was on the scene with her expensive clothes and trips to shopping malls, threatening to take Pri away, too.

A loud bleeping interrupted her: it was the bike's security block, alerting Ada to a car backing out of a driveway – a small blinking light on the map on her bike's display. As she stopped and waited for the road to clear, there was a rustle in the laurel oak casting a shadow over the sidewalk. Ada looked up and saw a small drone hovering in the branches. She assumed it was just another sec-drone, but when she looked closer she saw that there was no Gainesville PD logo on the machine's belly, and no ident number either. The unmarked drone's lens was trained on her like a rifle sight.

That didn't have to mean anything sinister, Ada told herself. Drones buzzed around all the time. Only a month ago, the school football team had sent out a drone programmed to bombard the crowd with fliers about their upcoming game. And if the *football team* could program a drone . . .

She pedalled away slowly. The leaves rustled once more, and out of the corner of her eye Ada saw a shadow inching along the sidewalk after her. The drone was definitely following her. Ada picked up speed, biking straight past the turning for her street. There was no way she was going to show the drone where she lived. Wait until she told her mom about this, Ada thought angrily. It was all *her* fault.

Ada's mom Sara was a scientist at the University of Florida, and an expert in artificial intelligence. Over two years ago she'd entered the Rodin Challenge, a special new competition organized by Global Advancement Projects (GAPs) – a worldwide agency that funded technical and scientific research. Sara had warned Ada to keep a careful eye out for any kind of surveillance from rival teams, but she'd laughed it off, thinking her mom was just being paranoid. It didn't seem quite so funny now. Had the drone been waiting for her outside the school gates? She'd been too distracted by her conversation with Pri and Kit to notice it.

Then, suddenly, she knew what to do. At the next intersection, Ada turned left, pedalling quickly down the street. Beyond the row of residential homes an arc of white light hovered like a giant halo above the Apollo Corp industrial park. She led the drone towards it, ignoring the locked front gate and veering off the street to a strip of wasteland that ran along the side of the solar-panelled factories and warehouses. When she and Pri were little, they'd discovered a rusted and broken section of the metal railings, with just enough room for them to squeeze through with their bikes. One of the factories had a door with a faulty ident panel, allowing them to sneak inside and make dens and play with their holo-pets while Apollo Corp's automated machinery churned out electrical parts along the conveyor belt. They might have grown out of holo-pets, but Ada hadn't stopped tinkering with the technology. And now she was going to play a game of a different kind.

Ada jumped down from her bike and wheeled it through the gap in the railings. The drone flew in low over the ground behind her – she took out her phone and snapped a quick picture before biking across the tarmac towards the warehouses. Banks of solar panels gleamed in the sun. Twisting round, Ada saw that the drone was weaving erratically in the air – as she had hoped, its visual sensors had been blinded by the brilliant glare. She had bought herself a few seconds' breathing space.

Cycling down a narrow alleyway between two of the warehouses, Ada jammed on the brakes beneath an overhang. She climbed down from her bike, her helmet softening into a hoodie as she pushed it back, then she held her phone at arm's length and took a selfie. Rifling through her backpack, she pulled out a cheap, pen-size projector she used for class and hooked it up to her phone. A couple of seconds was all it took to upload the selfie. Ada turned on the pen projector and found herself staring at a ghost. A shimmering image of herself stood in front of Ada – an identical fifteen-year-old girl, the same brown hair falling in front of her eyes, the same watchful expression on her face. It was like standing in front of a mirror.

Creeping to the corner of the warehouse, Ada carefully wedged the projector behind a drainpipe, aiming the pen so that her image was projected out into the middle of the tarmac. She caught her breath as a shadow darted out from above the shining solar panels – would the drone take the bait? If it had heat-seeking sensors, it would detect that the hologram wasn't real, and it would be Game Over. All Ada could do was pray that the machine didn't have that kind of tech.

The drone zoomed on over the hologram and paused in mid-air, its lens zeroing in on Ada's ghost. Ten seconds passed, thirty, a minute. Nothing moved. A small smile of satisfaction spread across Ada's face. Maybe having a holo-pet hadn't been so bad after all – she would have liked to have seen how Kit's precious Serenity could have helped shake off *this* unwanted admirer. Ada crept back to her bike and pedalled away, leaving the unmarked drone frozen in mid-air, hovering above her ghostly image.

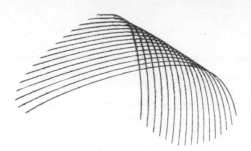

02: Castle

2052
The Luring residence, Gainesville, Florida, USA

Ada kept a careful watch on the sky as she cycled away from the industrial park. The streets were empty, American flags hanging limply in front yards. Ada's triumph at outwitting the drone had been replaced by a nagging unease. If one of her mom's GAPs competitors had sent the unmarked drone, why wasn't it hanging around the Machine Intelligence Lab on campus? What was it doing following Ada?

She turned left at the intersection and freewheeled to the end of the street, where she swung into the driveway of the last house in the row. As she hopped down from her bike, Ada pushed back her helmet and felt the material relax into the soft folds of a hoodie. She turned on her security block and stood in front of the ident panel by the front door. The door clicked open. Glancing one last time into the empty sky, Ada stepped into the hallway.

The house was quiet, the only sound the soft whirr of the air conditioning. As Ada tossed her backpack on to the floor, an electronic voice filled the hallway.

'Good afternoon, Ada.'

'Hey, Castle,' she replied. 'How's it going?'

'I am fine, thank you, Ada,' Castle replied. 'How was school?'

'Oh, you know,' she said.

There was a pause. 'I am afraid I do not.'

'It's a figure of speech, Castle,' Ada called out. 'It was school. It's the same every day.'

'Ah. I understand.'

Castle was the Luring's house AI. It monitored the lights, heating and household stores, and maintained the house security while they were out. Ada had been hearing its soft, reassuring voice since she was a little girl and couldn't imagine her home without it. She wandered through into the kitchen and opened the fridge. Rows of empty shelves stared back at her.

'We are running low on dairy, meat and other refrigerated goods,' Castle told her. 'I have placed a delivery order with the grocery store, but I am waiting for your mom to confirm payment.'

'Where is she?'

'Sara Luring is currently at the Machine Intelligence Laboratory at the University of Florida,' Castle told her. 'Would you like me to contact her?'

'Don't bother,' Ada said. 'Her Lab COMMS will be switched off anyway.'

'The Rodin Challenge is a very demanding project.'

Ada sighed. 'Her projects always are.'

Even she had to admit, however, that the Rodin Challenge was on another level. It required entrants to produce robots that could surpass human intelligence, to think at a new level altogether. Her mom had been working tirelessly on her robot Hawking for over two years, just in the hope of making the final three.

There was a loud crash from the next room. Wincing, Ada stuck her head through the doorway. The living room was in a state of disarray – the dining table littered with half-eaten fast-food cartons, electronic tablets and smart glasses, while the shattered remains of a vase lay across the wooden floorboards amid a puddle of water and strewn flowers. A small figure was crouched over the mess, trying in vain to fit the pieces of the vase back together.

'Kipp?' said Ada. 'What are you doing?'

The robot's head darted up nervously.

'I'm sorry, Ada,' he said. 'I was trying to clear up Dr Luring's papers before she came home, but I knocked something on to the floor.'

Years before the Rodin Challenge, Kipp had been Sara Luring's first robot. Ada had helped to build him, and she still remembered the first moment the little robot had waddled uncertainly into her room. Kipp's limited sensors meant he was always bumping into things and knocking them over, and he had an endless stream of questions about humans and the world. It was kind of like having a little brother, Ada thought. Only one that would never grow up.

'You shouldn't touch Mom's papers, Kipp,' she told him. 'She'll only get mad if she can't find something.'

Kipp cocked his head to one side, indicating puzzlement. 'She would be upset that I tidied up?'

'Mom has her own way of doing things,' Ada told him. 'It's OK – I'll get a broom.'

They cleaned up the mess together, mopping up the water and sweeping the fragments of the vase into the trash. Back in the kitchen, Ada dug out a tub of ice cream from the back of the freezer. She turned round to find Kipp watching her from the doorway.

'Are you OK, Ada?' he asked. 'You only eat ice cream when you're unhappy.'

'It's nothing,' she said. 'Pri wanted me to go with her and Kit to a party, but I told her I had to finish my project for the fair.'

Kipp looked puzzled. 'You finished your project last week, Ada.'

'I know. I lied.'

'Why?'

'Sometimes it's easier that way,' Ada told him. 'It's easier than saying I don't like Kit. It's easier than saying that it's my ex-boyfriend's party, and I don't feel like spending the night watching him slow-dance with cheerleaders.'

'It's Han's party?' Kipp's face lit up with a series of red and blue flashes. 'I liked Han. He was nice to me.'

'Yeah, well, Han's a nice guy.'

'I was sad when you broke up.'

'Me too,' Ada said.

'So why did you?'

'I don't know, Kipp,' Ada said sharply. 'Maybe all those trips to the cancer ward bummed me out.'

The little robot shifted uncomfortably. 'I'm sorry,' he said. 'I didn't mean to upset you.'

Ada looked away. 'It's not your fault,' she said. 'It's just . . . it doesn't get any better, Dad not being here. It still hurts.'

'We all miss Mr Luring. Especially your mom.'

'So why isn't she here? Why is she in the lab with her COMMS-Link switched off so I can't speak to her?'

'Because the Rodin Chall–'

'Screw the challenge!' Ada shouted. 'The truth is Mom would rather spend all day rewiring Hawking than talk to me about anything I'm feeling. Han was just the same – he was so scared of saying the wrong thing he didn't say anything at all. So I dealt with it the only way I can: alone. I figured he'd be relieved.' She laughed. 'Dumb move, right?'

'Maybe you should go to Han's party and try to talk to him,' Kipp suggested. 'It might make you feel better.'

Ada shook her head. 'It's way too late for that,' she said. 'If Han wanted me there, he should have invited me.'

She went upstairs to her room and closed the blinds, sitting down at her desk and pressing her thumb against the computer screen to unlock it. Her R8 feed flashed up in front of her. The most recent beat was from yesterday, a calendar reminder about the upcoming Science Fair that Thursday. Ada's R8 beats were so few these days that she might as well have been dead. She dug a spoonful of ice cream from the tub and swallowed it glumly. Han's lake-house party still seemed to be a secret, as Ada couldn't find a single mention of it anywhere online. Checking Kit's R8, she was confronted with a stream of beats, the latest of which was a selfie of Kit looking gorgeous down at the mall. She had her arm round Pri, who was beaming into the camera.

'You make a lovely couple,' Ada muttered. 'Hope you'll be very happy together.'

Licking the last of the ice cream from the spoon, she turned off her R8 and selected a memory stick from the stack in her drawer. The door opened and Kipp crept inside her room. He scrambled up on to the swivel chair beside Ada, hurriedly grabbing on to the desk to stop himself from spinning round. She shook her head, unable to help herself smiling. Inserting a memory stick into her machine, she watched as a program started automatically. Lines of computer code ran down the screen, and everything went black. Then the logo for Gainesville Police Department appeared.

The Queen of Tech, Pri had called her. She didn't know the half of it.

'The police?' Kipp groaned. 'Not again, Ada!'

She grinned. Taking her phone out of her pocket, Ada examined the photo of the malfunctioning sec-drone she had seen above the school and typed its ident number into the computer. The details for the sec-drone flashed up on the screen, and she selected an option from the drop-down menu directing it to the maintenance department.

'There,' she said with satisfaction.

'If the police catch you hacking into their system,' Kipp warned her, 'you could get into real trouble.'

'I'm *helping*, Kipp. Quit being a spoilsport.'

With practised ease, she navigated her way through the site until she found the schematics of the sec-drone nightly patrol routes. A map of Gainesville was marked with shaded rectangles – so-called 'dark zones', buildings such as churches and temples and army bases that the drones were forbidden to fly over. Ada copied over the latest updates to her bike's security block. Now, if she wanted to go for a night-time ride without anyone seeing her, her bike could map out a route.

Finally Ada accessed the police department's all-points bulletin alert system, where she uploaded the image of the unmarked drone she had taken back at the industrial park.

Kipp peered at the screen. 'What is that?'

'A weird drone that was following me today,' Ada told him. 'Maybe they'll think twice about stalking me with an APB on them.'

Kipp went quiet. She knew that he thought this was a bad idea, but over time the robot had learned to recognize her voice patterns – particularly the one that said she didn't want to be argued with. She was exiting the police department system when Castle's voice filtered out through the speakers.

'There is a new message for Sara Luring on the House COMMS,' it announced. 'Would you like to see it on-screen?'

'Sure,' said Ada.

She was expecting it to be the local grocery store, asking why her mom hadn't authorized payment for their order. But instead she found herself looking into a state-of-the-art boardroom, the walls filled with moving holo-images of robots. A young guy with spiky hair, glasses and a bright green shirt smiled at the camera.

'This is a message from Kevin Cruz, Head of Robotics at GAPs,' he said. 'I am delighted to inform Sara Luring that she has reached the final of the Rodin Challenge with her submission Hawking. All finalists are invited to GAPs HQ here in Kuala Lumpur, where their robots will be judged and the winner announced in one month's time. Congratulations, Sara!'

The message ended. Ada stared at Kipp in amazement. 'Did you hear that?' she said. 'Mom did it!'

She leaped out of her chair and picked up the robot, dancing round the room. Kipp panicked and pleaded with her to put him down, which only made Ada laugh harder. She spun him round until she felt dizzy, before finally releasing him and collapsing on the bed. Kipp staggered about for several minutes, his balance sensors disrupted. As the room revolved around Ada, a thought suddenly occurred to her. She sat up sharply.

'Castle?' she called out. 'Did Mom see this message?'

'Sara Luring's Lab COMMS have been switched off since eight thirty-five a.m.,' the house AI replied.

A slow smile crept across Ada's face. She closed her computer and hurried downstairs, only remembering at the last second to return the tub of ice cream to the freezer.

Kipp struggled down the stairs after her, stopping halfway when he saw Ada retrieve her backpack from the floor.

'Where are you going?' he asked.

'To give Mom the good news,' she declared. 'And you're coming with me.'

The robot hurried down the rest of the steps, almost tripping over his own feet. Kipp was so clumsy that Sara had had to program him not to leave the house alone, but he loved to go out with Ada. She said goodbye to Castle and heard the lock turn behind her. Ada got back on to the bike, her hood moulding and hardening round her skull. Kipp climbed up behind her, securing his hands round the frame so he wouldn't fall off.

Afternoon was fading into evening, red and purple streaks unfurling across the darkening sky. There was no sign of any drones. Ada cut through the suburbs and a local park, coming out among the labs and lecture halls of the University of Florida. She spent so much time on campus she knew it better than her own neighbourhood, picturing her intricate route through the squares and sidewalks in her head like the wiring on a circuit board. As Ada looped round a lake, passing a group of students throwing a football around on the grass, the outline of the Department of Mechanical and Aerospace Engineering filled the horizon.

'Nearly there, Kipp!' she called out.

But, as she rode into the square beneath the glassy gaze of the Engineering Department's banks of windows, Ada slowed. She twisted round in her saddle.

'What's wrong, Ada?' asked Kipp. 'Is it another drone?'

She frowned. 'Can you hear something?'

Somewhere on the swirling breeze, she was sure she had caught the sound of angry voices. But the square was completely still. Then, through the trees, she caught sight of a blinking red light. The shouting grew louder, and a line of people came marching across the concrete towards them. They were chanting and jabbing E-signs into the air – as they drew closer, Ada could make out their blinking slogans.

A ROBOT IS NOT A LIFE

HUMAN INTELLIGENCE = THE ONLY INTELLIGENCE

HI-AG: JOBS FOR PEOPLE NOT ROBOTS

'Uh-oh,' said Ada, her heart sinking.

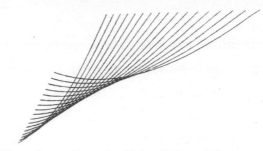

03: Ancient Civilizations

2052
University of Florida campus,
Gainesville, Florida, USA

The protesters marched on the Engineering Department with hoarse cries and fists clenched in the air, whistles and klaxons shattering the studious hush. Anti-robot slogans echoed round the square – Kipp shuffled closer to Ada on the back of the bike.

'What's going on?' he squeaked. 'Who are HI-AG?'

'The Human Intelligence Advocacy Group,' Ada told him. 'They're a group that campaigns to stop advances in artificial intelligence. They think the development of robotics threatens humans.'

She watched with growing unease as the marchers converged upon the entrance to the Engineering Department. Peaceful protests were one thing, but in recent months she'd seen HI-AG's campaign spill over into outright intimidation. Hateful messages and anonymous threats against scientists had floated to the surface on R8 –

an eminent Indian professor of robotics had been attacked outside his home in Kolkata, while unexplained explosions had damaged engineering facilities in Paris and Tokyo. HI-AG strenuously denied any involvement in such activities, but Ada knew her mom didn't believe them, and neither did she.

'I don't like the sound of these people,' Kipp said nervously. 'I think we should get out of here.'

'Agreed,' said Ada.

Still watching the protesters, she pushed forward on her bike. Immediately her security block bleeped a warning – Ada looked up to see someone stepping into her path. She jammed on the brakes, coming to an abrupt stop inches from them.

'Whoa!' she called out. 'Sorry, I didn't see you.'

'I'm no expert,' a voice replied coolly, 'but I think you might find it easier if you actually looked where you were going.'

Ada reddened. The woman was dressed casually: slim-fit trousers and a dark turtleneck sweater beneath her jacket, a backpack slung over one shoulder. Her eyes were an icy shade of blue, her blonde hair cropped close to her skull, accentuating her sharp cheekbones. At first Ada assumed she was a student on her way to class, but on second glance she realized that the woman was closer to her mom's age. A faint suggestion of perfume hung in the air around her.

'Sorry,' Ada mumbled. 'We gotta get out of here.'

'You're going to miss quite a show,' the woman said. 'Looks like someone in the crowd has a holo-projector.'

Ada turned back to the Engineering Department to see an image of a towering robot rear up over the windows, to a chorus of boos from the protesters. The robot had been fitted with mounted antimatter cannons, which it began to fire indiscriminately, filling the square with the sound of gunfire. Kipp flinched, covering his aural sensors with his hands.

'What are they *doing*?' Ada said angrily.

'Isn't it obvious?' the woman replied calmly. 'They're protesting.' Raising a camera pendant from around her neck, she held it up to her eye and began taking photographs of the besieged building.

'Against an engineering department?'

'I suppose it's what's being engineered *inside* the department that they have a problem with.' She nodded at Kipp. 'Machines like your little friend there.'

The robot shrank back fearfully.

'Kipp isn't a machine,' Ada said fiercely. 'And, if anyone tries to wave a sign anywhere near him, they'll regret it.'

'Strong words.' Glossy lips twitched with a smile. 'Are you going to fight them all by yourself?'

Something about the woman's tone was irritating Ada, and she was thinking up a suitably sarcastic reply when a beeping alarm erupted around the square. A sec-drone swooped over Ada's head and hovered in the air above the protesters, an electronic voice ordering them to shut down the holo-projector and clear the entrance to the Engineering Department. The crowd responded with defiant jeers and catcalls, a hurled stone narrowly missing the drone.

'This isn't going to end well,' the woman said. 'You might want to get out of here after all.'

'What about you?' Ada replied. 'Those "protesters" might not like it if they catch you photographing them.'

The woman aimed her pendant at the retreating secdrone and fired off a couple of pictures. 'Don't worry about me. I'm exactly where I need to be.'

'Ada, let's go!' Kipp urged.

The protesters surged forward with a roar, banging their fists against the windows of the building. Shaking her head, Ada climbed back on to her bike and rode towards the nearest exit. As she cycled out of the square and along the narrow alleyways between the university buildings, the shouts and the security alarms gradually began to fade.

'What are we going to do now, Ada?' Kipp said. 'We can't get into the Engineering Department with all those people outside!'

'You're absolutely right,' Ada agreed. 'Luckily for us, we're not going to the Engineering Department.'

She shot down an access ramp and cycled into a quiet, leafy corner of the campus. A run-down building with ivy-covered columns was tucked away by the perimeter wall, obscured by a row of trees. The tyres of Ada's bike crunched along a gravel path as she slowed to a halt outside the entrance of the building. Kipp relaxed his grip on the bike frame and dismounted, taking a couple of unsteady steps as he regained his balance.

'Those HI-AG people were really angry,' he said. 'Why do they hate robots so much?'

'That's a tough question,' Ada replied, her helmet melting back into a hoodie. 'Not everyone understands robots like me and Mom do. Sometimes people get frightened by stuff they don't know about.'

'They don't need to be frightened of me,' Kipp said. 'I'm not scary.'

'I know that, Kipp,' Ada replied. 'I'd tell them that if I could. I'd tell them you were the sweetest and funniest little guy I know.'

The small robot waddled up to the front entrance and studied the brass plate by the door. 'The Department for Ancient Civilizations? Are you sure this is the right place?'

'Trust me,' Ada said. She climbed up the steps and pressed the buzzer.

'Welcome to the Department for Ancient Civilizations,' a voice crackled out through the intercom. 'Please place your eye by the retinal scanner to confirm identification.'

When Ada looked into the small lens above the intercom, there was a series of short bleeps.

'Identification confirmed,' the voice said. 'Access permission granted. Please enter.'

The door swung open, and Ada ushered Kipp into a gloomy hallway decorated with oil paintings and marble busts on pedestals. Dusty glass cases were filled with arrowheads and shards of pottery. As she went along the deserted hallway, her sneakers squeaking on the wooden floor, it felt to Ada like she was creeping around some kind of ancient tomb, long abandoned by whichever civilization had built it. She went over to the elevator and called it down.

'This place feels old,' said Kipp, peering round the hallway. 'Where is everyone?'

'Anyone ever told you, you ask too many questions, Kipp?'

'You have,' the robot replied. 'Several times.'

'Go figure,' Ada said.

The doors opened and she stepped inside, pressing the button for the second floor. The elevator jerked upwards, and when the doors pinged open brilliant light poured inside. The dark and dusty corridors of the Department for Ancient Civilizations had been replaced by a brightly lit open-plan space broken up into small offices and labs by transparent glass screens.

Kipp jumped with surprise. 'This looks just like the Machine Intelligence Lab!'

'That's because it *is* the Machine Intelligence Lab, doofus,' Ada laughed. 'They moved it out of the Engineering Department when Mom started work on the Rodin Challenge. It was supposed to stop other research labs and corporations spying on her – I had to swear to Mom not to tell a soul before she'd even tell *me* where they'd moved it to.'

'So the HI-AG protesters . . .'

'. . . are protesting outside the wrong lab. Try not to tell them that, OK?'

'I won't, Ada,' Kipp said solemnly. 'I promise.'

They stepped inside the lab and an electronic voice asked Ada who she was here to see. When she replied 'Sara Luring', the glass screens shifted smoothly around them, forming into a corridor that led directly to a lab in the corner of the building. A woman in a white lab coat was working at an interface screen, her hands making sharp gestures in the air like an orchestra conductor.

'Hey, Mom,' said Ada.

Dr Sara Luring didn't look up.

'Mom!'

She turned round. With her angular frame, sharp gaze and shoulder-length black hair tied back in a loose ponytail, Ada's mom cut a tall, striking figure. At the sight of Ada and Kipp, she blinked over the top of her smart glasses.

'Oh, hi!' she said. 'I wasn't expecting to see you.'

'I know. We thought we'd pay you a surprise visit.'

'That's lovely, Ada, but I really can't chat right now,' said Sara, turning back to her interface screen. 'We're running some games protocols with Hawking – they're a crucial part of his development as an independent thinker.'

'That's OK, Mom,' Ada said easily, taking a seat at a workbench. 'I've had a busy day, too. I was followed home by an unmarked drone, so I illegally hacked into the police department system and posted an APB for it.'

'Sounds great,' said Sara, completely engrossed in her screen. 'Good for you, Ada.'

'Then we came here and a group of HI-AG goons attacked the Department of Engineering and got into a fight with campus security.'

'That must have been fun.'

'Also, some guy called Kevin Cruz sent a message to the House COMMS.'

'Mmmmm? Was he from the grocery store?'

'Actually, he was from GAPs.'

Dr Luring's hands froze in mid-air.

'GAPs?' she said quietly. 'What did he say?'

'You know, I'm not sure I remember . . .'

'Ada!'

'I'm kidding, I'm kidding!' Ada grinned. 'Kevin Cruz said that me and Kipp had been really good this year, and that as a reward you should take us with you when you go to Kuala Lumpur.'

Sara's hand flew to her mouth. 'We made the final?'

Ada nodded.

'This isn't a joke?'

'Check the message yourself!' Ada laughed. 'If you hadn't had your COMMS switched off all day, you would have seen it already!'

Dr Luring sat down abruptly on a stool. She took off her glasses and rubbed her face. There were dark circles beneath her eyes – Ada knew she had been struggling to sleep since her dad had died. She went over to her mom and put her arms round her.

'I'm proud of you,' she whispered. 'Dad would be, too.'

Sara nodded. Giving Ada a quick hug, she coughed and then stood up briskly.

'Where are we going?' Ada asked.

'Follow me,' Sara said. 'There's someone else we have to tell.'

A gap opened in the glass screens, allowing her to walk down a narrow passageway that ended at a locked door.

Sara pressed her palm against the ident-panel, turning it green. The doors slid open, revealing a small room with windows looking out over the university campus. A tall figure was sitting at a table, hunched over a chessboard. Powerful fingers toyed thoughtfully with a piece.

'Hawking?' said Dr Luring.

The figure turned its head towards her, revealing a sculpted human face with a grave, thoughtful expression. But, when it put down the chess piece and rose to its feet, it stood seven feet tall on proud metal limbs – a robot, towering above the room.

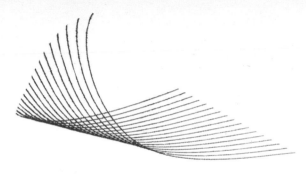

04: Apocalypse

3019
Rio de Janeiro, Brazil

Midday came blacker than night, churning clouds blotting out the sun and blanketing Rio in dust and smog. The city lay in ruins. Buildings were charred and hollow shells, the beaches scorched wastelands littered with dead birds and fish. An abandoned supertanker lay on its side in the bay, oil bleeding into the sea like black blood. On a mountain above the city, a giant statue leaned dangerously to one side, its hands stretched out in a hopeless gesture.

In the two months since Rio had been razed to the ground, not a single person had dared to return. But the city hadn't been completely abandoned. Inside the damaged statue, the sound of ringing footsteps echoed round a complex network of tunnels and chambers. A robot with broad shoulders and slender limbs strode beneath blinking strip lights. In binary code, his name was 01101011011100 00101101011011101101.

He was known as Kaku.

Passing through a set of automatic doors, the robot entered a vast, windowless chamber. He paused to admire his surroundings. The Reading Room was the library's pulsing heart, its walls covered in projections of pages of text. Thousands of words flowed down the walls every minute, tiny droplets in a never-ending waterfall. Looking to his left, Kaku could read a history of the Roman Empire under Nero; to his right was an account of the siege of Chicago during the Third World War. The entire history of the human race was contained within these walls, compressed and saved in the humming storage drives of the library's vast database.

Kaku had tended the library for decades, ever since its foundation following the Human–Robot Concords of 2875. He had spent most of that time alone, lost in his studies. Other robots found his interest in human history puzzling, but Kaku was perfectly content to work alone, with only his documents for company.

But all that had changed six months ago when the invaders had arrived and cloaked the world in death.

They descended without warning, a fleet of attack ships hurtling through a rip in the fabric of time from some distant universe. There had been no time to prepare or to organize Earth's defences. The alien craft could change shape at will, appearing from nowhere to lay waste to cities. No one knew what kind of creature piloted them, or what drove their insatiable appetite for destruction. They were called simply the Spawn.

The Spawn attacked with savage efficiency, killing

everything in their path. Once their attack ships had destroyed a city, rumbling mining vessels followed to blast the earth with explosions and pounding hammers and drills. It was as if conquering Earth was not enough – they wanted to rip the very skin from the planet.

The day the Spawn attacked Rio, Kaku could only watch helplessly as the city was engulfed in smoke and flames. The library trembled and shook as stray rounds of laser fire bit into it, chunks of masonry raining down on the floor of the Reading Room. Projection screens shattered; files containing precious ancient documents were wiped out in the blink of an eye. But, as the rest of Rio burned, somehow the statue remained standing.

In the face of the Spawn's brutal assaults, humans and robots alike had fled. Those who survived the first wave of attacks gathered in a few lonely outposts – Shanghai, Seattle and Algiers. Some headed for the Large Hadron Collider in Switzerland, the vast underground particle accelerator run by CERN, a gigantic supercomputer of unimaginable power that now devoted its run-time to finding a way to beat the Spawn. The Collider was the robots' main base of operations, and the centre of their resistance movement.

Kaku had stayed where he was, continuing his studies inside the Reading Room. He hoped to find something in human history – a battle tactic or a strategic move – that could help the robots win the seemingly unwinnable war. The odds appeared stacked against him, but among his fellow robots Kaku was known for making irrational decisions – what humans called 'feelings', or 'hunches'.

Now, as Kaku studied the words streaming down the wall, a new window flashed up on his visual panel. A COMMS-Link had been initiated from Mount Hood, a snow-capped volcano in the Pacific Northwest region of America.

LINK: 45.3735° N, 121.6959° W
01110010000111101001001010011111111000110101

In his visual panel, Kaku saw a white-tiled laboratory, precision spider arms hanging poised in the air. A five-armed robot stood over a metal operating table. It was Weil, a surgeon who repaired and modified damaged robots. He had been assembled at the same facility as Kaku, and the two robots had maintained COMMS-Link communications ever since.

A year earlier, Weil had been stationed above Mount Hood's timberline at a remote facility dedicated to the research of time travel. For years, CERN had opened wormholes in the time–space continuum, allowing robots to travel back into the past. Mount Hood had a time-jump unit of its own, directly connected to CERN. It had been closed weeks after the Spawn invasion: time-jumps required a massive amount of processing power, and in the midst of war CERN could not afford to shut down other parts of the system. Weil had been left in charge of a derelict facility manned by a skeleton crew of robots. He had complained bitterly about his posting, claiming his circuits were in danger of corroding through inactivity.

Yet, as Kaku examined the laboratory now, he saw that the operating table in front of Weil was covered with charred metal parts.

Data began to stream between the two robots at a subatomic level in their language, Quanta. They talked.

Casualties? Kaku said. What has happened?

We are under attack, Weil reported grimly, his five hands working on two damaged robots at the same time. Every building bar the time-jump facility is on fire. Defensive forces have been completely neutralized. Mount Hood has fallen.

To the Spawn?

To something worse than that. Look.

Weil patched Kaku through to a security camera mounted on the exterior of the laboratory. The compound was on fire, buildings cloaked in thick black smoke. Fallen robots littered the snowy ground in front of a burning barracks. Instinctively Kaku scanned the air for Spawn attack ships, but the skies were clear. Turning back to the barracks, he detected a sudden movement in the heart of the flames. Five figures were stalking through the fire, metal limbs glowing liquid red.

Robots? Kaku exclaimed.

He watched in disbelief as a small squadron emerged untouched from the raging inferno. Moving quickly and stealthily, the robots fanned out across the compound, training their antimatter guns on the doors and windows of the laboratory. The lead robot zeroed in on the security camera and took aim – for a brief moment, Kaku found himself staring down the barrel of a gun, before the picture cut out violently. He turned back to Weil.

I do not understand, Kaku said. Who are these robots? Where have they come from?

I have no idea, the surgeon replied. But they have taken this facility in a matter of minutes.

You must leave, Weil.

I will stay until there is nothing more I can do for my patients, he replied. Then I will go.

Where?

To the Collider, if I can. Spawn forces are massing outside, and we must protect it. All of us, he added meaningfully.

I am trying to protect it also, Kaku told him.

Hiding away in the library with your books?

I am not hiding.

You are not fighting.

Kaku didn't expect Weil to understand. Earth was doomed if CERN and the Collider fell, so it was only logical that the robots came together to try and defend it. Yet Kaku had seen first-hand the devastating way that the Spawn attacked. Sheer force would not be enough – the robots had to discover a new strategy to combat the alien invaders, if they were to have any hope of defeating them.

A giant explosion rocked the laboratory, overturning trays and sending surgical instruments to the floor with a loud clatter. Weil glanced towards the door. From deep within the building, Kaku could hear the ominous sound of gunfire echoing through the corridors.

I must go, Weil said.

Good luck, Kaku replied.

The COMMS-Link ended, and the laboratory disappeared from his visual panel. Kaku was struggling to comprehend what he had witnessed. It should be impossible for a robot to fire on another robot – violent acts were excluded from their programming. Yet he had seen for himself the armed attackers striding through Mount Hood. Why carry out such a brutal assault on a remote compound with no strategic value? Kaku needed to think. The Reading Room fell silent as he shut down all external operations, focusing his run-time on carrying out thousands of complex computations.

He thought.

After five minutes and forty-nine seconds, Kaku's indicator light flashed back to life. The time-jump unit. It had been shut down but not dismantled. If the direct link to CERN could be reinstated, then the attacking robots could use it to travel back to whenever and wherever they wanted. Kaku connected to Mount Hood via the library mainframe and checked the time-jump log. It was rebooting, a new date and a location being entered before his eyes. The year was 1489; the coordinates 45.8153° N, 14.1267° E. Seconds later, the log confirmed that the jump had been made. Whoever had attacked Mount Hood had vanished back in time.

Entering the coordinates into his GPS, Kaku viewed the robots' destination in his visual panel. In 3019, it was nothing more than a large mountainside cave looking down over a valley. But what about 1489? Cross-referencing his GPS with the library database, Kaku learned that the mountainside had once been home to a castle named Predjama. According to the database, in 1489 Lord Erazem of Predjama had been killed after a lengthy siege by forces belonging to Emperor Frederick III. In the bloody and war-torn history of humanity, it seemed an unremarkable event. A painting of Erazem, a fierce-looking warrior with cropped hair and a craggy brow, flashed up on the walls of the Reading Room. Kaku studied him thoughtfully. Mount Hood had already fallen; the robots who had attacked it had disappeared back in time. All that was left was to try and work out *why*.

He ran a search for Predjama Castle in the library records. Manuscripts began scrolling down the walls of the Reading Room, words falling like rain. Kaku spent hours poring over histories and legends, sifting the myths and memories for glimpses of the truth. Suddenly he ordered the search to pause. He focused on a medieval scroll written in an elegant inked script, the letters decorated with brilliant red, green and gold illuminations. It had been composed in 1502, by a monk at the Abbaye Saint-Jacques in France. This monk, Gauer, claimed to have once been a scribe for Lord Erazem and had survived the siege at Predjama Castle.

Kaku studied the text. While scanning Gauer's account of the siege, he had come across a phrase so unexpected he felt sure he had made a mistake in translation. But, when he ran the words through his lexicon database, he got the same result. There had been no mistake. Kaku straightened up, his circuitry humming with new possibilities.

The phrase he had found was 'mechanical men'.

Or, as he had translated it: 'robots'.

05: Visions

2052
Pazin Caves, Croatia

Geller knew it was only a matter of time before his dreams ended and the metal nightmares began. He had been asleep for centuries, frozen in a deep, unnatural slumber. For years, he had flitted from one dream to another, keeping a watchful eye out for a gleam in the darkness, ears pricked for a distant clanking footfall. But, as hard as he tried, he knew that the mechanical men would catch up with him eventually. They always did.

Now, as he dreamed, Geller found himself standing in a great castle under attack. Terrified men and women fled through choking clouds of smoke. Swords clashed; bodies stained the flagstones crimson; lifeless hands held in vain against gouged wounds. As he fought through the panicked throng, Geller could hear a woman's voice singing, a soft lullaby that somehow rose above the screams and the hungry crackle of flames engulfing the fortress. He followed the melody through the hallways and stairwells, a vague thread guiding him through a maze. When he opened a door at the end of the corridor, the uproar abruptly died out. The castle vanished, leaving Geller in an icy cave deep underground. A dark-haired woman was sitting cross-legged on the floor, singing softly to a white linen bundle in her arms.

'The Mechanical Men,
The Mechanical Men,
They came one day
And stole life away.

Far beneath the sun
We went underground
To the heart of the ankh
Where hope is found.'

As Geller listened to the woman sing, an unexpected wave of emotion came over him. He edged forward and crouched down beside her. She didn't seem to notice him, intent upon the bundle in her arms as she rocked back and forth.

'Hello?' Geller whispered. 'Don't be frightened. I mean you no harm.'

The woman ignored him, crooning something in a language he didn't understand. Following her gaze down to her arms, Geller realized with a start that the linen rags were empty.

A thin hand shot out and grabbed Geller by the wrist.

The woman glared at him. Her eyes were wild, set deep into a gaunt face; her skin stretched across hollow cheekbones.

'They are coming!' she hissed. 'Go, now!'

Even as Geller tried to pull away, he could hear the heavy tread of soulless feet striding through the cave. The robots had found him, his metal nightmares drawing near once more.

'Where?' he said.

The haggard woman pointed to the wall behind him. The rocks began to shift and mould before Geller's eyes, revealing a black portal.

'Come with me!' he urged.

She shook her head. 'It is too late for that. But you are the last of the wizards. If you die, all is lost.'

Geller hesitated.

'Go, child!'

She pushed him away, and he went stumbling towards the portal. Geller crossed the threshold into a chamber even colder and blacker than before. The cave behind him was engulfed in gunfire, a high-pitched scream piercing his chest like a sharp blade. Geller turned back, but he knew that he was too late, that the woman was already dead. He also knew, with the terrible clarity that dreams could visit upon the dreamer, that she was his mother. In desperation, he glanced down at the spell ring on his finger. Taking a deep breath, Geller severed the spell that was keeping him asleep.

He awoke with a gasp, opening his eyes to find himself

plummeting through the air, the ground racing up to meet him. His cry of alarm was cut off as he hit the floor, punching the breath from his lungs. He rolled on to his back with a groan.

Slowly the fog of sleep drifted away. The walls of a vast underground cavern rose up around him on all sides, seams of ore running through the earth like silver veins. Water dripped down from the ceiling, coating the rocks in a slick gleam. As he sat up, Geller caught a glimpse of his reflection in a stagnant puddle – a pale, thin face with straggly black hair stared back at him. His mouth was parched, his limbs numb from decades of inaction. Slowly, like an old man, he got to his feet.

The only light in the cavern came from above Geller's head, where a host of ghostly green clouds hung in mid-air. Inside each cloud lay a robed figure: they numbered nine in total, ancient men with white hair and mottled, wrinkled skin, paused on the threshold between life and death. None of them stirred at Geller's noisy reawakening, each lost in their own Suspension spells. The air in the cavern seemed to throb in time with the slow, silent beating of their hearts. Their hands bore the scars of centuries of spell-casting, deformed almost beyond recognition – fingers twisted and gnarled, knuckles swollen and misshapen.

Geller looked down ruefully at his own smooth, fleshy palms: the hands of a boy, not a wizard, for all the cool gleam of the spell ring on his finger. Despite being born centuries earlier, he had been awake for just sixteen short years – years devoted to learning the ways of magic and the art of spell-casting. This made him the youngest of the wizards by a long way. As far as Geller knew, no others had been born since the destruction of Predjama Castle, and the Book of the Apocalypse with it.

He rubbed his face, trying to lose the sour aftertaste his nightmare had left him. Even though he knew he would get into trouble if anyone found out he had broken his Suspension, he had no desire to go back to sleep. Forcing his stiff limbs into action, Geller hobbled across the floor of the Biding Cave towards a cleft in the rocks. He crouched down in a dark corner in the shadow of a jagged stalagmite and adjusted his ring, casting a Vision spell in search of Cavelos, the wizard Elder.

Geller's hands were clumsy with cold, and it took him several minutes before he was able to tease open a small hole in the air in front of him. Gradually he enlarged it until he was able to see into another cave, an underground study in which every piece of furniture had been carved from glassy black rock. It was like peering into the maw of a giant underground worm. One side of the cave was taken up with ornate bookcases lined with fragments of old parchment and ancient scrolls. The opposing rock face was dotted with buds of light – tiny Illumination spells that made the surfaces gleam and shine. Cavelos sat behind a black stone desk, poring over a scroll. The wizard Elder was dressed in the same dark robes as Geller, but with a hood that stretched down either side of his face to his chest. His eyes were so dark they verged on black; his skin, palest white. He read in absorbed silence, the only sound the occasional droplet of water coming down from the ceiling.

As Geller watched Cavelos work, his breath caught in his throat. The shadows at the rear of the cave parted silently and a man stepped through. He stood behind the Elder's desk, watching him thoughtfully.

'Greetings, Halpern,' Cavelos said, without looking up. 'I would prefer it if you knocked.'

Halpern gestured towards the mouth of the cave. 'And, if you had a door, I would be happy to oblige. As it was, I did not think I would take the wizard Elder by surprise with a mere Slip spell.'

They spoke in a language with a thick, layered mesh of syllables – Murmeln, the wizard tongue. A sardonic edge lurked beneath Halpern's scrupulously polite tone. He was taller than Cavelos, with jet-black hair, and a moustache and pointed beard that only served to accentuate his sharp features. In all his years spent underground, Geller knew Halpern only by reputation. He was a powerful wizard who spent most of his waking hours above the surface, gathering information about humans and hunting for traces of the iron knights who had attacked Predjama. There were rumours Halpern even had his own Suspension chamber hidden away in a city somewhere, instead of taking his place in the Biding Cave alongside the other wizards.

'It has been many months since last we spoke,' Cavelos said. 'You spend so much time among the humans, I fear one day I will mistake you for one.'

'We each have our ways of furthering the cause of wizardry,' Halpern countered. 'While you hide underground, surrounded by sleeping wizards and echoes of the past, I look to the future.'

'I am not *hiding*,' Cavelos said icily. 'I am waiting. One day the iron knights will return, and upon that hour we shall emerge from our place of refuge to strike.'

'That hour is now. It is high time we regained our place in the natural order of the world. We cannot cower in the shadow of Predjama forever.'

The Illumination buds flickered with irritation.

'Do not talk to me of Predjama,' Cavelos said. 'I was there; you were not. I alone have fought the iron knights – I have seen powerful spells bounce off their metal hides like summer rain, and felt their soulless gaze burn through me. There were but five of them, yet they slaughtered two armies before turning the Book of the Apocalypse to ash.'

'And then vanished into thin air,' Halpern added, stroking his beard to a point. 'With the world seemingly at their feet. I have scoured the seven continents searching for them, but they have left no trace.'

'They are out there somewhere,' Cavelos declared. 'In some dark hole of the future, they await us. Why else destroy our most sacred book and leave our numbers dwindling?'

Halpern smiled. 'Ah, the future. The magic word.'

'Explain yourself.'

'Elder, for years you have had me hunt the iron knights upon the surface. Yet I have come to wonder whether I have been looking in the wrong place. Even now, over five hundred years after Predjama, there is still not the technology to fashion the robots you describe, let alone in the days of Erazem. The only way I can make sense of it all is if the knights travelled not from some distant land but from some distant *time*.'

Cavelos's brow furrowed. 'What you are suggesting is impossible. Even wizards cannot travel through time.'

'Yet human technology continues to progress in leaps and bounds, with one dizzying innovation following upon the next. Who is to say what feats they might achieve in centuries' time?'

The question hung in the air, the Illumination buds waxing and waning as the Elder considered it.

'Let us pretend what you say is true,' Cavelos said eventually. 'How can we hope to defeat the iron knights if they hide in the future?'

'Like this,' Halpern said. 'Watch.'

He made a complicated gesture, expertly opening a small hole in the air before him. Geller peered through his own Vision spell into another and saw an office looking out over a crowded skyline of skyscrapers. Rain drummed against the window. A man in a brightly coloured shirt and glasses sat behind a desk, surrounded by glowing screens that shifted and changed around him.

Cavelos leaned forward. 'Who is this?'

'His name is Kevin Cruz,' Halpern explained. 'This is his office in the GAPs Tower, in the city of Kuala Lumpur, Malaysia. His company has laid down a challenge to scientists and machine lovers to construct a new robot, one that can think in ways that humans cannot.'

'An abomination!' said Cavelos. 'And yet if someone were to succeed . . .'

'. . . surely that would make it the first true robot, the blueprint for all the metal monstrosities that will come after it. If we can find this robot and destroy it, we can halt the march of machine intelligence in its tracks. We can rewrite history, stop the slaughter of Predjama from ever taking place and save the Book of the Apocalypse from destruction!'

His voice rang triumphantly round the cave. Cavelos sat back, tapping a finger on the surface of his desk.

'This is most interesting,' he murmured. 'Pray, how exactly did you hear about this challenge?'

'There are infinite ways to uncover humans' secrets these days,' Halpern replied smugly. 'Computers, social networks – much has changed since the days of castles and sieges.'

'So you often tell me,' Cavelos said. 'Do your computers and social networks tell you which robot will win this competition, or must we wait for the announcement?'

'There is a shortlist,' Halpern told him. 'Three names, being kept in the utmost secrecy. But, according to my sources, Kevin Cruz is one of only a handful of people in the world who knows their identity. I will lead a raid upon Kuala Lumpur and . . . *persuade* him to give us the names on the shortlist.'

As Geller watched from his cave, Kevin Cruz turned

away from his glowing screens and looked out over the wet city, blissfully unaware that he was being spied on – or that his safety, his very existence even, hung in the balance at that moment.

Cavelos nodded finally. 'You will select the other members of the raid yourself?'

'Only the best,' Halpern replied. 'Wizards I can trust. Rief and Nath and –'

He stopped at a raised hand from Cavelos. The Elder got up from behind his desk.

'What is it?' said Halpern.

Cavelos pointed at Kevin Cruz. 'Close it. Now.'

The window to Kuala Lumpur snapped shut. The watching Geller realized that he too needed to close his spell, but in his struggles to cast it he had teased open too large a spyhole for it to shut straight away. As the window shrank, to his horror he saw Cavelos turn round and stare into the corner of the study where Geller's Vision spell had formed. The Elder seemed to look through directly at Geller, his eyes narrowing. Crying out in alarm, Geller frantically tried to close the window, only for a hand to punch through the hole and grab him by the robes. He was helpless to stop himself being dragged through his own spell into Cavelos's study, where he was sent sprawling across the floor.

'It seems we have company,' Halpern remarked.

'Indeed it does,' Cavelos said coldly, staring down at Geller. 'Welcome, my son.'

06: The Last Wizard

2052
Pazin Caves, Croatia

Geller scrambled up from the ground, hastily brushing the dirt from his cloak.

'Forgive me, Father,' he stammered. 'I did not mean to –'

'Spy upon the private council of the wizard Elder?' Cavelos said. 'Bad enough that you break your Suspension, without compounding your error by attempting to eavesdrop using so clumsy a spell that I could not fail to notice you.'

Geller looked down at his feet, his cheeks burning.

'Come now, Cavelos.' There was a trace of amusement in Halpern's voice. 'The boy's spell-casting may leave something to be desired, but he is merely a child. How is he to better learn our arts if he sleeps all the time?'

'I'm not a child,' Geller said quickly.

'You are the Elder's son,' Cavelos reminded him, 'and the last of our kind. You wake at *my* command – no one else's.'

Geller took one look at his father's face and decided against arguing. There was no way he was going to mention his metal nightmares here, especially not with Halpern looking on.

'I am sorry, Father,' he said dutifully. 'I will go back to the Biding Cave, if that's what you want.'

Cavelos walked over to his bookshelves and inspected the scrolls, his hands clasped behind his back. 'You have heard Halpern's tidings,' he said. 'He believes that we can prevent the rise of the mechanical men by finding the scientist who builds the first true robot. Do you think he is right?'

'I – I do not know,' Geller stammered, unsure of the right answer. 'Maybe, if –'

'No "maybes". Go with him. Find out.'

Halpern blinked. 'To Kuala Lumpur?'

'Exactly so.'

'You would have me take a boy on a mission of such importance?'

'The *boy* is over five hundred years old,' Cavelos replied. 'It is high time he experienced the human world.'

'Then let him run in the fields or chase girls!' Halpern snapped. 'This is a wizard raid, not a child's errand!'

The Illumination buds in Cavelos's study turned red, shading the rocks the colour of blood.

'You have been in the company of humans for too long, brother,' Cavelos said. 'You forget the ways of the wizards. The Elder's will must be obeyed.'

'And, naturally, I will do his bidding,' Halpern said

quickly, smoothing his moustache. 'I merely worry about taking a novice wizard on a mission of such importance. How can we be sure that Geller will not jeopardize our undertaking?'

'He is my son,' Cavelos said stiffly. 'My blood flows through his veins. My power is his power.'

A smile flickered across Halpern's lips like a dying candle. 'So be it,' he said. 'Let him prove it.'

Worry gnawed at Geller as he followed Cavelos and Halpern through a series of underground tunnels. The wizards' cloaks rippled in the freezing draughts seeping out from the nooks and alcoves leading off from the passages. The Pazin Caves network stretched out for miles, its extent a mystery even to the oldest wizard. They headed now along a tunnel that sloped deeper into the earth and it grew even colder, Geller's breath forming icy clouds in the air.

'Hard to believe, is it not, Geller, that wizards once dwelled in palaces and castles, surrounded by the greatest finery?' Halpern said over his shoulder. 'Now we are forced to call these dank caves home.'

'Dank caves which have kept us safe for over five hundred years,' Cavelos replied.

'Safe? Our bloodline has dried up, most of our wizards too old to do anything but sit in Suspension. We must find a way to produce new wizards, else our line is threatened by extinction.'

'One bloodline, at least, remains strong,' Cavelos said proudly.

'And no doubt Geller will grow to be a mighty wizard. Yet he is only one. Unless he is the Malum reincarnate, it will not be enough.'

'You speak of the Malum as though in jest.'

'And? Would a human fear to jest about Father Christmas or the Tooth Fairy?'

Geller couldn't help himself. 'What's the Malum?'

Halpern laughed. 'You have not heard the tales? You surprise me, Geller! Why, the Malum is a majestic wizard taller than any robot, clad in a cloak of shadows. The mightiest human kings threw themselves prostrate before him; empires crumbled at the click of his fingers!' Halpern's voice faded into contempt. 'He is a myth, a fairy tale.'

'Wizards older and wiser than yourself have believed in the Malum, Halpern,' Cavelos warned. 'I hope for your sake you are correct.'

They had to be very far beneath the surface now. The passageway levelled off without warning, leading out into a vast, flat cavern lined with slippery pebbles. As he peered into the darkness, Geller saw the floor ripple and move before him. He was standing on the shore of a huge underground lake. Cavelos and Halpern waited for him at the water's edge.

'My son stands before us, ready to prove himself,' the Elder declared. 'What spells would you have him cast?'

'We have already seen his efforts at a Vision spell,' Halpern said. 'But I need to know if he can fight.'

'Fight?' Geller said. 'But how –?'

Cavelos waved him silent. He looked Geller up and down, apparently weighing something up.

'Very well, Halpern,' he nodded. 'You may attack him.'

Halpern came at Geller at once, flitting menacingly across the gloomy shore towards him. Eyes widening in alarm, Geller dropped to one knee and fumbled with his ring, making the frantic gesture for a Protection spell. A chain of small explosions went off in the air, forming a crystal arch in front of him. The barrier had barely materialized before a Damage spell crashed into it – it held with a shudder. Geller shook his head clear, desperately aware of the need to concentrate. It was the Damage spell they would be looking for: the only way he could prove himself. As Halpern circled his protective shield, feinting to cast again, Geller forced himself to focus on the lessons he had been taught.

Flick. Push. Wait. Visualize. Ignite.

He could do this.

Flick. Push. Wait. Visualize. Ignite.

He had to do this.

Darting out from behind the crystal barrier, Geller repositioned his casting ring and snapped his wrist, pushing his palm out and sending a Damage spell floating across the rocky shore towards Halpern. He snapped his wrist again, attempting to ignite it. A sharp shooting pain went through Geller's right hand, the ignition spark dying on his fingertips. Wincing, he could only watch as the dormant spell sailed harmlessly past Halpern and drifted out over the lake.

Leaving him totally unprotected.

Geller barely saw the spell that hit him – there was merely a blur of motion, and then something punched him in the chest, knocking him off his feet. The world tumbled and cartwheeled. Lifting his head groggily, Geller saw Halpern raise his hand, another Damage spell at the tips of his fingers.

'Enough.'

His father's voice, carrying across the shoreline. Halpern turned and flung his spell against the wall, igniting it with a thunderous explosion that shook the rocks and made the lake's still waters tremble.

'A truly fearsome display, Geller,' Halpern said drily, as Geller gingerly sat up. 'You will have the GAPs security droids fleeing for cover.'

'The boy needs practice,' said Cavelos. 'Who better to learn from than the mighty Halpern himself? Take him to Kuala Lumpur and give him the chance to prove himself.'

Halpern looked out over the lake for several seconds before turning back and sketching out a deep bow. 'As you command, Elder.'

He cast a quick, irritated Slip spell and stepped through the portal. Cavelos waited until the hole had closed before rounding on Geller.

'Twice now you have embarrassed me,' he said darkly. 'It is unbecoming that the Elder's son cannot cast simple spells properly.'

'I would have done better if you had warned me I was going to have to fight Halpern,' Geller protested. 'I'm lucky he didn't kill me!'

'If only your spells were as effective as your excuses. You should have stayed in Suspension.'

'I couldn't! The mechanical men –'

He faltered under Cavelos's searching gaze.

'You dreamed of the iron knights again?'

Geller nodded miserably. 'I tried to run from them,' he said. 'I always do. But this time they found me in a cave. Mother was there . . . She was singing some kind of lullaby, only there was only the two of us. And then the robots came. She made me go – I couldn't save her!'

His father let out a sigh. 'It is natural for a child to miss their mother,' he said. 'Yet you must understand, Geller, Mara died long before she took her last breath. The bloodshed at Predjama changed her, snatched away all reason. Even here, miles beneath the earth's surface, far beyond the reach of man or machine, she saw iron knights hiding in every shadow. The caves rang for days on end to her terrified screams. When it finally came, her death was a kindness. Humans are not like you and I, Geller. While you have slept, generations have lived and died like mayflies. Kingdoms have risen and fallen; the world has warred. Their knowledge, their science, their thirst for power grows by the day. As do their mechanical men.'

He crouched down beside Geller and placed a gloved hand on each shoulder, his dark eyes searching out his soul. 'It is natural for a child to miss their mother. But, my son, you are a child no longer. It is time for you to be a *man*.'

Geller felt a small thrill of power run through him.

'I won't let you down, Father,' he said solemnly.

'See that you do not. When you go to the surface, remember that danger can come in many forms, even those who call themselves brothers and wrap themselves in wizard cloaks. Halpern is ambitious and seeks to become Elder himself. Do not trust him.'

Geller nodded quickly. Cavelos straightened up, apparently satisfied, and strode away across the rocks and back up the tunnel towards the Biding Cave. Getting to his feet, Geller picked up a stone and hurled it across the silent water. He stared out over the lake.

Flick. Push. Wait. Visualize. Ignite.
Flick. Push. Wait. Visualize. Ignite.

If it meant standing here for another three hundred years, Geller told himself firmly, he would cast the spell properly. He thought about the robots attacking Predjama Castle and his mother. He pictured one of the brutal metal giants standing in front of him and felt a satisfying rush of anger through his bloodstream. Positioning his ring, Geller snapped his wrist and pushed his palm slowly forward. This time he kept the spell small, trying to maintain control of it. As it floated through the darkness above the lake, Geller flicked his wrist again and brought the spell to life.

A small flash lit up the cavern, sparks fizzing as they hit the water.

'Yes!'

Geller clenched his fist, shuffling his feet in a triumphant dance. With a bit more practice, he would be able to cast a Damage spell big enough to make even Halpern think twice.

But, as Geller shook his tingling fingers and prepared to cast another spell, his ears pricked up at a hissing noise coming from the rocks behind him. He whirled round and cast an Illumination spell, but the weak glow struggled to penetrate the inky shadows by the lake.

'Who's there?' Geller called out. He waved his hands dramatically, threatening to cast a spell. 'Come out and show yourself!'

The hissing grew louder, and a figure emerged from behind a craggy rock. Geller shrank back in fear. Stooped and shambling, the creature scuttled rather than walked. Robes hung from its bent and mangled skeleton like a shroud. Bone rebelled under paper-thin flesh, jutting out at unnatural angles. The skin was stretched painfully around its skull, threatening to tear at any second. Straggly wisps of hair hung from its chin, beneath a mouthful of rotten teeth. A pair of dark, watery eyes fixed on Geller. He wanted to run, but he was too scared. It felt as though the creature had pinned his feet to the floor. He opened his mouth to cry for help, but nothing came out.

With growing horror, Geller realized that the sound echoing round the lake was not a hiss but a single word, repeated over and over again.

'*Spawn . . .*'

Geller stared dumbly at the creature as it shambled closer to him, until he could see his terrified reflection in its huge black eyes. Its breath came in wheezes that rolled over him like a fetid wave.

'*Spawn . . .*'

The creature placed its left eye by Geller's, and he had the uncanny sensation that it was looking inside his skull. It sniffed twice, digesting his scent. He was paralyzed with fear.

'*Spawn . . .*'

The creature's mouth twisted into a grin, and it held up the mangled stump of a hand. Almost against his will, Geller reached out to touch it in greeting. When his hand brushed against blackened flesh, the creature collapsed, its skeleton crumpling and robes melting away to nothing. Geller cried out, stumbling backwards. One moment the creature had been before him, now it was gone, leaving nothing but a sour tang in the air where it had breathed. The young wizard dropped to his knees, the freezing waters of the lake lapping against his robe. Across the waves came a final whisper:

'*Spawn . . .*'

07: Games Protocols

2052
Machine Intelligence Lab, University of Florida, Gainesville, Florida, USA

'Good afternoon, Ada,' said Hawking, with a polite incline of his head.

For over two years, Ada's mom had spent evenings and weekends holed up in the university working on her robot, cancelling everything from movie nights to entire vacations at the last minute. Even after Ada's dad had got sick, her mom barely missed a day at the lab. It would have been easy for Ada to hate Hawking. But the tech junkie inside her couldn't help marvelling at him. It wasn't just his size and intelligence, nor the complexity of the science that had been required to construct him. Hawking was more than just a computer, a machine of metal, plastic and circuitry. He could talk and interact, his faceplate moulded into smooth human features that registered basic expressions. He was *alive*.

'Hey, Hawking,' Ada said, sinking into the seat opposite him. 'How are you today?'

'I am well, thank you.' Hawking gestured at the chessboard on the table. 'Dr Luring has just taught me the basic rudiments of chess. But I am finding the game somewhat perplexing. The king is the most important piece upon the board – when he falls, the game is ended. Yet he is also the weakest piece. Even a pawn can become a queen.'

Ada thought about this for a second. 'I guess it's like people,' she said. 'Sometimes they can look strong on the outside, but on the inside they're kinda soft. And the other way round.'

'Like me,' said Kipp, puffing his chest out.

Ada laughed. 'You're my knight,' she said. 'Because you're loyal and brave, and I never know where you're going to move next.'

'You're the queen,' Kipp declared. 'You can do anything. And you'll always have me to protect you.'

'Aw, thanks, little guy.'

Hawking considered the chessboard. 'So if I wish to win at this game,' he said thoughtfully, 'I must protect my king.'

'You heard Kipp,' Ada said, putting her arm round the little robot's shoulders. 'Gotta take care of the people who are important to you.'

'This is why we run these games protocols,' her mom added. 'By playing chess and backgammon and go, you can learn about humans and increase the efficiency of your problem-solving capabilities at the same time.'

Hawking nodded. Despite his vast processing power, he moved slowly and deliberately, like an old man, and could be easily confused. But, even though he was still getting to grips with the human world, the potential of his brain was astonishing.

'Ada's brought us some good news, Hawking,' Sara continued. 'You have made the final of the Rodin Challenge. We're going to Kuala Lumpur.'

'That is excellent news, Dr Luring,' the robot replied, with a bow of his head. 'Congratulations.'

'And to you,' said Ada's mom. 'Now let's see if we can win this thing, shall we?'

She swiped open her holo-screen and logged on to a computer program, a black knight chess piece flashing up on the screen. Spartak was the ultimate chess program, maintaining an open challenge site and playing thousands of simultaneous games around the globe even as it took on – and beat – the highest-ranked human grandmasters. To display Hawking's capabilities, Dr Luring planned to teach him chess and see whether he could learn to defeat Spartak. But first it was Ada's turn.

She sat down behind the white pieces as Kipp looked on, fascinated, bombarding her with questions. Hawking played in silence, concentrating intently. He had only just learned the rules to the game, but already Ada could sense his processing units calculating strategies. She won the first game – just – but shortly into the next one she found herself in deep trouble, her queen besieged by attacking pieces. As she pondered her next move, she was aware of her mom standing in front of her.

'Say hello, Ada.'

Ada looked up to find that her mom was filming her on

her smart glasses. She frowned, brushing her hair out of her face.

'Hi.'

'Aren't you going to smile for the camera?'

Ada held up her hand, shielding her face from the lens. 'What are you doing, Mom?'

Dr Luring switched off her glasses. 'All Rodin Challenge entrants have to document their work. And this is a pretty important day, wouldn't you say?'

'Yeah, but for you guys. It's not like I built Hawking.'

'Hey, you're an integral part of the team! You think I don't know how hard these last few months have been for you, especially with me having to work so much? I could never do this without you. There's only a month left until the final – after that, we can spend all the time together you want.'

'Sounds good,' Ada said cautiously. Her mom had made these kinds of promises before. 'You're still coming on Thursday night, though, right?'

Sara stared at her blankly. 'Thursday night?'

'The Science Fair? You know, the one I've spent weeks working on my project for? The one you promised you'd come to?'

'But, Ada, that was before we made the shortlist!'

'Mom!'

'OK, OK!' she said, holding up her hands. 'You're right. Of *course* I'll be there.'

'You swear?'

Dr Luring smiled. 'Hand on heart. After all, I need to

find out what you've been up to. You've been so secretive about this project.'

Ada glanced across at Spartak's home page. 'We're allowed to have a few secrets, right, Kipp?'

'Absolutely!' the robot replied enthusiastically. 'I haven't told Castle or Dr Luring anything about your project, or the drone . . .'

At the sight of Ada's furious glance, the robot hurriedly adopted an innocent expression. Sara gave her daughter an enquiring look over the top of her glasses.

'Drone?'

'It's probably nothing,' Ada said, trying to sound casual. 'I thought a drone was trying to follow me home from school, so I lost it in the industrial park. Maybe it had suffered some kind of glitch – you know what sec-drones are like.'

'Why on earth didn't you say anything?'

'I was going to! But then I found out about the Rodin Challenge and it kinda slipped my mind.'

'Really,' Ada's mom said disapprovingly. 'Let's hope the police take it a little more seriously when I call them.'

'I wouldn't worry about the police, Mom,' Ada replied, stifling a grin. 'I bet they're already on the lookout for it.'

Kipp opened his mouth and Ada nudged him with her foot, sending him staggering to one side. The robot grabbed hold of a table leg to steady himself, the chess pieces wobbling on the board. He hurriedly closed his mouth. Telling her mom about the drone was one thing, but if Sara learned about Ada's hacking she'd never let her near a computer again.

Once Dr Luring had initiated the games protocols, they left Hawking in front of the holo-screen considering his first move against Spartak and made their way out of the Machine Intelligence Lab. The sun had dipped below the campus roofs, shadows lengthening outside the Department for Ancient Civilizations. When Ada went to free her bike from the security block, she felt an uneasy prickle between her shoulder-blades. She turned round to see the woman from outside the Engineering Department sitting on a stone bench, her pendant camera pointed directly at Ada.

'Mom?' Ada said. 'I think we have company.'

As Dr Luring followed her gaze, the woman got up and walked over to them. 'Sorry if I startled you,' she called out. 'I recognized your daughter from earlier – we met outside the Engineering Department. I'm Lili Parker.'

'Dr Sara Luring,' Ada's mom said, warily shaking her proffered hand.

'I've been going round the university, trying to get reactions to the HI-AG protest,' Lili said, 'but no one seems to want to talk. I don't suppose you have a comment, Dr Luring?'

'A comment?'

An elegant woman in casual young clothes, as though trying to fit in on campus. The constant photographing. *'I'm exactly where I need to be . . .'*

'You're a reporter,' Ada said.

Lili held up her hands. 'Guilty as charged. I got a tip-off about the demonstration and came down here to see if I could get an exclusive.'

'I'm afraid I can't help you, Ms Parker,' Dr Luring said firmly. 'As you can see, the Engineering Department is a long way from here.'

The reporter examined the building looming up behind her. 'You would be an expert in ancient civilizations, right?'

Ada's mom blinked. 'Oh well,' she said, after a pause. 'I don't know about *expert* . . .'

'My husband used to adore that kind of thing,' Lili said. 'You know, Greeks and Romans. Wars and empires. The battle between the old and the new.'

She shot an arch glance at Ada, who once again had the irritating sense that she was being talked down to – as though Lili knew a joke Ada wasn't in on.

'I find it fascinating, too,' Dr Luring said politely, unlocking her bike. 'But, if you'll forgive me, it's been a long day and we were just on our way home.'

She placed a hand on Ada's shoulder, steering her past the reporter.

'The police broke up the demonstration, you know,' Lili called out. 'And arrested some of the protesters. Don't you think that says something about the right to free speech in this country?'

Ada's mom laughed with incredulity. 'Free speech? What about my daughter's right to walk safely through a university campus? HI-AG don't care about free speech; they're nothing but a gang of thugs.'

Lili flashed a smile. 'Can I quote you on that, Dr Luring?'

'Absolutely not.'

The reporter bowed her head, accepting defeat. Slipping

her pendant camera back inside her sweater, she walked away down the path, melting into the darkness beyond the trees. Dr Luring watched her go.

'How did you meet her again, Ada?'

'In the square, like she said. I had to swerve my bike to avoid hitting her. Kinda wish I'd carried straight on now.'

'Tell me if you run into her again, OK?'

Ada shrugged. 'She's just a reporter, Mom.'

'We don't know what she is.'

They rode out through the campus together, light sensors bursting into life like brilliant white flowers to illuminate their path. When they arrived home, Ada's mom settled the grocery bill and ordered takeout. As they ate pizza in front of the TV together, Ada could almost forget about robots and reporters, drones and international challenges. But it wasn't long before her mom's eyes began to shift back towards her papers on the dining-room table. Ada went to get herself a glass of water from the kitchen and came back to find her working at the table.

'I'm going to bed,' Ada said with a yawn. She put her arm round her mom and gave her a hug. 'Try and get some sleep, Mom. You look tired.'

'Mmmm.' Dr Luring was lost in her work again. 'Just a few more minutes.'

With a shake of the head, Ada headed up the stairs. 'Night, Kipp.'

'Goodnight, Ada.'

Upstairs, she checked the Gainesville Police Department system to see whether there had been any fresh sightings of the unmarked drone. But there were no updates. The first photos from Han's party were appearing on R8, beside excited posts littered with grinning emojis. As Ada looked through the pictures, memories came flooding back of her trip to Han's lake house the previous summer, when they had still been a couple: bright sunlight playing on the tips of the waves; Ada screaming as she jumped into the freezing lake; Han's laughter as they splashed about in the water together; damp footprints on the dock; goosebumps rippling across her skin as she dried herself; the thrill that ran through her when Han leaned forward to kiss her. They were memories Ada had locked away in her mind without even realizing, keeping them precious and safe. Because a week after that day at the lake house her dad came back from the hospital with some very bad news and everything changed.

A video feed flashed up on-screen – Ada couldn't stop herself from pressing play. She was plunged straight into the party, shouts and screams of laughter merging with the thumping music. A dazzling light show flickered out across the lake, neon-coloured lasers slicing through the darkness. On the jetty, people were drinking and dancing – the camera swung round in time to catch a boy leaping with a whoop into the water. Through the crush, Ada spotted Pri and Kit being chatted up by a couple of older-looking guys. The camera moved on, and she was about to stop the video feed when she caught sight of Han.

He wasn't alone: a pretty girl with bright-blue hair and a nose ring was nestled in the crook of his arm as he gazed up at the light show. Han whispered something in her ear, and she laughed. Then she leaned forward and kissed him on the lips.

Ada quickly closed her computer. There was a sick feeling in the pit of her stomach, which she angrily told herself to ignore. They broke up months ago. Han could do what he liked. Feeling suddenly exhausted, Ada lay down on her bed and turned out the lamp. But it was a long time before she fell asleep.

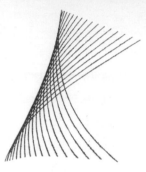

08: CERN

3019
Rio de Janeiro, Brazil

The stream of words had frozen on the walls of the Reading Room, the hush thickening and deepening. Kaku stared at Gauer's scroll in puzzlement. The five robots who had attacked Weil's Mount Hood facility had to be the iron knights who had attacked Predjama Castle in 1489. Killing indiscriminately – both human and robot alike – they had travelled back in time and destroyed two entire medieval armies.

Yet this could not be. For robots, *all* human life was sacred. The concept was hardcoded into their software. Even to contemplate taking a life was unthinkable. So what possible malfunction could have made these robots carve such a bloody trail of destruction? Why had they jumped to the Middle Ages, when humans still believed in magic and thought that comets signalled the end of the world? What was so special about Predjama Castle that had led to its doom? Kaku read the end of Gauer's scroll once more.

Without a heart to feel pity for their victims' screams, the mechanical men sliced and killed their way into the hallowed chambers of Lord Erazem's library. There they sought their prize, a volume of rare and arcane power. God forgive me, but I was unable to stop them from destroying it.

Opening a COMMS-Link, Kaku connected with a distant institution situated on the other side of the world, on the border of Switzerland and France.

The Collider.

LINK: 46.234167° N, 6.055278° W

011100100000111101001001010011111111000110101

In his visual panel, Kaku travelled through a huge network of tunnels buried deep in the ground beneath the Alps. As he followed the Collider's endless twists and turns, Kaku was reminded of the Midgard Serpent, a creature of human myth that grew so large it snaked round the entire world and grasped its own tail. According to the legends, when the serpent finally let go, the world would end. Kaku wondered whether the Collider's destruction would signal the same thing – the end of all hope for humans and robots alike.

At last he came out at the Control Centre, the operational hub of the Collider. It was a vast room with four circular banks of computers worked by mechanized robotic arms. When the particle accelerator first opened, it had taken two thousand humans to operate it, whole teams of scientists and engineers manning the Control Centre, working day and night to monitor the experiments. Now there was only CERN.

A huge shadow fell across Kaku's visual panel. Twice the size of other robots, CERN's form had evolved to suit its purpose. It had no head, just a slight moulded hump rising from its shoulders, with a single indicator light set in the centre. Its shoulders and upper chest were broad and gleaming, tapering to a narrow waist. Every time he opened communications with the Collider, Kaku felt CERN's processing power rush through his circuits.

Kaku. CERN's voice echoed inside Kaku's head, as strong and clear as a tolling bell. You wish to speak with me?

I bring word from Weil the surgeon, Kaku replied. The time-jump facility at Mount Hood has been attacked.

I am aware of this.

By robots.

There was a pause. Kaku could hear CERN's processors humming.

This is not possible, CERN said. Robots would not attack their own kind.

Kaku shared the footage from the laboratory security camera. Once more, he saw the robots stride forth from the flaming compound, weapons raised. As the lead robot prepared to shoot the camera, CERN zoomed in on her face and electronically mapped her features.

Running ident check, CERN declared. Ident check complete. Robot identified as 101000100110110100, or Angelis.

Who is she?

Team Leader, SSR Class – Safety, Security and Rescue. Angelis's team travelled to areas struck by natural disaster to locate and retrieve survivors.

CERN transmitted Angelis's activity log to Kaku's visual panel. Her team's list of operations spanned two hundred years, comprising earthquakes, forest fires and tsunamis. Fifty years ago, following the rescue of forty people from a malfunctioning nuclear reactor in South America, Angelis had been given the Nobel Cross for Valour, the highest honour a robot could receive.

She is a hero, Kaku said.

Her SSR team is the finest in its class, CERN told him. Its members combine speed and bravery with tactical and strategic capabilities. Each robot is fitted with antimatter guns and a reinforced exoskeleton capable of absorbing pressure up to 1,000 bars and temperatures in excess of 1,000°C. There is nowhere on Earth they cannot go.

Even the past, Kaku replied.

So it would appear.

The final entry in Angelis's activity log had occurred just days after the Spawn had begun their assault upon Earth. She and a team of four robots had travelled to Tokyo, which had been reduced to smouldering rubble by a detachment of Spawn attack ships, to hunt for survivors. The entire unit's COMMS-Links had gone down somewhere in the ruins, and it had been adjudged KIA – Killed in Action. Yet now the team had reappeared on a snowy mountaintop on the other side of the world, on a murderous mission to destroy robots and humans alike.

Angelis has spent her life protecting and preserving human life, Kaku said. What happened to her in Tokyo?

I cannot be sure. But I wonder if the Spawn found a way to corrupt her software.

To what end? What is this war about, CERN?

It is unclear. I have spent months trying to formulate an answer. Merely killing us and destroying our cities does not seem to satisfy the Spawn. Their mining ships dig and drill, burrowing deep underground. It is as though they are looking for something, something beyond even my imagining.

According to a manuscript I found in the library, Kaku said, Angelis travelled back to a medieval castle and killed all the men and women inside. Her SSR team sought a book, which they burned. Perhaps the answer lay within its pages. I must find out why. I must jump, too.

You propose to follow them? Kaku, you have seen what Angelis and her team are capable of. You are a librarian, not a warrior. If you try to confront them, they will destroy you.

I know, Kaku replied calmly. That is why I must travel to the Abbaye Saint-Jacques in 1502 and speak with the monk Gauer. He survived the attack on Predjama; perhaps he can tell me more about what happened that day. Maybe then I can understand why these robots have risked so much to travel back in time.

It is not that simple, said CERN. The SSR team have already returned to 3019, using up more of my processing power. If I were to send you back, I could not guarantee your return.

By their very nature, time-jumps were return tickets. Once one had been initiated, the return journey could only

84

be prevented by the Collider's complete destruction. No one had ever tried to jump on a single journey before. If there was a problem establishing a COMMS-Link with CERN across the centuries, Kaku would be stranded in the Middle Ages.

Angelis has returned to our time? he said. Where is she now?

I do not know. But I believe she is close. Look.

In his visual panel, Kaku found himself soaring like an eagle through the snow-tipped peaks of the Alps above the Collider. The horizon was dark with storm clouds. As Kaku banked and wheeled in the air, he realized that the clouds were in fact a fleet of Spawn attack ships, bringing a premature night down over the mountains.

The Spawn are preparing their assault, CERN told Kaku. If the Collider falls, then Earth will follow. You are proposing a time-jump that will further sap my resources, with only a minimal chance of success. It is an irrational proposition.

You are correct. But I believe it may be our only hope. Will you send me back?

Kaku waited. He did not compute the possible outcomes of his request – he did not think – but he did stay very still.

Stand by, said CERN.

Kaku's processing unit buzzed with excitement as the COMMS-Link went down. Moving quickly now, he connected to the library computer and activated Sleep mode. Heavy metal screens dropped round the machines, and the streams of data flowing down the walls abruptly dried up. As he went to leave the Reading Room, Kaku paused, suddenly aware that he might never be able to return to it. If his mission to the past failed, no one might ever set foot inside this library again. That said, if Earth truly was doomed, what did it matter?

The doors slid shut behind the robot as he left the Reading Room, climbing up a spiral staircase that ran through the statue's core. At the top of the steps, Kaku passed through a door that led out of the tunnels and on to the statue's arm. At one time he would have stood here for hours just looking out over Rio – its skyscrapers stretching up to the clouds, the glimpses of golden sands and blue water in between their gleaming banks of windows. But that was before the Spawn had attacked the city. The skyscrapers had been felled, leaving a stark forest of blackened metal spars jutting into the air. Rust-coloured clouds scudded in over the oily slicks in the ocean. A fire still burned in the remains of the football stadium, grey flakes of ash swirling in the hot breeze. No sounds of animal or human life reached Kaku. There was only a horrible absence.

CERN had told Kaku to stand by – he knew there would not be long to wait. But, as he looked out across the ruins of Rio, he realized something. The breeze was blowing southwards out to sea, but the rust-coloured clouds were moving north, *against* the prevailing wind.

Straight towards the statue.

Hurriedly Kaku opened a fresh COMMS-Link to the Collider.

What is it, Kaku? asked CERN.

My position is under threat.

Checking COMMS-Link security, CERN reported. Security has been compromised. Communications may have been monitored by enemy forces.

As the clouds neared, Kaku saw their rusted hues darken to an angry black. Their soft lines began to straighten and solidify before his eyes – shapes started to emerge. Flying craft hewn from dark, glittering crystal. Spawn attack ships. They had found him.

Spawn attack imminent, Kaku told CERN.

Preparing time-jump, the robot replied. Location: Abbaye Saint-Jacques. Year: 1502. And then, to Kaku's surprise, he added: Good luck.

As CERN reconnected and Kaku's hardware engaged, he felt data streaming towards him at a dizzying rate. From halfway across the world, CERN was altering the gravity around him, lifting the robot into the air. Despite the speed with which the Spawn were streaking towards him, it felt to Kaku as though time was slowing down. The air rippled like heavy water.

As he hung suspended in mid-air, the sky before him parted, revealing a glimpse of a lonely mountainside cloaked in darkness. CERN had opened the wormhole. Kaku's internal temperature plummeted, ice crystals forming across his metallic body. Tracer shots fizzed angrily through the air around him as the Spawn took aim, carving stone chunks from the statue. Yet Kaku felt strangely calm. His moment had come.

As the Spawn's craft descended in a furious flock upon him, the robot stepped through the wormhole and vanished in a hail of tracer fire.

09: Skybridge

2052
Bukit Bintang district,
Kuala Lumpur, Malaysia

A storm raged over Kuala Lumpur, rain lashing the streets and coating the parks and plazas in a grey haze. Trees arched their backs in the wind. The towering skyscrapers stood firm, lit up against the early evening sky with brilliant displays of red, yellow and blue lights. Their upper levels were linked by skybridges, enclosed tunnels that formed a whole new layer of the city hundreds of feet in the air.

Down on the ground, in the Bukit Bintang district of the city, the streets were thronged with shoppers and tourists. Halpern strode imperiously through the crowds, people stepping out of his way without even seeming to notice the tall wizard. Three other wizards arrowed through the streets of Kuala Lumpur in Halpern's wake like a flock of ravens, threatening to leave Geller behind.

Geller floundered behind them, lost in a sea of jostling elbows, overwhelmed by explosions of colour and noise.

Meat sizzled in street-stall woks, filling the air with delicious smells. Music blasted out of shopfront speakers. Everywhere Geller looked there were video screens: bright, happy faces talking and singing to the camera; news bulletins flashing up dramatic headlines. His senses were on overload, his heart racing in his chest. The silent alcoves of the Pazin Caves seemed impossibly far away.

Geller pressed on through the shadow of hotels and mega-malls, the lines of red paper lanterns strung up above the street shaking wildly in the wind. His hood was raised against the rain, but the storm hadn't done anything to lower the stifling heat and he was sweating beneath his cloak. He knocked into a tourist taking a photograph on their watch, mumbled an apology and hurried on.

Geller considered the three other wizards who were on this mission: dark-skinned Rief, ice-cool and aloof; the portly, sneering Nath; and the tall figure of Drahe. A chill had come over Geller when he first saw the cadaverous wizard in the green glow of the Biding Cave. There were rumours that Drahe had learned how to cast a Damage spell that could pass slowly through bodies like a painful electric current. There were also rumours that he took great pleasure in casting it. At least Geller didn't need to worry about keeping his distance from the other wizards – Rief, Nath and Drahe ignored him just like Halpern did. No one wanted him here.

When they reached the busy intersection at the end of the street, the wizards crossed without breaking stride, picking a path through the moving cars. Geller tried to follow suit, only to be greeted by screeching brakes and a blizzard of angry horns. Reddening with embarrassment, he backed away to the kerb and waited until the lights changed and the traffic halted. He had to run to catch up with the others, coming out on to a windswept and deserted plaza where puddles gathered on the black marble floor. To Geller, the surrounding skyscrapers looked like giant stalagmites hewn from metal and glass. The wizards stopped in the middle of the plaza to stare up at the building before them.

The GAPs Tower stretched into the sky, piercing the rainclouds like a needle. Unlike the other skyscrapers, with their video displays and neon lights, the building's walls were sheer and black, allowing it to melt into the night. A lone skybridge linked the GAPs Tower to the neighbouring skyscraper that kept it company in the clouds. Guards stood watch at the base of the building, assault rifles resting in the crook of their arms. As Geller craned his neck towards the summit, he caught sight of tiny lights orbiting the building.

'This won't be easy,' Rief said calmly.

'What were you expecting?' Halpern replied. 'The technological secrets within those walls are worth more than the gold and jewels that any bank vault could hold. The GAPs Tower might well be the most securely guarded building in the world.'

'What are those lights?' asked Geller, pointing to the top of the tower.

'Security drones,' came the short reply. 'Mindless robot cameras. They are as common as insects here on the surface.'

'So much for outside,' said Nath. 'What about inside?'

'Cameras and heat and movement sensors monitor every square inch of the building,' Halpern told him. 'We will be detected as soon as we set foot inside, triggering an alarm that will have those drones upon us in seconds. The mainframe security is automatically linked to the police department, who will immediately proceed to surround the building in support of the armed guards.'

'That could make questioning our target a little problematic.'

'True enough, brother,' Halpern said. 'Which is why we're not setting foot inside the tower. We will introduce ourselves to Kevin Cruz elsewhere.'

'Where?' A single harsh syllable: Drahe's voice.

Halpern nodded up at the skybridge. 'There,' he said. 'According to my sources, Kevin Cruz leaves the GAPs Tower at seven thirty in the evening and walks along the skybridge to a private entrance inside Jayaling House, where his apartment is located. Seven thirty every evening, like clockwork.'

'Or a robot,' Rief said darkly.

'The security inside Jayaling House is almost as tight as the GAPs Tower,' Halpern continued. 'So we only have the length of that walkway to attack. It is a small window.'

'You needn't worry about that,' Drahe said ominously. 'A few moments with me, and Kevin Cruz will be eager to tell us *everything*.'

'We will have to deal with his protection first,' said

Halpern. 'My sources tell me that Cruz is accompanied at all times by two body-bots – mechanized bodyguards. They are armed with state-of-the-art laser and taser stun guns. The element of surprise will be crucial.'

'Your sources seem to know a lot about GAPs and Kevin Cruz,' Geller said. 'Are you sure you can trust them?'

Four pairs of eyes swivelled towards him.

'That is no concern of yours,' Halpern said icily. 'Your father might be master of his precious caves, but here, in the world of the humans, I am Elder. Understood?'

Geller bit back a retort, and nodded. No sense in angering Halpern before the raid was even underway. He had promised Cavelos he wouldn't let him down.

'Still a while to go before seven thirty,' Rief noted, glancing round the plaza. 'We need to take up position somewhere closer to the target.'

'There is an observation platform on Jayaling House that overlooks the skybridge,' Halpern replied. 'I think we can assume in this weather that it will be empty. Remember this – if the Rodin Challenge scientists learn exactly who is hunting them, they will seek protection. Wizards have kept their existence secret for thousands of years – this is no time to break cover. Follow me.'

Halpern made a casting gesture and vanished from the middle of the empty plaza. One by one, the wizards Slipped up to the observation platform. When Geller followed, he found himself standing on a lonely ledge looking out over Kuala Lumpur's fluorescent skyline. Only the GAPs Tower and its skybridge remained dark.

Geller took up position on the edge of the platform, relieved that he had cast his first spell of the night successfully. His fingers were still sore from the hours he'd spent practising his Damage spell at the underground lake – he could only hope it had been enough.

The wizards waited, their hoods up against the rain, their cloaks flapping and billowing in the wind – five black gargoyles perched on the edge of a skyscraper. The storm grew in fury and intensity, until Geller had to fight to stop himself being blown off the observation platform. He had no idea what time it was, or how long remained until 7:30 p.m.

Finally, as his muscles were starting to cramp, lights came on inside the skybridge. Through the windows, Geller watched as the entrance to GAPs HQ slid open, and Kevin Cruz walked out on to the walkway. He was flanked by two heavily armed body-bots, metal exoskeletons with hideous, gleaming skulls.

'Here he comes,' Halpern said softly. 'Rief, Nath – take out the bodyguards. Drahe – prepare to go to work on Cruz. We need to be in and out of the skybridge within three minutes, not a second longer.'

'What about me?' whispered Geller. 'What should I do?'

'Stay out of our way,' Drahe said hoarsely. 'Or, when I'm finished with the human, I'll go to work on you.'

Kevin Cruz was already halfway along the bridge, walking purposefully towards the entrance to Jayaling House. It was time. With military precision, Halpern and his men cast their Slip spells into the skybridge. Geller was a second behind them, landing in a crouch in the brightly lit tunnel. Rief and Nath had already sprung to their feet and were taking aim at the approaching body-bots. But, almost immediately, Geller sensed something was wrong. Up close, there was something strange about Kevin Cruz. The engineer looked faint and ghostlike, blurred around the edges. As the wizards prepared to attack, an alarm went off, echoing round the skybridge like a high-pitched scream. Metal shutters slammed down either end of the walkway. Kevin Cruz simply disappeared, leaving the wizards alone with the heavily armed body-bots.

'What magic is this?' hissed Drahe.

'It's not magic, idiot,' Halpern snarled back. 'Cruz was a hologram. We've walked into a trap!'

He hurled a Damage spell at the body-bots, who shook off the explosion without flinching. As they prepared to return fire at the wizards, Rief, Drahe and Nath vanished. Geller hurriedly tried to follow them, but when he tried to cast the Slip spell he discovered he couldn't move his hands. It was as though they had been frozen solid. Panicking, he called out to Halpern. The wizard gave him a cold smile and Slipped off the skybridge. Suddenly Geller's hands could move again – fumbling with his ring, he prepared to cast.

'Freeze!' a metal voice ordered.

He looked up and found himself staring down the barrel of a gun.

10: White Lilies

2052
GAPs Tower skybridge,
Kuala Lumpur, Malaysia

Beneath Geller's feet, the walkway swayed and shook in the storm's furious grip. His ears rang from the shrieking alarm. The other wizards had abandoned him, leaving him to face Kevin Cruz's robots alone.

'Stay where you are.' The body-bot's voice was hollow and lifeless. 'The authorities have been alerted and will be here shortly. Do not try to resist. If you move, we will have no alternative but to fire.'

Geller was faced with an unpleasant choice: either wait for the police to arrest him, or try to cast a Slip spell before the body-bots could shoot. Capture by the human authorities would spell humiliation for both him *and* his father. Maybe that had been Halpern's plan all along. Looking down at his chest, Geller saw a cluster of red dots where the robots were training their weapons on him. He ran his tongue over dry lips. Maybe he'd get lucky – their weapons could malfunction, or maybe they'd miss. He took a deep breath and flexed his fingers.

The air shimmered and suddenly a hunched figure in black was standing beside Geller. It was the deformed creature from the Pazin Caves. The body-bots opened fire at once, only for their shots to bounce harmlessly off the crystal barrier that appeared down the middle of the skybridge. A Protection spell – and cast quicker than Geller could have believed possible. As Geller looked on in astonishment, the creature waved its deformed hand, almost carelessly, and one of the body-bots went hurtling backwards through the air like a puppet. The robot hit the window with such force it crashed through the reinforced glass and went plummeting down the hundred-storey drop to the plaza below.

The second body-bot responded with a furious burst of fire – Geller hit the deck as the Protection spell was peppered with shots. The sound of gunfire fought for supremacy with the howling wind slicing in through the smashed window. Rain poured inside the skybridge. The creature beside him waved its hand again, and the body-bot let out an electronic scream of distress. Peering through the crystal barrier, Geller saw the robot reel away, its gleaming skin bubbling. It looked as though it was being eaten away from the inside, circuits fusing and metal melting. The body-bot slumped to the ground, sinking into a molten pool of its own remains.

The alarm shut off, replaced by a loud rasping noise that echoed inside Geller's skull. It took him several seconds to realize that it was his own breath. He climbed to his feet to find the creature waiting for him. Its mouth contorted into an ugly leer, which Geller guessed was its version of a smile. As it fixed its black, watery eyes upon him, Geller had the sense of an ancient, overwhelming power.

'You saved me,' he whispered. 'Why?'

'*Spawn* . . .' the creature hissed.

'I don't understand!' Geller said. 'What is spawn? What do you want?'

The creature shuffled along the skybridge until it was standing under Geller's nose, cloaking him in its fetid breath. Moving with unexpected speed, it reached out and clamped its stumps round Geller's hand. White-hot pain seared his palm, as though a nail had been driven through it. Geller screamed, bile flooding into his mouth. He dropped to his knees. The pain was so intense he thought he was going to black out.

Then, without warning, his hand was free. Through the tears in his eyes, Geller looked up and saw that the creature had vanished. He stared in disbelief at the sizzling remains of the second body-bot. His palm was red-raw, his hand shaking uncontrollably. As he picked himself up, Geller could see the blue flashes of the security drones as they hurtled across the skyline of Kuala Lumpur. Fighting to control his trembling hand, he opened a shaky doorway to the Pazin Caves and dived through it.

Geller broke the surface of the lake, spluttering and fighting for breath. The water was shockingly cold, his wizard robes threatening to tangle up his legs and drag him under.

He kicked out, splashing in what he hoped was the direction of the shore. The cavern was utterly black, offering no clue to the way to safety. Just as he was starting to despair, Geller felt his foot graze against rocks, and he was able to find a foothold to steady himself. He waded free from the water's frozen clutches and collapsed on the shoreline.

Thanks to his wounded hand and his eagerness to escape the skybridge, Geller's Slip spell had landed him straight in the underground lake of the Pazin Caves. A few feet further out from the shore, and it might have been a fatal error. Shivering in his soaking robes, Geller tried to cast an Illumination spell to light up his position. But, as he made the gesture with his aching hand, a shape loomed up before him. Geller's mouth dropped open.

It was a robot. In spite of its human-like features, its lifeless eyes gave away that it was definitely *not* human.

Instinctively Geller scrambled backwards on the rocks. Almost as quickly as it had arrived, the mechanical man disappeared, and he found himself staring at a woman in a white lab coat. Looking down at his damaged palm in disbelief, Geller realized that it was projecting images into the air before him.

'Hi, my name is Dr Sara Luring,' said the woman in the lab coat. 'I work here at the Machine Intelligence Lab of the University of Florida.' The camera switched back to the robot. 'And this is Hawking, my robot. We are celebrating today because we've just found out that Hawking has been selected for the final of the Rodin Challenge, which I think you'll agree is fantastic news.'

A slow smile crept across Geller's face. Maybe the mission to Kuala Lumpur hadn't been a total failure after all.

'Say hello, Ada,' he heard the woman say, laughing.

'Hi,' a girl's voice said reluctantly.

'Aren't you going to smile for the camera?'

A teenage girl stared back at Geller. He was used to harsh faces and deformed hands, aloof figures in black cloaks. But Ada was his age, with smooth skin and dark hair that she brushed out of her eyes as she frowned into the camera. Even though she looked uncomfortable, Geller thought that she was startlingly pretty. Ada held up her hand in front of the camera.

'What are you doing, Mom?'

When his father and Halpern had talked about the GAPs scientists, Geller had only thought about the terrible machines they were trying to create. He had never imagined them as real people with families, and daughters with dark hair. Laughing, Dr Luring stopped filming, and the lake fell into silence.

Geller sat still for several minutes, suddenly numb to the icy-wet clothes against his skin. Slowly, tentatively, he cast a Vision spell in search of Ada Luring. In his mind's eye, Geller roamed invisibly through the classrooms and corridors of the University of Florida, following the spell as it sought out his target. Drifting away from the university, Geller was transported through the unfamiliar streets of a city called Gainesville, coming to a halt by the gates beneath a sign that said SCOTT MEMORIAL HIGH SCHOOL. A bell rang, and the doors of the nearest building burst open.

Young people streamed out. Geller peered anxiously through the throng, looking for the girl with the dark hair and serious expression.

Then, suddenly, he saw her. She seemed to move out of step with the other students, lost in some secret thought. Holding his breath, Geller followed Ada as she walked into Gainesville. She stopped at a florist's and bought a bouquet of white lilies, which she took to the local cemetery. At a grave marked 'Robert Peter Luring', Ada kneeled and laid the flowers by the tombstone. She bowed her head, and Geller could see her lips moving. When she straightened up again, her eyes were glistening.

Geller felt something rising up from deep within himself, a surging power of some mysterious nature that he could not identify or explain. It was a power that belonged to him and him alone, elevating him from the cold caverns that encompassed his world; a power somehow connected to a girl he had only just seen for the first time, and had never spoken so much as a word to.

As Ada wiped her eyes on her sleeve, a dark shadow fell across her.

'Pretty girl.'

Geller sprang to his feet. 'Father!'

The waters of the lake seemed to flinch. Cavelos stood behind him on the rocky shore, his face expressionless as he watched Ada dry her eyes.

'How did you find me?' Geller asked.

'I was told my own son had been lost during a raid,' Cavelos murmured. 'Did you not think I would seek you out? As it transpired, I did not even have to leave the caves. Halpern and the others will be surprised, I think.' He nodded at Ada. 'Who is she?'

'Her name is Ada,' Geller replied. 'Her mother is Dr Sara Luring – her robot, Hawking, has made the final of the Rodin Challenge. I think she may be the scientist we are looking for.'

He half expected his father to laugh with disbelief, or grow angry at his presumption. But Cavelos merely nodded.

'I was told your mission was a failure.'

'It was,' Geller said. 'As far as Halpern knew. When we broke into the skybridge and Kevin Cruz turned out to be a hologram, he abandoned me. But then this . . . thing appeared from nowhere and saved me from the body-bots. It put something in my palm – when I tried to cast a spell, it triggered some kind of message from Dr Luring. But I didn't see it until after I got back to the caves, I swear!'

Cavelos frowned as he inspected Geller's left hand.

'Describe the creature that saved you,' he said.

'It was very old,' Geller said quickly, 'and very ugly. It moved like all its bones had been broken. But it had these horrible black eyes that seemed to look right inside me, and it cast the strongest spells I've ever seen.'

'Incredible!' Cavelos gasped.

'What is it, Father?' asked Geller.

'The creature you describe is no "thing", Geller. It is the Malum!'

He stared at Cavelos in astonishment. 'But Halpern said the Malum was a myth!'

'Halpern has not read the scrolls I have. While he rubs shoulders with humans, I have studied the arcane histories of wizardry. There can be no denying the truth of your description. The Malum dwells deep underground, far below even the Pazin Caves. Such is his power, he can take the form of one or a hundred identical wizards. An entire army of wizards, Geller! With them at our beck and call, we could smash the iron knights to smithereens.'

'But if the Malum is so powerful, Father,' Geller said hesitantly, 'why has he waited all these centuries to appear?'

'Does that matter now?' Cavelos's eyes shone with excitement. 'He is abroad, Geller – and you are the only wizard to witness him! Do you know what this means?'

'I don't know what any of this means!' Geller replied, bewildered. 'What does he want with me?'

'That is the question, my son. Did he say anything to you?'

'Just one word,' Geller replied. 'Over and over again: spawn.'

'That was it? Nothing else?'

He shook his head.

'Tell me again what happened. Tell me what you saw.'

'I can try,' Geller said uncertainly. 'What do you want to know?'

There was a glint in Cavelos's eyes. 'Everything,' he said.

11: The Brood

2052
Pazin Caves, Croatia

The Biding Cave was sinking into darkness, its green clouds evaporating as the sleeping wizards roused themselves from the Suspension spells. One by one, they lowered themselves to the cavern floor, where they huddled like rooks: old and stooped, with rheumy eyes and crooked skeletons beneath their black robes. Yet, for all their physical infirmities, their awakening had unleashed a crackling of ancient power that made the vast dimensions of the Biding Cave seem somehow inadequate. Spell rings glinted, the air thick with the meshed syllables of Murmeln.

From his vantage point on a rocky ledge jutting out over the cavern, Geller felt a tremor of excitement run through him as he watched the wizards stir. For the first time in over half a millennium, the entire brood had been summoned to wake – and it was all because of him. His father stood beside him, his hand resting on Geller's shoulder. Geller's chest swelled with pride. Below them, a small group of wizards stood apart from the rest: Halpern and his cohorts, hanging back in the jaws of a cave filled with stalactites. As Geller looked on, Halpern's glinting eyes searched up through the gloom towards him, his fingers stroking his beard to a fine point.

Before their gazes could meet, the final wizard reached the ground, evaporating the last wisp of glowing green light and plunging the Biding Cave into night. Cavelos waited, his breath forming pale clouds in the air as the expectant murmur grew beneath them. Finally he strode to the edge of the outcrop and raised his hands. Fizzing sparks erupted from his spell ring, falling in a brilliant golden rain on the wizards below.

'Welcome, brothers!' Cavelos called out, his voice resonating round the rocky walls. 'Many years have passed since our last gathering.'

'Too many, Elder Cavelos,' an ancient wizard replied, in a voice whittled thin by the passing centuries. 'To be Suspended for this long is little better than death.'

'I agree, brother Angrom,' replied Cavelos. 'Yet we needed to conserve our strength until we could put a face to our enemy.'

'And is that moment upon us?' Angrom asked eagerly.

'I believe so. Tidings of great moment have been delivered to me that I would share with all of you – tidings delivered by my son, Geller.'

As Geller stepped forward into the iridescent light, he had the satisfaction of seeing Nath and Rief exchange a horrified glance. Halpern nodded grimly, while Drahe glowered with open hatred. Geller didn't care – they couldn't touch him now, not with his father beside him. Cavelos opened a Slip spell down to the cavern floor and Geller accompanied him through the portal. The wakened wizards shuffled closer, inspecting him through failing eyes, hungrily flexing their deformed fingers.

'He is young,' Angrom whispered. 'A babe in arms.'

'Yet the blood of the Elder flows through him,' Cavelos replied steadfastly. 'I sent our strongest wizards on a raid to learn the name of our enemy, but they failed, claiming that Geller had been taken by the humans. But instead here he stands before us, bearing the crucial knowledge we need.'

Halpern hurried forward, pushing through the wizards to stand at their head.

'This is news indeed, Elder,' he said. 'No doubt all our brothers are delighted at Geller's safe return. How, pray, did he come by this information?'

Geller grinned. 'The Malum showed me,' he said.

A feeble cry went up from the wizards, ancient throats straining with croaks of amazement. Halpern laughed with disbelief.

'That is impossible!' he said. 'The Malum is a myth. Must we stand here and listen to a child's fairy tales?'

'Do you call my son a liar?' Cavelos's voice was deathly quiet.

'What must I call him, to deny what he says? Have him summon forth the Malum again, and I will bow to them both. But I cannot just accept the boy's word upon this matter.'

'The Malum comes at no one's bidding, Halpern. But Geller can show you the scientist we must eliminate – whose name you failed so spectacularly to retrieve yourself. Cast another Vision spell, my son, and show us the Lurings.'

Geller looked up to see Cavelos waiting expectantly. Taking a deep breath, he stepped forward and opened a Vision spell in search of Ada. Bright, antiseptic light poured through the hole he had created; on the other side, Ada sat at a table inside a laboratory, surrounded by flickering screens. She leaned forward, arms folded, gnawing on her lip as she considered a chessboard in front of her.

'We're going to have to find a new game to play,' she said glumly. 'I'm getting tired of having my ass kicked.'

Geller carefully enlarged the Vision spell to reveal her opponent at the other side of the table. A sea of hisses rose up from the depths of the Biding Cave. It was Hawking, the giant mechanical man – the vision of whom had terrified Geller down at the underground lake. He loomed over Ada, his human-like features impassive as she moved a piece.

'My apologies, Ada,' Hawking said. 'Although, now I am beginning to understand this game, I am finding it most engrossing.'

At the sound of the robot's electronic tones, Angrom let out a wail of woe. Geller was plunged back into his Suspension dreams, the clammy shadow of his metal nightmares falling over him once more as he stared at Hawking. It was only the sight of Ada that kept him from shutting off his spell.

'Behold!' Cavelos declared. 'The face of our enemy reveals itself. It is learning to think beyond the confines of the human brain; in its unnatural movements, I see the iron knights that tore the Book of the Apocalypse from our grasp. This is the robot we must destroy, and the scientist responsible for its unnatural existence.'

Frail voices rose in agreement, only to lapse into sullen silence as, inside the laboratory, a screen slid to one side and Dr Luring appeared. As Hawking pushed a piece across the board towards her king, Ada glanced over at her mother.

'What's up, Mom?'

'That was Kevin Cruz on the Lab COMMS,' Dr Luring replied. 'There was an attack on the GAPs Tower last night.'

'What kind of attack?'

'Looks like some sort of failed kidnapping. Kevin thinks it may be related to the Rodin Challenge. GAPs have been worried about HI-AG agents infiltrating their organization for years. He's warning all the finalists to take care.'

Ada rolled her eyes. 'Thanks for the heads-up, Kev. Who'd have thought HI-AG might be a problem?'

'It's not funny, Ada.' Dr Luring slumped down on to a stool and removed her smart glasses, massaging the skin beneath her eyes. 'First a drone follows you home, then HI-AG appear on campus, now this. I don't know . . . maybe I should withdraw from the competition.'

'Are you kidding me?' Ada swivelled round in her chair. 'You can't give in to these losers now, Mom. Look how close you are to winning this thing! No one's going to be able to match Hawking.'

Back in the Biding Cave, Cavelos turned to Halpern. 'HI-AG?'

'A group of humans who protest against the development of robots,' Halpern told him. 'It would appear they are taking the blame for our raid.'

'Humans?' Cavelos snorted. 'How are they explaining the fact you vanished into thin air?'

'Does it matter? So long as they have no idea of our existence.'

United in simmering hatred, the wizards watched as Ada tipped over her king in defeat and shook Hawking's hand. Geller's moment of triumph had evaporated, the consequences of what he had done only now becoming clear to him. He had been so desperate to please his father, he hadn't considered what he might be exposing Ada to – what would she think if she could see the malevolent audience that spied on her now?

A chorus of reedy, ailing voices grew around Geller, chanting simple words of evil intent: 'die', 'kill', 'all must die'. Even when the Lurings began to shut down their screens and Geller closed the Vision spell, the air bristled with threats.

'The enemy has revealed itself, brothers,' Cavelos declared. 'The time to strike is upon us. Tonight Halpern will lead a new raid, this time on the city of Gainesville. Come the morning there will be no trace of Dr Luring or her monstrous mechanical offspring.'

Halpern bowed. 'And the girl?'

'Whatever it takes to ensure complete success,' Cavelos replied. 'I will not tolerate another failure.'

'No!'

The word flew out from Geller's mouth before he could stop it. The wizards drew back, startled. Cavelos shot him a black look.

'It appears I am not the only wizard with an interest in human matters,' Halpern said lightly. 'Although Geller seems interested in one human in particular. Perhaps it would be wise if he stayed here this time, rather than risk jeopardizing a second raid.'

'You're a liar!' Geller's face was hot with anger. 'It wasn't my fault the raid on GAPs failed. *You* were the one who got your information wrong. That's why you tried to stop me from escaping, so I'd take the blame. Only the Malum saved me.'

The Biding Cave rang to the sound of Halpern's incredulous laughter. 'Is it not incredible, the power of this boy's imagination?' he said mockingly, appealing to the other wizards. 'Go on, Geller, tell us another tale of make-believe for our entertainment, this time with elves and dragons and – aah!'

There was a sickening crack, and Halpern cried out with pain. He hunched over, clutching his left hand.

'My fingers!' he shrieked. 'You go too far, Cavelos!'

His knuckles had popped out from their joints, fingers bending at unnatural angles. The Elder's hand was still raised in the air, a further spell ready at his fingertips. A shocked murmur rippled through the assembled wizards.

'What choice do you leave me, Halpern?' Cavelos replied. 'You have spent so much time on the surface you have forgotten the ways of the wizards, the respect that should be afforded to the Elder and his bloodline. Think on that, as you reset the bones in your fingers. You will be ready for the raid?'

'Count on it,' Halpern rasped. He slunk away out of the Biding Cave, still clutching his shattered hand. After a brief hesitation, Rief, Nath and Drahe hurried after him. In the aftermath of Cavelos's assault, there was a palpable air of consternation – to attack another wizard's spell-casting hand was the most grievous insult imaginable. The remaining wizards huddled together, talking rapidly in low tones and warily eyeing Geller.

'Come with me,' Cavelos said abruptly.

He opened a Slip spell through to his study – when Geller stepped through the portal after him, the Illumination buds inside the chamber darkened to a violent purple. His father snapped the spell shut, rounding on him.

'*Never* question me in front of the others again,' he said. 'Or I will put you in a Suspension spell from which I guarantee you will not awaken.'

'Halpern's going to kill Ada!' Geller protested.

'You saw the girl helping her mother in the laboratory. Even if we eradicated Dr Luring and the mechanical man, who is to say Ada will not carry on her work?'

'But she's just a girl!'

'Exactly, Geller! A human girl, whom you have never even met. What should it matter to you whether she lives or dies?'

Geller folded his arms. 'We shouldn't kill people just because we can.'

'The iron knights slaughtered hundreds at Predjama in a matter of minutes! Think of it not as a life taken but a thousand saved. The rise of the robots must be stopped, my son.'

'Then lead the raid yourself and take me with you,' Geller said boldly. 'You warned me yourself: Halpern can't be trusted.'

'Halpern knows the surface better than anyone, and his hatred of the mechanical men is second to none,' Cavelos replied. 'I can trust him to take care of the Lurings at least. Halpern's obsession with the humans has blinded him to the fact that the real power lies here in these caves. The Malum is abroad, Geller. You will stay with me and help me find him.'

'I don't care about the stupid Malum!' Geller cried. 'We have to –'

Cavelos raised his hand and Geller went flying backwards through the air, slamming into a bookcase. It felt as though an invisible hand was pressing down on his ribs, pinning him to the wall and kneading the air from his lungs.

'Father . . . !' he gasped. 'Can't . . . breathe . . .'

The Elder crossed the chamber and stood before him. A gloved hand reached up and grasped Geller's face, turning it from side to side. As Geller fought for breath, his father studied him without a flicker of emotion in his eyes.

'The more I look at you,' Cavelos mused, 'the more I see your mother. Mara was nothing more than a serf when I found her, ignorant as a farm animal, her hands red-raw from scrubbing pots and pans in the castle kitchens. And yet I gave her the honour of carrying my child. I had such high hopes for you, Geller! But, almost from the moment you were born, you have been a disappointment to me. Even now, centuries later, I find myself having to protect you, as though you are still the swaddled babe we carried wailing out of Predjama. Perhaps I should find you a kitchen to work in; perhaps you would be of more use labouring at the stove than with a spell ring upon your finger.'

Geller tried to speak, but all that emerged from his mouth was a feeble gurgle. Black spots exploded in front of his eyes. Cavelos gazed at him for what felt like an age before turning away abruptly – the spell broke around Geller, sending him crashing to the floor where he curled up into a ball, taking in shuddering gulps of air. As he lay wheezing, Cavelos sat down at his desk and began studying a manuscript.

'Leave this place now,' he said, without looking up. 'When the raid departs for the surface, we will begin our search for the Malum.'

Geller forced himself to rise, pulling himself up by a bookcase shelf. As he left the study, stumbling over rocks and blinking back tears, he could feel something hardening inside his chest, like a cold block of iron. The wizards had lost themselves in the darkness of the Pazin Caves; they thought Geller was weak because he hesitated to take a human life. But as he slunk away from his father's study, his lungs still burning in his chest, Geller decided he would show them – Halpern *and* his father.

He would show them how strong he really was.

12: The Blind Brother

1502
Abbaye Saint-Jacques, France

High up in the French mountains, a bell was tolling midnight. As it struck for the twelfth and final time, the air shifted in the middle of a wood above the snowline, and a figure appeared. Kaku moved slowly and stiffly, his limbs encased in ice. He craned his neck, examining the trees around him, barely able to believe what he saw. His sensors were telling him the year was 1502. He had done it. He had travelled through time.

After the ashen stench of Rio's ruins, the Alpine air was unbelievably cold and pure. Steam rose up from Kaku's body as the coating of ice began to melt. He checked his COMMS-Link and heard only a faint hissing noise. CERN was a millennium and a half away – if he couldn't generate another time-jump, Kaku faced a very long and lonely wait until the future became the present.

His limbs shed their icy casing as he strode through the

forest, leaving a trail of sizzling footprints in the pristine snow. His sudden appearance had brought unwanted attention: scanning the trees, Kaku's visual sensors picked out several pairs of glinting eyes. Wolves. They kept their distance as they padded through the snow after him, unnerved by the robot's lack of scent. Kaku was relieved. He had the firepower to deal with the pack if they attacked, but the report of his antimatter gun would alert the whole mountain to his presence.

He came to the edge of the trees and saw that he had reached his destination. The Abbaye Saint-Jacques stood on a steep crag overlooking a mountain pass, a cluster of buildings behind steep stone walls. Kaku could make out the chapel and a great hall with towers rising up into the night sky like giant stone fingers. He switched to infrared visual sensors, and the buildings came alive with bright red shapes. Most of the monks were resting in their rooms in the towers above the great hall, although a handful still paced the hallways. More shapes were moving in an outbuilding by the castle wall – horses, sheltering in the stable.

Satisfied Kaku wasn't a threat, the wolves retreated growling into the wood. The robot strode out from the trees, quickly covering the short distance to the abbey. He made his way round the perimeter to the outer wall of the stable and climbed it, his powerful fingers biting into the stone and finding purchase where a human could not. At the top of the wall, Kaku dropped down on the other side, landing with a squelch in a mixture of snow and mud. A horse whinnied softly in the stables. The abbey slumbered in the darkness, a single light burning in a window on the second floor. Zooming in, Kaku saw a monk sitting at a reading desk, surrounded by parchment. That had to be the library. Kaku's processing unit was piecing together a schematic of the abbey, trying to pin down where he could locate Gauer the scribe.

Keeping to the perimeter wall, he edged round the courtyard until he reached a side door leading into the abbey. Kaku opened it and stepped inside, a sharp draught slicing across the flagstones to greet him. According to his sensors, the corridor was clear all the way to the hall. Kaku was going to have to be very careful to stay out of sight. A single glimpse of him would cause mass panic inside the monastery. It was five hundred years before the first robot would be built – the monks would think he was a creation of the Devil. And, unlike Angelis's rogue SSR team, Kaku could not just kill anybody who got in his way.

He strode along the corridor, aware of his footsteps ringing out in the silence. As he passed an alcove, Kaku glimpsed a book lying open on a reading stand beneath a stained-glass window. He paused, then ducked through the low doorway. Picking up the book, he turned the pages as carefully as if they were butterfly wings. It was a medieval Bible, written in Latin. He had never seen a more beautiful book. Analysing the penmanship, he came up with a match to the manuscript he had read in his library in 3019. Gauer was here all right.

Lost in admiration, the robot was startled when his aural sensors picked up the sound of footsteps approaching. He replaced the book and drew back into the alcove, his red indicator light glowing in the darkness. A line of monks filed past in the corridor, their heads bowed. They were making for the chapel, presumably to say their midnight prayers. Kaku shook his head, knowing he was lucky to stay undetected – he could not allow himself to be distracted again.

When the corridor fell silent, Kaku emerged from the alcove. Using his infrared scanners to monitor the now-deserted towers, he tracked a solitary figure walking slowly out of the library and into the room directly above it. Natural quarters for a scribe; worth investigating. Sonorous chants swirled up from the chapel as Kaku followed the figure up the staircase. He passed the entrance to the library without a glance, worried what further temptations might lie within.

On the next floor, Kaku pushed open a door and found himself looking inside a small, cold room. There was no furniture save for a bed and a shelf of books. Moonlight poured in through a narrow window. An old man was lying in bed, a wooden stick resting against the wall by his hand. When Kaku stepped inside the room, the old man's head snapped upwards, revealing two milky white pools where his irises should have been. He was blind.

'Who is it?' he croaked. 'Do not try to pretend you're not there. I could hear you creeping up the stairs. Name yourself, sir!'

Kaku ran the man's speech through his lexicon database until he found a match. Medieval French, with the trace of a foreign accent.

'I am Kaku,' he replied in the same language. 'I have travelled many miles in search of a man who lives in this abbey.'

'The hour is past midnight. It is no time for visitors.'

'My quest is of the utmost urgency,' Kaku told him. 'I am looking for a scribe named Gauer.'

The old man barked with laughter. 'Then look no further, Kaku the Stranger. I am Gauer. Tell me, what brings you to my room in the middle of the night?'

'A manuscript,' Kaku replied. 'Telling the tale of the siege of Predjama Castle.'

The old man hissed, shrinking back in his bed. 'What dark magic is this?' he wheezed. 'The manuscript of which you speak is secret. I have not shared it with a living soul. No one shall see it until I die!'

'I have seen it,' Kaku said firmly. 'I know that you were the only survivor of the attack on Lord Erazem's fortress. I wish to learn more about it.'

Gauer didn't reply. He cocked his head.

'What is it?' said Kaku. 'Do you hear something?'

'It is what I do not hear that troubles me,' the scribe replied. 'My eyes no longer see, but my ears can hear a snowflake fall upon the stable roof. You are silent. I cannot hear you breathe.'

The old man snatched up his wooden stick and swung it at Kaku, catching him off-guard. The stick hit his chest with a loud clunk. Gauer dropped his stick and let out a moan of fear.

'The iron knights!' he wailed. 'At last you have found me! Lord have mercy upon my soul!'

'You are wrong,' Kaku told the old man quickly. 'Please, do not alarm yourself. I cannot harm you.'

It was a good thing that the rest of the monks were down in the chapel praying, out of earshot of Gauer's cries. The old man fell silent, his hands trembling as he reached out and touched Kaku's arm.

'But you are not flesh and blood,' he whispered. 'How can I trust you?'

'I am different from the iron knights of which you speak. They have fallen under some kind of terrible spell. I am trying to stop them.'

'Hah!' The old man's face creased with scorn. 'If the wizards cannot stop those devils, what makes you think you can?'

'Wizards?' repeated Kaku, puzzled. 'There is no such thing.'

Gauer gave him a toothy grin. 'Oh, isn't there now? Maybe you don't know everything after all, Kaku the Stranger. There has been magic on earth since the earliest days of humankind. But wizards prefer to keep themselves hidden, shying away from the pages of history. There was one such wizard at Predjama named Cavelos. He was an advisor to Lord Erazem, and he cast Protection spells around the castle that repelled the enemy's siege engines.'

'I cannot believe this is true,' Kaku said steadfastly. 'I

have studied human history for many centuries, and I have never come across evidence of real magic or the existence of wizards.'

'Which is exactly how they wanted it. They do not share their secrets with any humans.'

'So how do you know of them?'

The old man laughed. 'How do you think?'

Kaku paused to consider the question. 'You are also a wizard,' he said finally.

Wheezing, the old man adjusted the ring on his finger and held out his hand. A small flame danced into life on his palm. 'Correct, Kaku the Stranger – although not a very powerful one, I confess. My skills with the quill outdid my skills with the casting ring, and I concentrated my energies on becoming a scribe. Cavelos, my son, was a different matter. He is a very great wizard. Perhaps too powerful for his own good.'

Kaku stared at the flame dwindling on Gauer's palm, his processing unit struggling to make sense of what he was witnessing.

'If this is true,' he said slowly, 'if magic truly does exist, then the world is not as I had thought it. This wizard, Cavelos – was he the reason the iron knights attacked Predjama?'

Gauer shook his head. 'It was the *book* – the Book of the Apocalypse. The key to the secrets of magic, written in Murmeln, the language of wizardry.'

Kaku crouched down beside the scribe. 'Tell me more,' he urged. 'Tell me what happened at Predjama.'

'The Emperor's men were attacking the castle when the iron knights arrived,' said Gauer. 'Five of them, tall as trees and clad in rusting armour. They shrugged off swords and arrows as though they were twigs, killing anyone who crossed their path. When they began to climb the castle walls, I took my apprentice Matthias to Erazem's library, where we found Cavelos, his consort Mara and their baby. Cavelos planned to take the Book of the Apocalypse and escape from the castle, but the knights tracked us down. In desperation, I gave the book to Matthias and showed him a secret passage into the mountain.'

Kaku leaned forward. 'And then?'

Gauer let out a deep sigh. 'When the knight attacked me, I thought my time had come, but Cavelos saved me. He cast a powerful spell that stunned the knight. Together with Mara and the baby, we headed into the mountain after Matthias. It did not take long for us to find him. His body was lying on the floor of the passageway, the Book of the Apocalypse by his side – or at least what was left of it. The book had been burned beyond repair.'

'They destroyed it? Why? Did they not want to learn the secrets of magic for themselves?'

'You tell me, Kaku the Stranger,' Gauer replied. 'The minds of mechanical men are beyond my comprehension. All I know is, whatever their reasons, they were willing to slaughter two whole armies to do it.'

'I have tracked these iron knights from the beginning of their journey,' Kaku said. 'They have travelled further than you can possibly imagine.'

'Cavelos was furious when he found out what they had done,' Gauer told him. 'He turned on me, cursing me in the foulest tongue. If Mara hadn't begged for my life, I truly believe he would have killed his own father. Instead, he banished me to the surface, while he disappeared into the earth with Mara and his child. It was night by the time I emerged from the tunnels, but I didn't stop running. I travelled for days upon end, convinced that the iron knights would chase me down. Finally, exhausted, I collapsed outside the gates of this abbey. The brothers here brought me inside, and I have never left.'

Straightening up, Kaku went to the window and looked out over the snowy mountain pass. 'I came here seeking answers,' he said. 'But I only have more questions.'

'Such is often the way, on the path to enlightenment,' Gauer replied. 'We may be fashioned from different material, but I sense that we are kindred spirits, you and I. Let me share another secret with you.' The scribe leaned forward in his bed. 'There was a copy!'

Kaku turned back from the window. 'There is another Book of the Apocalypse?'

'Made with my own hand, secretly copied out in Erazem's library at night.'

'You did not tell Cavelos?'

Gauer laughed. 'He would have killed me if I had! It was an act of sacrilege: there can only be one Book of the Apocalypse. But it was such a mysterious, beautiful thing; I could not bear that there was only one of it. Perhaps you might understand that.'

'I have seen your work,' Kaku told him. 'You are more than a scribe. You are an artist.'

The scribe smiled faintly, nodding with satisfaction.

'Where is this copy now?' the robot pressed. 'Is it in the library? I must know what lies inside it. I must know the secret the iron knights were so determined to destroy.'

'I do not have it. I gave it to Cavelos's son, the last of the wizards.'

'The baby?'

'I feared that Cavelos's thirst for power was so great he could not be trusted with the book. So I hid it in a place beyond even his reach, where in time his boy would be able to retrieve it. I shared the book's secret with his mother, Mara. She loved Cavelos, but she too could see the danger of his ambition. She promised that, when the boy was old enough, she would point him in the right direction. What greater gift could he be given? Look.'

Gauer reached up to the shelf above his bed and pulled down a book. Opening it at the last page, he took out a piece of parchment and handed it to Kaku.

'The final page of the Book of the Apocalypse,' he said reverently. 'I had to copy it out time and again until I finally got it right. The runes are different to Murmeln, more complex. It is as though the author changed language for the final page.'

In the tower above the chapel, the bell tolled a single time, marking one o'clock. But Kaku didn't hear it. He stared at the parchment scrap Gauer had handed to him, his circuits furiously trying to work out how it could be possible. For the scribe was right – this piece wasn't written in a wizard tongue, even if there was such a thing. It was written in Quanta.

The language of the robots.

13: Knight to King 4

2052
Scott Memorial High School, Gainesville, Florida, USA

A tiny hovercraft rose up towards the ceiling of the high school gymnasium, narrowly missing the flashing electronic sign announcing the 'Scott Memorial Science Fair 2052' as it buzzed through the air. The bleachers had been retracted for the night, basketball hoops folded away into the walls. Rows of booths had been set up across the gym, one for every student who had entered the Science Fair. Parents and teachers wandered the aisles admiring the projects, a crackle of anticipation in the air as the judges began circling the room.

All around her, Ada could see cool projects and bright ideas. There were working dioramas of volcanoes spitting tiny flames into the air, a glowing hologram model of the solar system and kaleidoscope projectors bathing the walls with brilliant colours. Ada's booth looked empty in comparison: just a chessboard and robotic arm, a holo-screen and Kipp. But that wasn't what was troubling her right now.

She craned her neck and scanned the crowd. It was 7:55 p.m. Her mom was late. According to Castle, Dr Luring hadn't left the Machine Intelligence Lab since 6:12 a.m. that morning, but, despite leaving three messages, Ada hadn't heard anything back. Her mom must have switched off her Lab COMMS again. Nothing was more important than Hawking, Ada thought bitterly. Not even her own daughter.

'Don't worry, Ada.' Kipp waddled over to her side. 'Dr Luring will be here soon.'

Ada sighed. 'No, she won't.'

'But she promised she would come.'

'Promising is easy, Kipp. It's *doing* that's the hard part. I was dumb to even think that she'd make it.'

'Maybe something happened at the lab.'

'Or maybe she's just too busy with Hawking to care,' Ada muttered. 'Dad would have come. He never let me down.'

'Hey, stranger.'

Ada blinked. Han was leaning against the counter of her booth. He looked the same as he always did – baggy clothes, trademark designer glasses and a messy hairstyle that Ada knew took him ages in the mirror to perfect. It took her a second to register that it actually was Han, and not some holo-Han sent over by his friends as a practical joke. Aside from the occasional 'hey' in the hall or the canteen, they hadn't spoken since the break-up.

'Hi,' she managed.

'How are you doing, Kipp?' Han called out. 'Not falling over too much?'

'I'm doing my best!' Kipp replied brightly. 'Thank you, Han.'

He fidgeted with his glasses, a sign she knew meant that he was nervous. '*Sooooo* . . .' he said, 'I thought I might see you at the lake house.'

'Oh,' said Ada, caught off guard. 'I didn't think . . . the party seemed like a big deal and I only heard at the last minute . . . and I had to get ready for this, so . . .'

'I missed you.'

He said it so quietly she almost didn't catch it. She'd spent weeks dreaming up clever things to say in case she and Han spoke again, but they'd been wiped clean from her brain. She was flustered, could feel her cheeks reddening. It was almost unfair – why had Han picked now, of all moments, to come over and talk to her?

'I saw the pictures on R8,' she said pointedly. 'You looked like you were having an OK time to me.'

Han glanced up at her. 'It was your idea to break up, Ada. Not mine.'

'I know.'

He paused. 'You remember when we went up to the lake house together, just you and me? I can still hear you screaming when you jumped in the water.'

'I didn't jump,' Ada said, her mouth twitching with a smile. 'You pushed me, remember?'

'I had fun that day,' Han said. 'I had fun a lot of days with you.'

'Me too. I'm sorry the fun had to end.'

'Jeez, Ada, your dad died!' Han sighed in exasperation. 'Ada, I wanted to be there for you.'

'And do what? He died, and that was that. There was nothing anyone can do. I've spent eight months wondering if I'd ever talk to you again, but now you're here and all I can think about are the things I've been trying to forget. Can you understand that?'

Han nodded. 'I'm trying to,' he said. 'Anyway, I just wanted to say hi. Catch you around, I guess.'

He thrust his hands in his pockets and slouched away down the aisle, sidestepping Mr Pirelli as the physics teacher bustled towards Ada's booth. The judges were coming. Ada took a deep breath, putting Han's look of resignation to the back of her mind. She ran over to her holo-screen and turned it on with a swipe.

'And this is Ada Luring, one of our strongest students,' Mr Pirelli said proudly. He was a short, middle-aged man with thinning hair, and her favourite teacher in the school. The judges smiled at Ada, who grinned back, trying to banish all thoughts of Han from her mind.

'Please tell us about your project, Miss Luring,' said the lead judge, a grey-haired lady holding a tablet.

'My project is a game,' Ada said, slipping into the speech she had rehearsed in her head. 'A chess game, against Spartak, the ultimate grandmaster chess program. And I'm going to beat it. Well, technically, I'm not going to beat it. My robot Kipp is.'

As the judges cast an appraising eye over Kipp, he

snapped to attention, almost toppling over in the process. The grey-haired lady made a note on her tablet. 'And how does he propose to do that?'

'With the program I've created, we can tap into the power of CERN and use the supercomputer to drastically enhance Kipp's processing power and tactical awareness.'

'CERN?' cut in Mr Pirelli. 'The particle accelerator in Switzerland?'

Ada nodded.

'Well, this should be fascinating,' he said. 'Please proceed.'

Kipp hopped up into a chair beside the chessboard, facing the robotic arm. Ada booted up Spartak's challenge program and displayed the board as a projection on the back of the booth. When she was sure Kipp was ready, Ada took a deep breath and started to run her program. Through the robotic arm, Spartak moved a white pawn forward. Ada's program initiated contact with CERN, and suddenly the levels on her holo-screen rocketed upwards.

Kipp moved a black knight out beyond the row of pawns.

As the game progressed, word must have spread through the gym, as a small crowd began to gather round Ada's booth. She kept careful watch on the levels on the holo-screen – too much power from CERN would overwhelm Kipp's system. But she couldn't resist allowing a little surge, and watching as her robot attacked Spartak's defences and captured a white bishop. Ada risked a glance at the judges and saw one of them nod, impressed.

Behind the judge's shoulder, a light flashed. Ada blinked

and caught sight of a head of cropped blonde hair. A pair of glittering blue eyes gazed at her. As Ada stared in astonishment at Lili Parker, the reporter lifted the pendant camera from around her neck and took another picture.

There was a loud clatter, followed by a groan of disappointment from the crowd. Turning back to the chess game, Ada saw to her dismay that the levels on her screen had gone haywire. Kipp had been overwhelmed by the power surge, knocking the pieces from the table all over the floor and stretching to save the black queen. Swiping shut her holo-pad, Ada ran over and caught the robot just before he fell off his chair. Chess pieces lay scattered around the booth like fallen soldiers.

'I couldn't do it, Ada,' Kipp said miserably. 'I tried to control it, but there was too much power. I'm sorry.'

'Hey, it's OK!' she said. 'It was my fault, not yours.'

She looked up to find that the crowd was drifting away; Lili had vanished. Ada hurried over to the judges, who had already finished making their notes.

'That was unfortunate, Miss Luring,' the lead judge said sympathetically, tucking her tablet under her arm. 'For a moment there, I thought you were going to do it.'

'I still can!' Ada tried desperately. 'Just let me put the pieces back and restart the game –'

She trailed off as the judges moved on to the next booth. Slumping into a chair, Ada covered her face with her hands and groaned.

'Well,' Mr Pirelli said brightly. 'That was . . . interesting.'

'That was a *disaster*,' lamented Ada.

'A fairly accurate summation,' Mr Pirelli agreed. He smiled. 'On the other hand, failure is an integral part of the scientific process. Not even Einstein got it right first time.'

He winked, and went after the judges. Ada got down on her hands and knees, and began picking up chess pieces. Maybe it was a good thing her mom hadn't showed up after all. What would everyone think if the daughter of Dr Sara Luring couldn't even program a robot to win a measly game of chess? It was all Lili's fault. The reporter had no right to be there, sneaking around, taking photos and distracting people. What did the Science Fair have to do with the HI-AG demonstration anyway?

She stood up and marched out of the booth.

'Wait!' Kipp called out. 'Where are you going?'

Ada ignored him, elbowing her way through the crowded aisles. To her left, the judges were admiring a diorama; the air was filled with bursts of applause, electrical bleeps and whirring noises. But, when Ada turned the corner into the next row of booths, the gym seemed to fall quiet. Lili Parker was standing directly in front of her beneath the hologram of the solar system, the planets revolving round the blazing sun in a ghostly glow. As the crowd shifted around her, Ada suddenly realized that the reporter wasn't alone. Her hand was on a girl's shoulder, who was pointing up to the planets.

The girl was Kit Somers.

Examining the two of them now, Ada couldn't believe she hadn't seen the family resemblance sooner: mother and daughter shared the same cold beauty, the same maddening half-smile and sense of superiority. Their last names were different, but maybe Lili had kept her maiden name for work, and Kit was named after her dad. Or maybe Lili had just lied about it. She *was* a reporter after all.

Kit slipped her arm through her mom's, pulling her along the aisle to another demonstration. Ducking out of sight, Ada returned to her booth and pulled out her phone.

'OK, Lili Parker,' she said under her breath. 'Let's see who you really are.'

She typed the reporter's name into a search engine, and got a page full of hits, most of them links to articles Lili had written. It appeared she had worked for newspapers the length and breadth of the country: from Alaska to Iowa, Pennsylvania to New Mexico. But it was the story at the bottom of the page that drew Ada's eye. It was dated five years previously, from a local newspaper in South Carolina:

CROWDS REMEMBER LOCAL CAMPAIGNER

Mourners gathered at Charleston Cemetery for the funeral of Kenneth Somers, following his death in a traffic accident last Friday. Mr Somers, 39, was the chapter head of the South Carolina branch of HI-AG and a vociferous opponent of developments in AI technology. He lost control of his vehicle on the highway outside of Jacksonboro, when the windshield was struck by a malfunctioning sec-drone.

Beneath the article there was a photograph of the mourners. Lili and Kit stood at the graveside, flanked by mourners dressed in black. Ada stared at it in disbelief.

'What is it?' said Kipp.

'Kit's dad was a member of HI-AG!'

Kipp looked puzzled. 'What does that mean?'

'It means you need to start packing up. We're getting outta here.'

Ada left her robot carefully putting away her computer and ran through the gymnasium in search of Pri. She found her friend by one of the other booths, gazing into space as her father Dev inspected the volcano diorama.

'Do you think there's any chance that volcano might actually explode?' Pri mused. 'Being covered in ash and molten lava's got to be better than standing here pretending to be interested while my dad lets his Inner Nerd out. He's *so* embarrassing . . . hey!'

Ada grabbed Pri by the arm and dragged her behind the stand to the retractable bleachers.

'What's the big emergency?' said Pri. 'You look like your head is about to explode!'

'Have you seen Kit's mom?'

'I know, talk about glamorous. Still, she is Kit's mom so, like, duh!'

Ada thrust the newspaper story in front of her friend. 'That's not all she is.'

Pri scrolled down through the report. '*Okaaaay*,' she said.

'That's all you've got to say? You know what HI-AG is, right?'

'A fitness workout?'

'Pri!'

'I'm kidding, I'm kidding!' Pri said defensively. 'My mom might not be some brainiac scientist like yours, but I'm not *completely* stupid, you know. HI-AG are those guys who think we shouldn't build any more robots.'

'Right. So don't you think it's a bit of a coincidence that Kit's mom is hanging around the university campus at the exact same time my mom is finishing work on Hawking?'

Pri laughed. 'You can't be serious.'

Ada's voice dropped to a whisper. 'The other day an unmarked drone followed me home, and then Lili Parker magically turned up outside my mom's lab and started asking a ton of questions about HI-AG and free speech. I think *she* was the one behind the drone.'

'Back up for a minute,' Pri said. 'You think Kit and her mom moved to Gainesville so that they could spy on your family?'

'Yes!'

Pri sighed and handed Ada her phone back. 'I get it, OK? You don't like Kit. I thought maybe you two might become friends, but I was wrong. But that doesn't mean you have to make up some big conspiracy theory about Kit's mom, Ada. That's not cool.'

'Conspiracy theory?' Ada stared at her. 'You don't believe me?'

'Of course I don't believe you! You sound like a crazy person!'

Ada laughed bitterly. 'I don't know why I tried to tell you about this. Ever since Kit arrived, you've changed.'

'Want to know the truth, Ada?' Pri said angrily. '*You* changed, not me. I know you went through hell when your dad died, but now all you want to do is sit in front of your computer. That might be fun for you, but it isn't for me – I want to go shopping and hang out at the mall and check out cute boys. So does Kit, and that's why we're friends. Not everyone's like you, Ada. Not everyone cares about robots.'

'So I have to be interested in hair and make-up for us to be friends now?'

'No, but maybe you need to stop turning your nose up at anything that doesn't take a physics PhD to understand.'

'Maybe *you* need to check out a library for once instead of the mall,' Ada retorted. 'Then I wouldn't have to spend all my time explaining stuff to you.'

'Go find a robot to hang out with then,' Pri said sharply. 'If I'm too stupid for you.'

Ada watched her friend march back to her dad, fighting the urge to throw her phone against the wall. The night had turned into a complete disaster – her mom hadn't bothered to show up, she'd messed things up with Han again, her project failed and now she'd fallen out with her best friend. Was there any way she could make things worse?

She trudged back to her booth to find that Kipp had managed to replace the chess pieces to their last positions. But, instead of playing, the robot was huddled in the corner of the booth, standing protectively over the rest of Ada's things. The reason for his concern was standing at the front of the booth, inspecting the chessboard.

'Just what I need,' Ada said sourly. 'What do you want?'

Lili Parker didn't look up from the board. 'Knight to king four.'

'What?'

'Your next move. Knight to king four. It puts white in all kinds of trouble.'

'Thanks for the advice.'

'The human brain – the most reliable piece of technology there is. Maybe you should tell your mom that. I did some checking, and I'm not sure she's a doctor of ancient civilizations at all. Precisely the opposite, in fact.'

'You're not the only one who can use a search engine,' Ada retorted. 'I know exactly who you are, too, Ms Parker. You didn't get a tip-off about the HI-AG demonstration – you knew it was going to happen. Hell, you probably helped them plan it.'

'HI-AG had legitimate concerns that needed to be voiced,' Lili said coolly. 'If the scientific community won't take responsibility for the risks they are taking, they need to be shown the error of their ways.'

'By attacking university departments and stalking me and my mom?'

'You need to stop before anyone gets hurt. You don't understand the technology you're meddling with.'

'Really,' Ada said sarcastically. 'You think you know more about robots than my mom?'

'Maybe not about circuits and programming,' Lili

137

replied. 'But when it comes to the damage these machines can do, the harm they can cause, I know more than you ever will. Which is why you need to listen to me.'

'Thanks for the advice. We'll bear it in mind.'

'I wish you would. I wish your mother was here so I could talk to her, too.' She looked round the gym. 'But I guess she couldn't make your demonstration. It's a shame – all the other parents are here. Was Dr Luring too busy with her robot?'

Shooting Lili a look of pure hatred, Ada grabbed Kipp and her things and hurried out of the gym.

14: Alarms

2052
Gainesville, Florida, USA

'Slow down, Ada!' cried Kipp.

They sped through deserted streets beneath an unbroken black strip of night. Using the sec-drone patrol routes that Ada had secretly downloaded from the Gainesville Police Department's system, her bike's security block was able to plot an unmonitored path through the streets. Dark zones suited her mood perfectly. She had reprogrammed the security block, disabling the speed limiter and adding nano-turbines to give her some serious – and seriously illegal – acceleration. All she needed now was the right place to use them.

When she reached the Apollo Corp industrial park, Ada turned off the road, bouncing over the ground and slipping in through the gap in the railings. The factories and warehouses stretched out into the shadows, dormant solar panels giving off a dull gleam. She pedalled as fast as she could, trying to outrun all the things that were eating at her: unmarked drones and Lili Parker . . . her crumbling friendship with Pri . . . her mom's obsession with Hawking and the Rodin Challenge . . . Ada wanted to leave all of them trailing in her dust.

'Hang on, Kipp!'

She guided her bike in between two warehouses and found herself looking down a long strip of tarmac. Ada hit the nano-turbines. The force of the acceleration snatched the breath from her lungs, and she had to cling on to the handlebars as the bike shot forward. The warehouse walls melted into a blur.

'Ada, no!' Kipp shouted.

As the bike hurtled towards the end of the row, Ada guided it to a loading ramp and took off, exploding up into the air. For a few glorious seconds, she was airborne, weightless. Then the bike hit the ground – hard. Ada fought to keep the vehicle upright, the impact of landing jarring her wrists. Blue sparks flew up from the tarmac as she slammed on the brakes, battling the nano-turbines until they slowly ran out.

She pulled up, her breathless laughter ringing out around the industrial park. Brushing her hair out of her eyes, Ada twisted round in the seat. A trail of tyre marks was scorched across the tarmac behind her.

'Are you OK, Kipp?'

'I think so,' the robot replied groggily. 'Are you?'

'I don't know about OK,' she said. 'But better, yeah.'

She rode back through the gap in the railings and headed home. Her security block switched to standard night-mode procedure, bathing her bike in a rotating sphere of blue light that rolled clockwise from top to bottom. From the seat, it was like looking out through deep ocean water. Ada freewheeled down the hill before sweeping into her road, past the identical houses and their neat green rectangles of lawn. When she reached her house, she steered her bike up the driveway and hit the brakes. Her helmet reformed into a hoodie as she climbed off the bike and shut down the security block. Kipp followed slowly behind her.

The front door clicked open at the touch of her hand, recognizing her. The holo-lights in the hall had been dimmed, the house still.

'I'm home!'

There was no reply. Ada kicked off her shoes and wandered through into the living room. The table was covered in robot blueprints and takeout cartons as usual, but there was no sign of her mom.

'Castle?' Ada called out. 'Is Mom home yet?'

'Good evening, Ada,' the house AI replied. 'Sara Luring is currently at the Machine Intelligence Laboratory at the University of Florida.'

'Fine,' Ada muttered. 'She can stay there, for all I care.'

'Did the Science Fair go well?' Castle enquired.

'Not really.'

'I am sorry to hear that.'

Ada trudged upstairs to her room and collapsed on to her bed. She lay on her back, staring up at the white ceiling. There was a series of soft thuds on the stairs, and then Kipp appeared in the doorway.

'I don't like seeing you so sad, Ada. What can I do to make things better?'

'Can you go back in time and stop me being an idiot?'

He shook his head.

'Then nothing,' she said, pressing a pillow over her face with a groan.

A high-pitched bleeping noise went off around the house. Ada sat bolt upright, throwing her pillow to one side. It was the house alarm.

'Castle?' she called out. 'What is it?'

'Sensors indicate –'

The lights in the bedroom went out, and both Castle and the alarm fell silent. A prickle of unease ran down Ada's neck.

'Indicate what, Castle?' she said. 'What's wrong?'

Silence.

Ada went over to the window. The lights were still working in all the other houses down the street. Even if there had been a power outage, Castle had a reserve power supply in case of emergencies. If the house computer detected a system error, it would automatically reboot itself. It never just stopped working.

Kipp joined her at the window. 'Ada, why is Castle not responding?' he asked.

'I don't know,' Ada replied. 'But I don't like it.'

She found herself wishing that, just this once, her mom had come home at a normal time. Castle's main interface panel was downstairs – she could try to manually reboot the computer from there, and hopefully it would come back online. Ada moved quickly and quietly out of her bedroom, Kipp sticking closely behind her. As she crept down the stairs through the slanting shadows, it felt as though the house itself was holding its breath. At a small sound she froze, gesturing at Kipp to do the same. She waited.

And heard a soft footfall in the hallway.

There was someone else in the house with her, trying very hard not to be heard.

Geller crouched in the branches of a gnarled oak tree by the house next door to the Lurings, hidden from view behind a soft fringe of Spanish moss. The sky darkened as the neighbourhood settled down for the night. Car doors slammed and screen doors banged shut. Dogs barked to be let inside. The scent of flowers carried on the warm breeze.

Geller felt almost dizzy with his own daring. He had waited until Halpern's raid left for the surface before seeking out a distant cave out of sight of the rest of the wizards. If Cavelos wanted to scour the underground network for signs of the Malum, he could do it on his own. Opening a small window in the darkness, Geller had Slipped out of the Pazin Caves to within sight of Ada's house.

His heart racing, he had scrambled up into the branches of the tree, scanning the street for signs of magical activity. Damaged fingers or not, Halpern was still a formidable wizard, and he would not be alone. If they found Geller, he would be dragged in front of the other wizards for punishment. Cavelos wouldn't be able to save him even if he wanted to. Geller could be placed in Suspension, banished, or maybe even worse. Yet there was no way he could just abandon Ada to Halpern and his cronies.

As Geller stared out over the street, a loud meow in his ear made him jump. He whirled round, almost toppling out of the tree. A ginger tabby cat was perched on top of the nearby garage, staring at him inquisitively.

'Shhhh!' Geller pleaded, pressing a finger to his lips. The tabby arched its back and let out an angry hiss. Geller hurriedly cast a low-power Suspension spell, and watched as the cat's eyes drooped shut and it slumped on the garage roof, fast asleep.

He turned back in time to see a bike bathed in a bright blue orb come swooping down the street towards him. The breath caught in Geller's throat. A dark-haired girl cycled past his hiding place and turned into the driveway of the Luring house. It was Ada. There were spots of colour in her cheeks, but her expression was preoccupied, troubled even. To Geller, the shadows only made her look even more beautiful. In one breathless moment, he realized the inadequacy of the Vision spell, what a shallow picture it painted when compared with the real thing. At once he felt a power rising within him; it was as if he was stronger, the possibilities of his spells increasing.

Turning off the blue orb, Ada jumped from her bike and then she and a small dog-like figure disappeared inside the house. Geller checked that the coast was clear before shinning down the oak tree. He ran across the lawn and leaped over the wall, his cloak billowing out behind him.

Landing softly on a path running round the side of the Luring house, he dropped into a crouch beneath an open window. He opened a Vision spell and watched Ada walking around inside her house. She was talking with a disembodied electronic voice, which Geller guessed was some kind of invisible computer inside the building. There was no sign of Sara Luring, but for all Geller knew she could be heading home that moment – with Halpern and the other wizards behind her. He had to get inside, and quickly, but the raid on the GAPs Tower had taught him to be wary of human security systems.

Adjusting his ring, he cast a Control spell, seeking out the computer Ada had been talking with. He had never tried to control a computer before, and initially he was baffled by the electronic pulsing of its processor. Yet, as he probed its cold, artificial mind, to his surprise Geller found that he could exert his will over it as easily as a human's. Ordering the computer to turn off its security system, Geller gave a satisfied grin and climbed in through the open window.

A piercing alarm shrieked into life, sending him toppling into the house.

Geller forced the computer to shut down completely, plunging the house into darkness. The wizard mouthed a Murmeln curse under his breath. So much for not drawing attention to himself. He crept through the living room into the hallway, a Damage spell tingling at the tips of his fingers. At the bottom of the stairs, he peered up into the gloom.

'Protect the queen!'

There was a metallic gleam in the darkness, and something came hurtling down the stairs at Geller. He released his spell.

'Kipp, no!'

Ada's voice, from the top of the steps. Distracted, Geller missed the ignition of his Damage spell, which drifted harmlessly into a wall. His attacker crashed into his belly, knocking the wind from his lungs and sending him stumbling back into the wall. He fought back, shoving his assailant away to the floor with a crash. Footsteps flew down the stairs and a second figure jumped on top of him. They toppled to the ground, entwined. A fist caught him a glancing blow on the temple – wincing, Geller rolled his attacker over and pinned them to the ground.

And found himself face to face with Ada Luring.

She opened her mouth to scream. In desperation, Geller cast a light Control spell on Ada to keep her quiet. Her throat muscles twitched, but no sound came out. Geller's fingers were burning – controlling Ada and the house computer at the same time was testing his power to the limit.

'I am going to let go now,' he told her. 'I'm not here to hurt you, I promise. Please don't scream.'

Ada nodded quickly, her eyes wide with alarm. Geller released her wrists and got to his feet before lowering the Control spell. She let out a shuddering breath and rolled over, coughing.

'Take anything you want,' she croaked. 'Just don't hurt Kipp.'

'Who?' said Geller.

He realized she was referring to the first attacker, who was still lying on his back, desperately trying to right himself. Kipp, Geller noted with a slight shudder, was a robot. Ada crawled over and wrapped a protective arm round him.

'You don't have to worry,' Geller told her, holding out his palms in a reassuring gesture. 'My name is Geller and I only want to talk to you.'

Ada rubbed her throat. 'I tried to scream but nothing came out,' she said. 'How did you do that?'

Geller took a deep breath. 'I used a Control spell.'

'A spell?'

'Yes.'

'You're a magician.'

'A wizard.'

She shifted slowly away from him until the wall was at her back, her eyes flicking towards the front door.

'If you think this is funny, you've got it totally wrong,' she told him.

'I know it isn't funny. I'm serious.'

'Why were you creeping around my house in the dark?'

'I told you, I wanted to talk to you!'

Geller rubbed the back of his neck in frustration. His first meeting with a human girl wasn't turning out at all as he had hoped. He thought Ada would be grateful that he had come to help her, but all he had done was frighten her and now she didn't believe a word he was saying. Halpern and the others could swoop in on them any minute, and Geller's fingers were already burning from casting so many spells in quick succession.

'We're running out of time,' he said, a note of desperation creeping into his voice. 'I must speak with Dr Sara Luring. Will you tell me where she is?'

Ada's eyes narrowed with suspicion. 'What do you want with my mom?'

'To save her life!' Geller exclaimed. 'Unless you start listening to me, she's going to die. And so are you.'

15: Blackspot

2052
Gainesville, Florida, USA

Ada stared at Geller.

'What do you mean, we're going to die?' she said.

'There are others like me,' he explained. 'Wizards. They're coming to destroy Hawking and kill you and your mother.'

'How do you know about Hawking? Mom's project is secret.'

'I've been watching you at the laboratory,' he confessed. 'Through a spell. All of the wizards have seen you working on the robot.'

Ada should have laughed in his face, or maybe screamed for help. First this weird-looking boy had broken into her house and told her he was a wizard – which was of course *impossible* – and now he was telling her that people were going to kill her.

Geller's eyes flicked between her and Kipp, waiting to see how they would react. His face was thin, framed with unkempt black hair that reached down to his shoulders, his skin so pale his veins were almost visible. But there was nothing weak or fragile about him. He was *different*.

Ada shook her head. 'None of this makes any sense,' she said. 'Why would anyone want to hurt Mom?'

'The wizards believe that the winner of the Rodin Challenge will be the first true robot,' Geller told her. 'All other mechanical men will follow after him, including those that wage war and kill humans. They think that destroying Hawking will help them regain the power they have lost.'

She wasn't sure which was scarier: the absolute conviction with which he spoke, or the fact that she believed him. Geller's story may have sounded crazy, but hadn't he also shut down her vocal cords without touching her? And how did he know about Hawking? Ada could feel Kipp trembling in her lap and her head was filled with frantic warnings – *don't listen to him, he's crazy, a complete whack job; he broke into your home and attacked you; he thinks he's a WIZARD for Chrissakes!* But something about Geller, his simple sincerity, made Ada feel strangely reassured that he meant her no harm. And, if there was only the slightest chance that what he was saying was true, she had to make certain.

'OK,' she said. 'You can speak to Mom. But I need to talk to Castle first.'

Geller looked confused. 'Who's Castle?'

'The house computer. You're the one who shut it down, right?'

'Oh right! Let me release it.'

Geller made a gesture with his hand, and gradually the lights inside the house came back up. It was a pretty smart trick, however he was doing it.

'System back online,' Castle announced. 'Unauthorized intruder remains on the premises. Shall I call the police, Ada?'

'Not yet,' she said, pointedly eyeing Geller. 'Can you call Mom? Use the emergency code if you have to.'

'The Lab COMMS at the University of Florida have been disabled,' Castle reported. 'I have no way of reaching Dr Luring.'

'Disabled?' Ada looked at Geller. 'Did you do that, too?'

He shook his head quickly. 'I don't even know what a Lab COMMS is,' he said.

'Then I guess we'd better go see Mom in person.' Ada ran over to the hallway, slipped on her shoes and put her hoodie on. 'Come on, Kipp!'

The robot waddled after her, keeping as far away from Geller as possible.

'Shall I alert the authorities that there is a problem at the university?' Castle asked.

'And tell them what?' Ada replied. 'Mom's Lab COMMS isn't working and I'm worried because a wizard's told me she's in danger? Let me see what's going on over there – if I see anything I don't like, I can call Gainesville PD myself. In the meantime, keep trying Mom!'

'Understood. Take care, Ada.'

Ada was halfway out of the door when a thought struck

her. She put her palm on Geller's chest, stopping him in his tracks.

'Hold on,' she said. 'How do I know that this isn't a trap? You tell me Mom's in danger, so I lead you straight to her. If these friends of yours are so keen to kill her, what are you doing here warning me?'

Geller thought for a second. 'They're not my friends,' he said. 'Halpern, Drahe, even my father . . . they think I'm weak because I'm not like them. They don't know me, and they don't know you either.'

'And you do, do you?'

She thought she saw Geller flush slightly in the gloom. 'I think there might be things we have in common,' he said. 'Things we could share.'

His reply, hesitant and almost embarrassed, caught Ada off guard. Looking at Geller's face now – with its open, almost hopeful expression – she wondered whether he was even capable of lying.

'OK,' she said, removing her palm from his chest. 'Guess that'll have to do for now. But, if I find out this is all some elaborate practical joke, you're in big trouble.'

She marched out into the driveway and activated the security block on her bike.

'Kipp will ride with me,' she told Geller, climbing into the seat. 'But you can borrow my dad's bike. It's in the garage.'

Flicking her hoodie over her head, Ada looked back and saw the wizard still standing in the doorway, an uncertain expression on his face.

'Bike?' he repeated.

'You know, two-wheeled vehicle with pedals?' Ada rolled her eyes. 'Tell me you know how to ride a bike.'

'I'm a wizard,' Geller said. 'I don't need to.'

'But how are we supposed to get to the lab if you can't ride?'

'There are other ways.'

'Like what?'

A ghost of a smile crossed Geller's face. He held out his hand. 'Trust me,' he said. 'My way is faster.'

It was only a matter of three or four steps. Keeping a firm grip on Kipp's hand, Ada walked forward through the portal Geller had created and emerged into a quiet square on campus. But in those few paces everything changed. Everything that she had thought possible was turned upside down in an instant, her old life left behind her, like the house still visible through Geller's spell. Ada gazed around at the university buildings, unable to believe her eyes. The sheer scale of what had just happened had left her speechless.

Geller followed her through the portal, closing it up with a simple gesture. She stared at him, spots of bright colour in her cheeks.

'How. Did. You. Do. That?'

Geller shrugged. 'I told you,' he said simply. 'I'm a wizard.'

Questions were exploding like fireworks inside Ada's brain. Part of her was still desperate to deny what had just happened, to work out a logical explanation for it. Perhaps Geller had hypnotized her, and she had been in a trance for the whole journey. But, if that was the case, how had she been able to glimpse her home through a shimmering window in the air behind her?

'This is unbelievable,' she said finally.

'I know it must seem strange to you.'

'*Strange?*' She could hear the hysterical edge to her voice. 'That's one word for it. I thought you were downright crazy. But if you're telling the truth about this then my mom . . .'

Geller nodded. 'We should go.'

Ada led them through the deserted square, the automated lighting staying dark as they hurried towards Dr Luring's lab. Disorientated by the Slip spell, Kipp was struggling to keep up. There was a loud squawk and a thump of plastic against metal – Ada turned round to see the little robot lying prone in a flower bed.

'Kipp?' she said. 'Are you all right?'

The robot groaned. 'I think I banged my head.'

He was lying in the dirt beside a damaged sec-drone, its belly ripped open, exposing sinews of torn wiring. Ada hauled the dazed Kipp to his feet and checked he was OK before kneeling down to examine the machine.

'What happened?' said Geller, glancing up into the air. 'Did that thing just fall out of the sky?'

'Hard to say,' Ada replied. 'Sec-drones don't usually crash. If I had to guess, I'd say something jammed its signal.' She straightened up. 'Mom's lab is just round the corner. She'll be able to explain it.'

They turned left at the entrance to the College of Medicine, cutting down a walkway that led to the Department for Ancient Civilizations. But, at the sight of a second sec-drone lying on the pavement, Ada skidded to a halt.

'I'm guessing that's not a coincidence,' Geller said.

'The lighting sensors aren't working either,' Kipp piped up. 'This path shouldn't be dark.'

Geller frowned. 'What does this all mean?'

'Let's see.' Ada began ticking off her fingers. 'Lights out. Lab COMMS down. Sec-drones jammed.' She slowly circled round, scanning the darkened campus buildings. 'They're creating a blackspot.'

'What is that?'

'An area where there are no electronic communications. A kind of bubble of silence. So you can't call for help.'

Geller frowned. 'Are you sure, Ada? Wizards don't care about Lab COMMS or sec-drones. We can Slip in and out of places.'

'Well, *somebody* went to a whole lot of trouble to make sure they wouldn't be seen. And if it wasn't your guys then it must have been . . .' Ada's jaw tightened. 'HI-AG. Of course. That's why Lili Parker was acting so smug at the Science Fair: she *knew* that my mom wasn't going to be there!'

'Wait, slow down. Who is Lili Parker?'

'A reporter with links to HI-AG, a pressure group who hate robots,' Ada explained. 'Kinda like your wizard pals, but without the magic powers.'

'I know who HI-AG are,' Geller said quickly. 'Are they trying to stop your mother building Hawking, too?'

'They would be if they knew where she worked, but they think her lab is still in the Engineering Department on the other side of campus.'

'Lili Parker doesn't,' Kipp said. 'She saw you coming out of the Department for Ancient Civilizations, remember?'

Ada swore and started running down the walkway, aware of Geller matching her stride for stride. They entered the next square together, the Department for Ancient Civilizations looming out of the darkness. Through the line of trees, Ada could make out several figures creeping towards the building. She went to cry out, only for Geller to pull her back and press a finger to his lips.

'Allow me,' he said.

He made a gesture with his hand, and a fine mist drifted out from the ring on his finger. When it reached the figures in the trees, they stopped in their tracks. Ada's eyes widened.

'What did you do?'

'I Held them,' Geller told her. 'They won't move again until I release them.'

'Awesome!'

'It won't last forever, though,' he warned. 'Better find your mother.'

Ada hurried up the gravel path towards the Department for Ancient Civilizations. The frozen figures were as still as statues, their faces hidden behind cheap robot masks, and they held bolt-cutters and wrenches in their hands.

Ada shook her head. 'Figures,' she said. 'Cowards.'

'What do you think they would have done if they got inside?' Geller asked.

'Knowing HI-AG, take Hawking and chop him up for scrap metal. Do me a favour, leave them here for as long as you can, OK?'

Ada walked up to the front entrance and pressed the buzzer, placing her eye to the retinal scan at the intercom's instruction. The door clicked open with a series of beeps.

The hallways of the Department for Ancient Civilizations were shrouded in dust and darkness, not at all what Geller had been expecting. It certainly didn't look like the kind of place where anyone might build a robot. He rubbed his throbbing hands as he followed Ada and Kipp down the hallway, examining the ancient weapons in their display cases in the hope of finding something he might be able to use against Halpern. A glass cabinet on the wall was coated in dust, obscuring its contents. Geller stopped and wiped it with his sleeve.

A misshapen skull with watery black eyes appeared in the glass, its mouth twisted into a hideous smile. Geller yelped in fright.

'What is it?' Ada called back.

He looked into the cabinet again, and saw only his own reflection staring back at him. The Malum had vanished.

'Nothing,' he said. 'Sorry. I thought I saw something.'

Ada muttered something under her breath, ushering Kipp away to the elevator. When the doors opened on the second floor, Geller found himself looking into the same lab he had seen in his Vision spell. The windows were dark and the overhead lights switched off, the only illumination coming from the ghostly screens flickering in mid-air. A different kind of magic to the spells of the Pazin Caves, but, to Geller's eyes at least, magic all the same.

As Ada stepped out of the elevator, the transparent panels in the air rearranged themselves into a corridor. Dr Sara Luring came hurrying towards them.

'Ada!' she exclaimed. 'I've been trying to contact you all evening, but there's a problem with my Lab COMMS! Something's happened with Hawking that you wouldn't believe –' She stopped, noticing Geller for the first time. 'Who's your friend?'

'This is Geller, Mom,' Ada told her. 'Are you OK?'

'I'm fine. I'm better than fine, in fact. I need to show you something. Just you, Ada,' she added, her eyes warily flicking to Geller. 'Sorry.'

'Mom, you can trust him. He's a bit of an expert on robots, actually.'

'Ada, I don't –'

'Please, Mom. Trust me if nothing else.'

Dr Luring hesitated, then led them over to a screen, turning it on with a swipe of her finger. Peering over Dr Luring's shoulder, Geller found himself looking through a camera into a small room. Hawking was sitting at his chessboard, quickly moving the pieces around the board. Ada leaned closer to the screen, brushing a lock of hair behind her ear. At that moment, Geller thought, she looked a lot like her mother.

'What is he doing?' asked Ada. 'Is he playing Spartak?'

'Not since this morning,' Dr Luring replied. 'Hawking was three moves away from checkmating Spartak when he just . . . stopped. He didn't move for hours, and I thought there had been some kind of circuit malfunction. But then he started doing this.'

As Geller watched, he realized that the robot was laying his black chess pieces out on the board, lining them up to make a shape across the chequered tiles.

'What is that?' he said, curious despite himself.

'I have no idea,' Dr Luring said happily. 'Some kind of symbol or glyph. But it sure ain't chess.'

'I thought you wanted him to play Spartak,' said Ada.

'Don't you see? Hawking's moved *beyond* chess. He's starting to think at a level beyond human intelligence, beyond our comprehension. We're going to win the Rodin Challenge, I know it!'

Ada shook her head. 'That's great, Mom, really happy for you,' she said. 'But I *really* need you to listen to me. We have to get out of here. Right now.'

'Why?'

Ada jerked a thumb at Geller. 'He came to the house with the craziest story, but you've really got to listen to him.'

The screens parted once more, and a tall shadow appeared in the gap between them. Geller paled and took a step back, once again plunged into the terrifying recesses of his nightmares in Suspension. Hawking strode into the laboratory with eerily graceful steps, his face as real and as expressive as a human's.

'Is everything all right, Dr Luring?' he enquired.

'We're fine, Hawking, thank you.'

'There are people standing outside the building,' the robot reported. 'They do not appear to be moving, like pieces on a board. Is this a new game of which I am unaware?'

Ada's mom looked puzzled. 'What people?'

'It's HI-AG,' Ada told her. 'They know you're here; they're the ones who blocked your Lab COMMS.'

'Why aren't they moving?'

'Because Geller put a spell on them, Mom! We can explain, but let's do it somewhere else, please! Forget HI-AG – there are wizards after you!'

'You'll explain right now,' said Dr Luring, folding her arms. 'You expect me to believe this preposterous talk of wizards and spells –'

Geller held his hand up sharply. 'Shhh!'

Dr Luring fell into a startled silence. Geller's skin was tingling, magic sparking at the tips of his fingers. He closed his eyes, straining his ears to hear some kind of telltale noise. But it was as though all sound had sucked from the building, leaving it a vacuum. He swallowed nervously.

'Geller?' said Ada. 'What is it?'

'We're too late,' he whispered. 'They are already here.'

16: First Strike

2052
Machine Intelligence Lab, University of Florida, Gainesville, Florida, USA

As Geller surveyed the laboratory, there was a loud ping behind him. He whirled round, a Damage spell at his fingertips, only to see the triangular light above the elevator flashing and pointing down to the ground floor.

'Uh-oh,' Ada muttered.

'What is it now?' Dr Luring said crossly. 'Ada, who *is* this boy?'

Geller dragged two desks together to form a makeshift barrier, never once taking his eyes off the light above the elevator. As he watched, the flashing triangle flipped round to point upwards.

'They're coming,' he warned.

'Can't you just magic us out of here?' Ada asked him.

'Now hold on a minute!' Dr Luring folded her arms again. 'No one's magicking me *anywhere* until I get an explanation of what's going on here.'

'Later, Mom!' Ada said urgently. 'Is there another way out?'

'There's a service exit, but –'

'Go!' Geller said. 'I'll hold them off as long as I can.'

Ada gave him a dubious look, and then nodded. Grabbing her mother by the arm, she pulled her away, gesturing at Kipp and Hawking to follow her. The two robots obliged, the smaller of the two waddling to keep up with Hawking's sleek, muscular stride. Geller ducked down behind the desks, his eyes fixed on the elevator doors. He had promised Ada he would delay the other wizards, but he had no idea what kind of spells his aching fingers were capable of casting. Still, no going back now. Adjusting his casting ring, Geller aimed a Damage spell at the smooth metal doors.

It seemed to take an eternity for the elevator to arrive at the second floor, the doors opening in slow motion. When the metal shutters finally parted, Geller blinked with surprise. The elevator was empty. He twisted round, ready to call back the Lurings as they hurried for the service exit. A sudden, terrible thought struck him.

'Wait!' Geller cried. 'It's a tr–'

A huge explosion ripped through the Machine Intelligence Lab, lifting Geller off his feet and sending him flying into a filing cabinet. Glass panels shattered, fire engulfing the room. Dimly, Geller heard a loud scream – was it Ada? Alarms wailed for assistance, automatic sprinklers raining down upon the flames. His head swimming, Geller could only watch as Halpern came striding through the choking smoke, cloaked figures scurrying in his wake. At the sight of Geller, Halpern's eyes narrowed.

'You!' he hissed.

Geller threw himself to one side, narrowly missing a Damage spell as it punched a hole through the metal cabinet. He scrabbled behind a desk on his hands and knees, a monitor erupting into flames above his head. In desperation, Geller flung a weak Damage spell in Halpern's direction, but it failed to ignite. With an icy chill, he realized that he was going to die.

A strong hand reached down behind the desk and grabbed him, twisting his arm viciously behind his back and pulling him to his feet. Tears of pain sprang to Geller's eyes.

'Careful,' Rief muttered in his ear. 'You might hurt someone.'

They were all there, Geller saw to his dismay: Rief and the pudgy, grinning Nath, Halpern and the tall figure of Drahe lurking in the shadows behind him. With his ring hand twisted up behind his back, there was nothing Geller could do to fight them off. Halpern picked up a circuit board from a workbench and inspected it under the light of a soft Illumination spell. Dropping the board on to the floor, he smashed it beneath his heel.

'How brittle this mighty technology is,' he murmured. 'I don't know why Cavelos is so scared of his mechanical men. If I had been at Predjama, the Book of the Apocalypse would still belong to the wizards, and we would have spent the last five hundred years living as kings.'

'Say that to my father's face,' Geller said defiantly. 'He will break more than your fingers.'

Halpern nodded, amusement in his eyes. Then he struck Geller across the face with the back of his hand.

'Be silent.'

Geller looked away, his cheek stinging, his mouth hot with blood.

'Your precious father *isn't* here, is he?' jeered Nath. 'There is no one to protect you, whelp. No one to stop Halpern taking you apart bit by bit.'

'I would not waste my magic,' Halpern said dismissively.

'Allow me,' came a deathless voice from behind him.

Drahe stepped forward, rolling up his right sleeve. Geller struggled in Rief's grasp, straining to keep away from the skeletal hand reaching out for his neck. Icy fingers closed on his flesh, and a sickening wave of pain flooded through his body. Geller screamed.

The windows behind him exploded as a bright object crashed into the laboratory like a falling star. Glass sprayed through the air, tables and screens shattering. The force of the impact shook the building's foundations to its core, scattering the wizards. Geller and Drahe went tumbling to the floor, the gaunt wizard cracking his head on the corner of a processor and knocking himself out cold. Shuddering, Geller scrambled free from the wizard's clutches.

In the middle of the devastated laboratory crouched a gleaming figure. Silently it rose to its feet.

A new robot stood before Geller, a full head taller than Sara Luring's creation, which was already an awesome, fear-inspiring presence. This robot's broad chest was covered in glistening ice particles and it had heavy weaponry mounted on its arms. Unlike Hawking, this mechanical man had clearly not been designed to resemble a human in any way, shape or form. Its face was a blank metal plate with a single flashing red light. Slowly turning its head, the robot surveyed the room.

'Abomination!' Halpern yelled. 'Destroy it!'

Nath darted out from behind a screen and hurled a Damage spell at the robot, connecting with its right shoulder and sending it staggering backwards. In response, the robot's arm-mounted guns glowed a deep orange. It took aim at the ceiling above Nath and fired a powerful blast, sending a pile of debris crashing down on the wizard's head.

Geller dragged himself behind a bank of computer screens and drew his knees up to his chest, his body throbbing in pain. He had to get to Ada. With Drahe and Nath neutralized, Halpern and Rief circled the new robot, taking it in turns to hurl Damage spells in an attempt to contain it. But their target was moving too quickly for them, scuttling around the lab on its long metal legs. As Geller risked a glance at the screens, Rief cast a new spell and the robot slowed. The wizard was trying to Hold it. Geller had managed to trap the HI-AG members using the same spell, but they were only humans. Rief paled with the effort, his forehead glistening with sweat as he fought to control the robot.

The arm-mounted guns glowed orange once more, and

the screens around the dark-skinned wizard shattered. Rief ducked out of the way.

'The robot is too strong!' he wailed to Halpern. 'We must retreat!'

'Stand your ground!' Halpern snarled. 'We do not flee this time!'

But, even as he spoke, Rief was retreating towards the elevator. The panicking wizard was making no attempt to protect himself, yet despite the barrage of fire exploding around him he managed to make it to safety unharmed, hammering on the elevator buttons until the doors closed.

'Geller, help!'

At the sound of his name, Geller whirled round and peered through the smoke. Over by the shattered windows an ashen-faced Ada was staring at the giant robot in astonishment. Geller scrambled towards her, keeping low to avoid the shots and spells echoing round the lab. She took him over to the service exit, where he found a fretful Kipp crouching by Ada's mom. Dr Luring was propped up against the wall, her hand pressing a bloody wound in her shoulder. Pieces of burnt and twisted metal surrounded her. Amid the debris, Geller spotted a charred metal torso and a blackened faceplate.

'Hawking . . .' Dr Luring sobbed. 'He's dead!'

'Shhh, Mom!' Ada said, stroking her hair. 'It's OK.' She shot Geller a worried look. 'We need to get her out of here.'

'I can carry her!' Kipp volunteered.

Ada shook her head. 'No, Kipp, you can't.'

'Allow me.'

Geller looked up to see the huge robot standing over him. His deep voice seemed to come from his chest, resonating through the metal and moulded plastic of his body.

'Who are you?' said Ada, a tremble in her voice.

'I am Kaku. You are Ada Luring.'

She stared at him. 'How do you know my name?'

'Now is not the time for explanations. Later, when you are safe.'

'What happened to Halpern?' Geller asked. 'Did you kill him?'

The robot's red light passed coldly over him.

'I did not kill anyone,' he said. 'The final wizard retreated when he realized this was not a battle he could win. But he may return with others, or the authorities may come. We must leave. You are also dressed in the guise of a wizard – are you friend or foe?'

'Geller's a friend,' Ada said quickly. 'He came here to save us.'

Kaku nodded. 'Then he may come with us.'

'Wait a minute,' Geller said quickly. 'Who says I want to come with you? I know what robots like you are capable of. How do I know you won't turn those guns of yours on me?'

'Kaku just saved your life!' Ada replied. 'He saved all of us. We need all the friends we can get right now. Come with us, Geller. Please.'

She reached out and squeezed his arm. Geller nodded reluctantly, aware that he could not leave her at that moment, no matter who she called a friend. Kaku kneeled down and picked up Sara Luring with a surprising gentleness, before throwing the remains of Hawking over the other shoulder. Levelling his guns at the wall, the robot blasted a hole through it. Clanking forward, he ran across the lab.

'Hey, wait!' Ada cried.

Kaku leaped out into the night, a bright gleam in the shadows, plummeting down the two-storey drop before landing in an athletic crouch, Dr Luring and Hawking's remains still safely in his grasp. Ada laughed with disbelief.

'How are we supposed to follow that?' she said.

'The service exit,' Geller replied, taking her hand. 'Come on.'

Together with Kipp, they ran through the smoke and headed down the back stairs, coming out through the fire doors into the square. Shocked faces were watching from windows around the square, cameras pressed against the glass. In the distance, sirens wailed.

An angry shout echoed across the square – Geller whirled round to masked figures marching out of the trees. His Hold spell had worn off. As he forced his aching hands to try to cast another spell, a huge explosion ripped through the Department for Ancient Civilizations, swallowing up the HI-AG agents in a cloud of smoke and flames. Glancing behind him, Geller caught a glimpse of Halpern in the shadows, his face bathed a fiery red as he gazed at the burning building, before Ada dragged him away and they ran for their lives through the darkness.

17: Public Enemies

2052
Santa Fe Swamp, north-east of Gainesville, Florida, USA

In the heart of the Santa Fe Swamp, a creek wound its way through the boggy ground like a black serpent. Ada splashed through the shallow water, her feet snagging on curled tree roots. Kipp laboured behind her, slipping and sliding through the creek. The moon was a white spotlight in the sky, distant sirens blaring out like hunting horns. They'd left Gainesville behind them, several miles to the south-west. Yet Ada's mind was still trapped inside the Machine Intelligence Lab, the moment the explosion had lifted her and her mom from their feet and left Hawking in pieces.

She remembered little about their escape from the campus – a confusion of alarms and flashing lights, people shouting and running and calling for help. The giant robot Kaku led them unerringly through the chaos, cutting through backyards and alleys and selecting only empty streets. Every now and again, he held up his hand and moved back into the shadows, and Ada would catch a glimpse of an emergency vehicle hurtling through the next intersection. Whatever kind of technology Kaku was drawing on, he made sure that nobody saw them.

The robot headed north, shadowing a state road out of Gainesville and making for the line of mangrove trees on the horizon. The last time Ada had visited the Santa Fe Swamp was on a fifth-grade field trip, and in the darkness the insect-ridden groves felt alien and threatening. Geller hovered beside her, his pale face grave with concern. Ada knew he wanted her to say something, anything, but she didn't have the words at that moment. A couple of hours earlier, she would have laughed at the idea that there were even wizards. But now she had seen the destructive power of magic with her own eyes, had felt a building explode around her.

Further along the creek, Kaku's red indicator light flashed in the darkness as he scanned the swamp. The huge robot was still holding Sara Luring above the water, Hawking's head and torso slung over his shoulder. Kaku hadn't spoken a word since the battle at the university. No one had dared to question the robot, or even ask where they were going. Part of Ada wondered whether she should have insisted that they take her mom to the hospital. But it was almost as though Ada was watching herself wade through the creek from somewhere high up in the trees. She wondered whether she was suffering from shock.

The creek twisted to the left, and Ada spotted a wooden

cabin on the bank overlooking the water. Paint peeled from rotten wood, the windows were blinded by dirt and cobwebs. A small dock jutted out into the creek – when Kaku took a giant stride out of the water and placed his foot on the rotten planks, Ada winced, expecting to hear a loud crack. But to her surprise the dock held, and Kaku strode soundlessly over to the cabin door and pushed it open.

'*This* is where he's taking us?' Geller whispered. 'Are you sure this is a good idea?'

'What choice do we have?' Ada said, biting her lip. 'He's got Mom!'

She helped Kipp out of the creek and pulled herself up on to the dock. If anything, the inside of the shack was even more rundown than the outside. It was so low-tech it could have been a museum exhibit. The surfaces were thick with dust, stuffing exploding from the bellies of rotting chairs. Flies buzzed lazily around the ceiling. Ada flicked a light switch, but the bulb above her head stayed dark. The air was muggy and oppressive.

Kaku laid Dr Luring gently down on the sofa and carried Hawking's charred remains through into the next room. Ada kneeled down beside her mom. Sara's forehead glistened with sweat and her skin was deathly pale. Despite the ugly wound on her shoulder, she had barely made a murmur throughout the journey to the cabin.

'Mom,' Ada said. 'For a minute back there, in the lab, I thought . . . we tried to get to you in time, but we weren't quick enough. I'm sorry.'

Her mom reached out and gripped her hand. 'You have

nothing to apologize for, Ada Luring, do you hear me?' she said, in a fierce whisper. 'This is all my fault, my obsession. I wasn't there when you needed me the most, and I am so sorry for that. When your dad died, I just felt so lost . . . I wasn't sure I could ever find my way home again. Can you forgive me?'

Tears were running down Ada's cheeks. She nodded quickly.

'It's OK, Mom,' she managed. 'It's all gonna be OK.'

They hugged then, a hug that Ada had needed desperately without even realizing it. At that moment, no one else in the room – in the world – mattered or even existed. It was just her and her mom. Eventually they pulled apart, laughing at each other as they dried their eyes. Kaku returned from the next room and began to tend to Dr Luring's damaged shoulder, skilfully patching up the wound. Ada's mom stared at the robot as he worked, lost in admiration.

'Look at you,' Dr Luring whispered. 'You're magnificent. I can't begin to conceive of the technology that created you.'

Kaku bowed his head respectfully. 'You are what created me, Dr Luring. You created all of my kind. Your work on Hawking brings about all of the robots.'

Ada's mom closed her eyes. 'Hawking is destroyed.'

'Which means my father and Halpern have won,' Geller said.

Kaku shook his head. 'This is not necessarily true.'

'Hawking's in pieces!' Ada said. 'How can you say that?'

'Because I am still here. If the development of technology had been halted or disabled, I would be erased from existence.'

'Wait a minute.' Ada's mom struggled into a sitting position. 'Where exactly are you saying you come from?'

'My home lies a thousand years into the future,' Kaku said gravely. 'The year 3019.'

Dr Luring stared at him in astonishment. Geller burst out laughing.

'I am not joking.'

'Of course not. You can just travel through time,' replied Geller sarcastically.

'You make it sound simpler than it is, Geller.'

'Even wizards can't do that!'

'I do not know about the limits of magic. But we have technology capable of making time-jumps.'

'Kaku, the implications of what you're saying . . . if this is true . . .' Ada's mom looked overwhelmed. 'This is the most important scientific advance in the history of existence. There is so little of this I understand and I have so many questions. Why here? Why now? Why us?'

'I have travelled back into the past in order to save the future,' Kaku told her. 'Earth is in grave danger.'

'What kind of danger?' asked Ada's mom.

'The planet has succumbed to brutal invasion. It will be destroyed unless I can stop it.'

The robot's words hung heavily in the stale air.

'And I thought it was just me thinking the world was ending,' Ada said quietly.

The cabin fell silent as they struggled to digest what Kaku had told them, an atmosphere of incomprehension and unease taking hold. When her shoulder had been bandaged, Dr Luring got up from the sofa and went through to the bedroom to examine what was left of Hawking. Geller pulled back the moth-eaten curtains from the window, peering out into the swamp.

'Are you sure we are safe here?' he asked.

'For now,' Kaku replied. 'Until we can assess the condition of Dr Luring. The swamp makes it harder for the police to track our electronic trail.'

Geller looked confused. Ada pulled out her phone. 'These devices all give off a signal that the police can trace,' she explained.

'Shouldn't you throw it away then?'

'Maybe,' she said. 'But it's also our only way of seeing what's going on back in Gainesville.' She used her watch to log on to her R8 and let out a low whistle.

'What is it?'

Ada scrolled down her screen. 'My R8 has just *exploded*,' she said. 'I've never seen anything like it. I'm getting hundreds of beats per minute. Everyone's talking about what happened at the Machine Lab.'

'How do they know you were there?'

'People started filming the department building when the fight broke out. We're officially famous.'

Clicking on a newsfeed, Ada watched from a building across the square from the Department for Ancient Civilizations as an explosion punched a hole in the second floor. Kaku leaped out through the smoke, to a chorus of shocked cries and murmurs from the people watching. The robot strode across the square, past the wounded bodies stretched out across the grass. A few seconds elapsed, and then the camera zoomed in on Ada as she emerged with Geller from the rear of the building. The picture froze on a close-up of her face, an old school photo flashing up alongside beneath Ada's name. No wonder her R8 was going crazy.

'They are making us look like criminals!' Geller protested. 'Can't they see that *we* were the ones being attacked?'

'It gets worse,' Ada said grimly. 'They're saying two people died in the square during the explosions. I guess they must have been from HI-AG. Hold on a minute.'

She checked HI-AG's R8 and clicked on their latest video upload. Lili Parker was being interviewed by reporters on campus, standing in front of a police holo-cordon.

'This tragedy is the inevitable result of unauthorized and dangerous experiments with artificial intelligence,' she declared. 'Five years ago I lost my husband to an out-of-control robot – how many more innocent people must die before we realize that every machine is a potential killer? Tonight the HI-AG organization has suffered casualties of a war started by scientists like Sara Luring, who care more about machines than human beings. I *demand* that the police track down this metal murderer and its accomplices and bring them all to justice!'

Lili's voice echoed round the cabin. Ada paused the feed

and closed her phone. 'They're blaming you,' she told Kaku.

'I am not a murderer,' the robot replied calmly. 'It was the wizard who made the building collapse. Robots cannot kill people.'

'Hah!' Startled, Ada saw that Geller's face had reddened with anger. 'What about Predjama Castle? Was it wizards who killed all the people there?'

Kaku shook his head. 'No, it was not.'

'Hundreds of people were slaughtered,' Geller said hoarsely. 'Cut down where they stood, like stalks of wheat. My mother died because of what happened that day. Don't tell me that robots cannot kill people.'

'Your anger is understandable, Geller,' Kaku replied. 'But you should not blame all robots for what happened at Predjama.'

'What are you all talking about?' said Ada, bewildered. 'Pyjama what? What castle?'

'Predjama Castle,' Geller said, staring coldly at Kaku. 'It was my birthplace, a medieval fortress. Robots attacked it and killed everyone inside – it was only thanks to the magic of my father, Cavelos, that we survived. But the sight of the slaughter drove my mother mad. She died soon afterwards.'

'A medieval fortress? Geller, how old are you?'

'I was born the year the castle fell,' he told her, 'in 1489. But I've been asleep in a Suspension spell most of the time since.'

'So let me get this straight . . .' Ada said slowly. 'Kaku is from the year 3019, and you're nearly six hundred years old.' She rubbed her face. 'And I'm officially going crazy.'

'Listen to me, Geller,' Kaku urged. 'Robots are not programmed to attack humans. It is not that they choose not to: they *cannot*. It would be like a human trying to fly or breathe underwater.'

'So who attacked Predjama then? Ghosts?'

'It was an SSR team led by a robot named Angelis. They were trained in search-and-rescue techniques and had devoted their existence to saving human lives, not taking them. But something happened to Angelis and her team that altered their programming and made them able to kill. I believe they have been corrupted by alien forces known as the Spawn, which invaded Earth six months ago.'

At the mention of the word *Spawn*, Geller started. He opened his mouth to say something, then closed it again.

'Wait,' said Ada. She was having to work very hard just to keep up. 'If these Spawn are attacking Earth in the future, why did they send robots back to Predjama?'

'They sought to destroy the Book of the Apocalypse, a powerful volume that contained the secrets of magic within its pages. The SSR team burned it to ashes.'

'Which is how we ended up living in an underground cave,' Geller finished glumly.

'The only logical conclusion is that there was something in the book that the Spawn feared,' Kaku told him. 'Something they feared so much they would send Angelis and the SSR team back a millennium and a half just to destroy it.'

'Do you even have wizards in the future?'

'If there are practitioners of magic, they have kept their existence a secret,' said Kaku. 'The first I learned of the wizards was when I travelled back through time after Angelis to 1502. I spoke with a scribe named Gauer who had survived Predjama. He revealed that he was also a wizard, if one of little power. According to Gauer, there was a copy of the Book of the Apocalypse. He hid it with the son of his own son, Cavelos.' Kaku turned to Geller. 'Which would seem to be you.'

Ada looked at Geller in amazement. The young wizard swallowed. 'There must be a mistake,' he said. 'Gauer must have been lying. There is no copy of the Book of the Apocalypse. Even if there was, I do not have it!'

'You are certain?' Kaku said.

'Of course I am!' Geller said defensively. 'I think I would know if I had the Book of the Apocalypse in my keeping! I've been asleep for over five hundred years in a cave. Apart from my clothes and my spell ring, I do not have a single possession.'

'Wait a minute.' Ada's forehead was creased with thought. 'Something doesn't add up. Kaku, you didn't know that Geller was the baby Gauer was talking about. So why did you come here looking for him?' The answer occurred to her even as she asked the question. 'It wasn't him you were looking for.'

'You are correct,' Kaku said approvingly. 'I did not travel to Gainesville in search of Geller. Gauer showed me the final page from the Book of the Apocalypse, written in a different language which had apparently baffled wizards for centuries. But I could decipher it – it was in Quanta, the language of the robots. As I translated the passage, I came across a name, a name which led me here all the way from the sixteenth century.'

A shiver ran down Ada's spine. 'Whose name?' she said softly.

The robot turned to look at her, uttering a single word. 'Yours.'

18: Future Tense

2052
Santa Fe Swamp, north-east of Gainesville, Florida, USA

'That's impossible!' Geller exclaimed. 'The Book of the Apocalypse has been in the hands of wizards since the dawn of time. It was destroyed in 1489! How can it mention Ada?'

'I cannot explain how it came to pass,' Kaku replied. 'But Ada Luring is named on its final page.'

Ada shook her head. 'There must be another Ada Luring then. Someone important.'

'CERN ran a probability test before sending me from 1502 to 2052. We could not afford to carry out another time-jump unless we were sure. It is you.'

'Then it's a mistake in the book,' Ada said stubbornly. 'Has to be. It was a copy this Gauer showed you, wasn't it? He doesn't even speak Quanta. Maybe they meant Mom, and the symbol for Sara is really similar to Ada.'

'The probability of such an error would make that

extremely unlikely.' There was a note of puzzlement in the robot's voice. 'I do not understand why you are so keen for this to be wrong.'

'Of course you don't understand!' Geller said scornfully. 'You're a robot. You do not care about human feelings.'

'Stop it, Geller!'

He blinked at the sharpness of Ada's tone.

'You're not helping,' she told him. 'I need peace and quiet to try to figure this mess out.'

She slumped into a battered chair and stared up moodily at the ceiling. It felt as though she had been given jigsaw pieces from ten different puzzles and told to put them together. Nothing seemed to fit.

'OK, Kaku,' she said slowly. 'Answer me this. You found this page from the Book of the Apocalypse in 1502, right? But how can anyone know my name hundreds of years before I'm even born? It doesn't make any sense!'

'Only if the book was written then.' Unexpectedly, it was Kipp who answered. He flinched as everyone swivelled to look at him.

'What do you mean, Kipp?' Ada asked.

'Kaku travelled back in time. Maybe someone writes this book in the future and then takes it back to the past with them.'

'An interesting supposition,' Kaku said thoughtfully. 'It would also explain how the final page of the book was written in Quanta. Well done, Kipp.'

Kipp looked bashfully at his feet. 'I've never had a supposition before,' he said.

'If this is true, the entire source of wizard power was written in the future and delivered back to the beginning of civilization,' said Geller. 'Just thinking about it makes my head hurt.'

'Time travel is complex,' Kaku said solemnly.

'Tell me about it,' Ada groaned.

The bedroom door opened and her mom emerged, cleaning her smart glasses on her shirt. The colour had returned to Sara's cheeks, and some of her old purpose with it.

'Kaku?' she said. 'Can you come here, please? I need your help.'

'Is there a problem, Dr Luring?'

'I've examined Hawking, and I'm wondering whether there's a chance his processing circuits may be salvageable.'

'You gotta be kidding me, Mom!' said Ada. 'You're *working*?'

'The whole point of this attack was to destroy Hawking,' her mom shot back. 'If I can save him, don't you think it might be worth a try?'

'It could be the only reason I am still in existence,' Kaku said. 'If Hawking truly is the forefather of all robots. It would be an honour to assist you, Dr Luring.'

He strode into the next room, ducking through the low doorway. Ada shook her head.

'Your mother really cares about Hawking, doesn't she?' Geller said, absent-mindedly massaging his knuckles. 'It's almost like he is real to her.'

'More real than me sometimes,' Ada replied. 'Or at least it feels that way. I'm sorry to hear about your mom.'

Geller nodded. 'I never really knew her,' he said. 'I was only a baby.'

'My dad died last year,' Ada said, almost blurting the words out. 'Maybe it would have been easier if I hadn't known him.'

'I would give anything to have more memories,' Geller said. 'To better know my mother's face, to see her smile. All I have is a lullaby she used to sing to me. And even that was about robots.'

'Sounds like your mom and mine had more in common than I thought,' Ada muttered. 'Mine doesn't shut up about robots either.'

They both smiled.

'This is weird,' Ada said. 'I don't talk about my dad with Mom, or even my best friend. Yet I'm telling you, and you're a complete stranger – not to mention a freaking *wizard*. Hey, you haven't put another spell on me, have you?'

Geller ruefully rubbed his casting hand. 'Don't worry, you are safe,' he said. 'I need time before I can cast again.'

'Time? Why?'

'Magic comes at a cost,' he told her. 'Spell-casting damages fingers, deforms them over time. I have never cast spells as powerful as the ones I did tonight.' He held his hands up to the light. 'Do they look different to you?'

Ada was about to laugh but stopped at the look on Geller's face.

'They look fine,' she said. 'Like normal hands. Do they hurt?'

Geller nodded. 'My bones ache.'

She gingerly took the young wizard's thin hands and clasped them between her own, trying to rub warmth into the cool fingers and knuckles.

'Does that help?' she asked.

He looked away shyly. 'Yes,' he said.

Ada's phone buzzed, making the pair of them jump. She frowned when she checked the screen. 'Why is Kit calling me?'

'Who's Kit?' Geller asked.

'Lili Parker's daughter – who also happens to go to my school.'

'Don't answer it!'

'She's using an emergency code. It must be serious if she's calling me – I don't think she even likes me.' Ada received the call. 'Hello?'

'Ada, thank God!' Kit sounded hysterical. 'I'm so worried!'

'Hey, it's OK – calm down!' Ada said. 'What is it?'

'It's Pri!' said Kit. 'I'm worried something's happened to her. I've been trying to get hold of her all night, but she's not replying.'

'She's probably just asleep, Kit. It's pretty late.'

'She's not at home, Ada. Her dad called me, asking me if I'd seen her. He's really worried. And the worst thing is I think I know what's happened to her!'

'What do you mean?'

There was a long pause on the line. 'After the fight on the campus, and those protesters dying, my mom got really mad,' Kit said quietly. 'She asked me whether Pri would know where you were, and when I said she wouldn't know anything she started yelling and stormed out of the house. I've never seen Mom like that.'

Ada paused. 'Is this a joke, Kit? Because it's not funny.'

'Ada, you have to believe me. Please! I know I haven't been a good friend to you. I haven't even been nice to you. I'm so sorry.' Kit gasped and her voice cracked. 'I've got no one else to turn to.'

Ada's blood ran cold as Kit cried on the other end of the phone. 'Don't worry about that now. You really think she's got Pri?'

'You don't understand how much she hates robots, Ada.' Kit gulped. 'She blames them for my dad's death and will do anything to stop them. I'm scared for Pri, but I can't tell the cops. I know you don't like her, but it's my *mom*, Ada!'

'Don't worry about it,' Ada said, trying to sound calmer than she felt. 'I'll take care of this. It'll be OK.'

'I'm sorry!'

'It's not your fault,' Ada said reassuringly. 'Pri will be all right, I promise.'

She hung up the phone. Kit was always so cool and collected. Her panic made Ada's skin crawl and her gut twist with fear for Pri. There was no time to lose. She crept over to the door to the next room, peering through the crack. Her mom and Kaku were hunched over Hawking, completely absorbed in their work. Ada turned back to find Geller watching her curiously.

'What was that all about?'

185

'Nothing,' Ada said quickly. 'Come on, Kipp.'

'It wasn't nothing,' Geller said. 'Where are you going?'

Ada was already in the cabin doorway. 'This place is too stuffy – I need some air. I won't be long.'

'Are you insane?'

'Shhhh!' Ada's eyes flicked back to the next room. 'I have to go somewhere, all right? My friend's in trouble, and I don't have time to get a permission slip from my mom. So either help me or get out of my way.'

Geller weighed up his options.

'So be it,' he said finally.

The cabin had barely vanished from view before Geller began to regret his decision. What was he thinking? There were all kinds of powerful forces after them – wizards, the human authorities, maybe even the rogue mechanical men Kaku had talked about. And then there were the Spawn. Geller couldn't believe it when the robot had mentioned their name, echoing the word the Malum had hissed at him over and over again. But why did the Malum care about what happened to Earth a thousand years into the future, when according to Kaku there weren't even any wizards left? The sheer scale of everything made Geller's brain hurt. There was also the added complication of Ada: her dark, serious gaze, her quiet sorrow; the touch of her hands around his own. Now she was striding purposefully back through the swamp towards Gainesville, Kipp hurrying along behind her. What if Halpern returned with even more wizards? What if this time Cavelos came with him?

'This is a really bad idea,' Geller told Ada.

'You said that already,' she replied. 'About ten or eleven times. Go back to the cabin if you're scared.'

'What happens if this is a trap? All you've got is Kit's word for it, and you know who her father was. You should have at least told Kaku.'

Ada gave him a sideways glance. 'I thought you hated robots.'

'I don't trust them. But I think Kaku wants to protect you, and the way he fought Halpern and the others earlier . . .' He shook his head. 'It's like having an army standing by your side.'

'Seriously, Geller, the last thing I need right now is an army,' Ada said. 'Enough people have died tonight already. Everybody in Gainesville is looking out for a ten-foot robot – if Kaku takes one step outside this swamp, we'll have sec-drones on us in a flash. He's better off in the cabin with Mom. We'll go back as soon as I know that Pri's safe. They'll be so busy working on Hawking, they probably won't even notice we've gone.'

'You can't really think that is true.'

'I don't expect you to understand,' said Ada. 'How could you? You've spent your whole life underground. Pri is my *best friend* – that means something, something important. I can't just sit around if she's in trouble.'

'Right,' Geller said. 'I'm the cave boy. I can't comprehend what a friend is so I shall shut up.'

'Don't get mad – I didn't mean it like that!' Ada sighed. 'Look, the last time I saw Pri we had a fight, OK? I got mad and said some stuff I shouldn't have and now she's in trouble. I gotta make it right.'

'Then let me cast a Slip spell to Gainesville! Why are we walking?'

'You need to rest those hands of yours,' Ada told him firmly. 'If we get into trouble, I don't want you running out of magic.'

'*If?*'

They carried on in silence, even Kipp keeping his thoughts to himself. Geller's feet were cold and wet from splashing through the creek. After centuries cloaked in the cool silence of the Biding Cave, the night-time swamp seemed furious with noise – croaking toads, chirruping insects, the distant roar of larger beasts. It felt like there were eyes everywhere silently watching them. As they crossed a patch of marshland, the soft ground sucking at their feet, the moon came out from behind a cloud. Geller scratched his head. He could have sworn that they had walked through this clearing ten minutes ago.

'Are you sure we're going in the right direction, Ada?' he said. 'I think we are walking in circles . . . Ada?'

Geller whirled round. Ada and Kipp were nowhere to be seen. One minute they had been right beside him, now he was standing alone in the clearing. As he peered through the darkness, a warning tingled through Geller's fingers.

He blinked and found himself surrounded.

A ring of cloaked figures had appeared in the trees around Geller. They moved as one, stooped and shambling, their black, watery eyes fixed upon him. *The Malum can take the form of one or a hundred*, Cavelos had told Geller, *an entire army of wizards*. Geller tried to yell a warning to Ada, but the Malum made a gesture and nothing but air came out from his mouth. He clutched at his throat, panic threatening to overwhelm him. The clearing pulsed with the sheer power of the Malum's magic. Geller knew, with hollow certainty, that it could easily block any spell he tried to cast. Trembling, he stood helplessly as the ring of identical wizards shuffled closer around him, leering and hissing as they went.

'*Spawn . . . Spawn . . . Spawn . . .*'

As one, the Malum raised their hideously gnarled hands and cast a spell. The ground opened beneath Geller's feet, and he went tumbling into a deep black void.

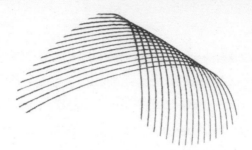

19: The Eve of Defeat

3019
The Collider, Franco-Swiss border

The robot surgeon Weil hurried through underground corridors alive with alarms and pulsing red warning lights. Sparks erupted from damaged wall panels; every now and again, a far-off explosion rocked the tunnel. Weil strode onwards, the three extra arms snaking up from his back forming a protective shield above his head.

Barely a week had passed since his arrival at the Collider, following a long and arduous flight from Mount Hood. Weil had been lucky to escape the compound alive. The attack by the SSR team had caught him completely by surprise, Angelis and her robots melting out of the snow to torch the buildings and mow down the research crew in their tracks. As gunfire echoed through the corridors, Weil barely had time to warn Kaku over the COMMS-Link before laying down his instruments and fleeing his surgery.

He'd raced up a smoke-clogged stairwell and crashed

through an access door at the top, coming out on to the roof. As he charged across the solar panels, the door banged open behind him, and the air became electric with antimatter fire. A round caught one of his arms, knocking him off his stride. He stumbled onwards, ducking and zigzagging through the barrage until the roof's edge lurched into view. Weil jumped.

For a few seconds, he had felt completely, blissfully free – weightless even. As gravity tried to claw him back to the ground, Weil activated the nano-turbines beneath his skin, powering him away from the laboratory and sending him soaring up into the skies. An angry burst of gunfire pursued him from the roof, but Weil was already spiralling into the safety of the clouds. He had caught a final glimpse of the burning compound, the ground strewn with dead robots, before it disappeared from view.

There were rumours that nearby Seattle was still holding out against the Spawn, but Weil knew he had to see CERN. He flew east across the North American continent, on a bearing towards the Atlantic Ocean. He saw for himself the devastation that the invaders had wrought upon the planet – the huge craters in the blackened ground, the burning forests, the mile-long oil slicks in the lakes and oceans. Weil was a surgeon. His task was to repair robots, not destroy them. But the war had changed him. Now he felt a strong urge to return the same damage to their attackers that had been done to them. Not just to the Spawn, but the SSR team, too. To take what humans called revenge.

Across the Atlantic Ocean, Europe was wrapped in a black fog – the land a patchwork of destruction, whole cities transformed into giant tombs filled with decaying remains. As Weil neared the Collider, he detected movement in the dark skies ahead of him and took evasive action to avoid patrolling Spawn ships. He approached from the south, flying low through the scorched desert of concrete and metal that had once been the city of Geneva. When the Collider's main entrance came into view, Weil opened up an emergency COMMS-Link requesting entry. The three-feet thick titanium doors had yawned open in reply, allowing him inside.

Somehow Weil had reached his destination – yet it felt as though he had only delayed the inevitable. The war against the Spawn showed no sign of turning, the situation worsening with every sunrise. Seattle fell two days after Weil arrived at the Collider, Algiers the day after that. The Spawn continued to raze cities to the ground, bringing in their heavy drills to attack the earth beneath the rubble, like rodents burrowing deep below the surface. And, although CERN continued to channel his run-time into searching for answers, still the robots had no idea why.

Now, the explosions were getting louder and closer as Weil hurried through the Collider's narrow passageways. As hard as the defending robots and humans were fighting, security breaches were being reported across CERN. At this rate, it wouldn't be long before Spawn craft would be hurtling through the tunnels. Weil turned left, heading into the room he had been given as a makeshift surgery. The brightly lit chamber was littered with robot parts. As Weil began collecting up his surgical tools, a message came over his COMMS-Link. It was being transmitted from Lausanne, a ruined city on the shores of Lake Geneva to the north-east of the Collider.

When he opened the message on his visual panel, Weil saw Angelis standing with her arms folded in the ruins of a building. The rest of her SSR team stood around her, weapons at the ready. They had fallen victim to some kind of decay, rust eating away at their faces and breastplates. Reddish-brown scars criss-crossed their bodies. But Angelis stood as proudly as ever.

LINK: 46.5197° N, 6.6323° E

0111001000011101001001010011111111000110101

Robots of CERN. There was a harsh metallic edge to Angelis's voice, as though that too was corroding. For years, our team laboured in ruins such as these, pulling humans and robots from piles of rubble and buildings consumed by flame. But now we stand side by side with the forces of destruction. The Spawn gather to take the Collider. The defence of Earth has failed – resistance is useless. Put down your arms. You have two hours to comply.

The message ended abruptly. There was no chance to reply, no negotiations. Just an order. Weil's circuits fizzed with anger. He finished packing up his surgical tools and left his surgery, aware that in all probability he would never be able to return to it. As Weil stomped along the tunnel towards the particle accelerator's Control Centre, he opened a COMMS-Link to CERN.

LINK: 46.204391° N, 6.143158° E

0111001000011110100100101001111111000110101

CERN responded immediately: Weil.

CERN. Have you seen Angelis's message?

It was sent to all the robots inside the Collider.

We must destroy her, Weil said fiercely. Angelis, the SSR team, the Spawn. We must destroy them all.

We must STOP them. But I will not destroy another robot, no matter what their crime.

You do not hate them?

I pity them, CERN said. They are trapped in a nightmare from which they cannot awake. Can you not see the rust that has them in its grip? It is the stain of the Spawn, like pustules on a plague victim. The SSR team are dying, Weil.

Let us hope they die faster.

You are angry. It is to be expected.

Weil didn't know how any robot could stay calm. Then again, CERN wasn't just any robot.

I am abandoning my surgery, he reported. The Spawn assault is imminent. What is our plan?

I have simulated every possible outcome of this battle, replied CERN. I cannot see a way we can win. Our only hope is Kaku.

Kaku? Weil repeated, surprised. What can he do?

I sent him back in time to learn what Angelis and the other

robots were doing travelling to the past. It would seem they wished to destroy a book. A very powerful book, a book of magic.

There is no such thing as magic, CERN.

So we have always believed. But it would appear the Spawn knew more than we did. Kaku has made another jump to 2052, where he is searching for a teenage girl called Ada Luring, who was named in this book of magic.

You really think a girl from the past can help stop the Spawn?

I do not have a better alternative.

These time-jumps must be diminishing your power, CERN.

I have enough for one more jump. But if Kaku cannot find this girl, or she cannot help us, we are lost.

Weil could barely believe what he was hearing. CERN was the most powerful robot in the history of Earth, capable of carrying out millions of complex calculations every second. Yet, when the world needed him to come up with a brilliant battle strategy or devise a fearsome new weapon, here CERN was talking about magic books and teenage girls! Had the pressure to beat the Spawn corroded his processing unit? CERN seemed to think that the planet's fate rested on Kaku's shoulders, but the librarian was a scholar, not a warrior. Weil could only hope that his old friend could rise to the challenge when it really counted.

The tunnel shook, pieces of metal sheeting dislodging themselves from the ceiling and crashing down around Weil. The Spawn offensive was intensifying. Maintenance bots scurried through the tunnels, desperately trying to put out fires and to repair damaged circuitry. As Weil watched, a fuel tank exploded, sending a maintenance bot flying across the corridor and crashing into the wall. The surgeon scooped up the bot with one of his tentacle arms without breaking stride.

At the end of the tunnel, Weil came to a set of electronic doors, passing through them into the Control Centre. The room was dominated by four islands, raised circular banks of machinery that controlled the different accelerators that made up the Collider. Robotic arms stretched out from the banks, tapping away at the keyboards. Wall screens provided second-by-second updates and read-outs from the machinery – Weil noted that several of the screens were showing nothing but black static. He wondered how long it would be before the whole room fell dark.

CERN was striding about the four islands, his shadow stretching the length of the Control Centre. Weil couldn't help but feel awed by the other robot's presence. CERN worked the instruments like a virtuoso, making thousands of tiny adjustments a second. Even at the height of war, he would keep the particle accelerator running. The only way to stop him would be to destroy him.

Welcome to the Control Centre, Weil, said CERN, without turning round. I have ordered our brothers and sisters to draw back here to defend it from the Spawn. I fear we may have need of your skills before this day is ended.

I am here to fight, not to heal, said Weil. There is no word from Kaku?

No.

Then we will have to fight with what we have. I bring reinforcements.

Weil carefully placed the injured maintenance bot down on the floor and turned back to the doorway, opening a fresh COMMS-Link to utter a single command. The door slid open, revealing a line of grim-faced robots. They limped and shuffled into the Control Centre, a scarred battalion assembled from mismatched parts. Some were missing arms; others had three legs. All of them were armed. Weil had worked through the night to piece them together from robots who had fallen to the Spawn's assault.

You have been busy, CERN said approvingly.

We cannot let the Spawn win. We must fight.

It will not be enough, said CERN.

It will have to be, Weil replied.

20: The Black Doorway

2052
The Ankh

Geller woke with cold stone beneath his head and darkness all around him. He sat up with a groan. His mouth was dry and his mind cloudy, as though he had been freed from a centuries-long Suspension spell. Sharp pains sliced through his skull as he turned his head and looked around.

'Hello?' he called out. 'Is anybody there?'

His voice sounded pitifully small and thin – Geller had the sense that he was sitting in the middle of a vast chamber. He struggled to his feet, his memory returning to him in sharp, painful fragments. The battle at the university, the flight to the swamp, the Malum surrounding him in the trees . . . With a chill, Geller wondered whether the ancient wizard had ambushed Ada, too. Gainesville couldn't have felt further away. Geller knew he was underground: he could sense the earth's ceiling far above him. But the atmosphere was different from the Pazin Caves. The air was colder and drier and *older* somehow. The wind made a mournful whistle as it echoed round the walls.

Blindly feeling his way forward, Geller inched across the floor. The wind grew stronger and more high-pitched – just as he was about to place his foot down, he felt fresh air beneath it and hurriedly stepped back. He was standing on the edge of a steep drop. Crouching down, Geller found a chipped piece of flagstone on the floor and tossed it into the darkness, waiting to hear it hit the ground. But all he heard was the keening wind. Slowly and carefully, Geller followed the edge of the floor, marking out its limits and searching in vain for a bridge or a door out of the chamber. He wasn't sure how long it took – this deep beneath the earth, it felt as though time couldn't reach him. Twice the platform edge took him by surprise, his foot straying dangerously close to thin air. Eventually Geller reached the conclusion that staying still was a safer option than exploring.

Or, better yet, Slipping out of here and trying to find Ada.

However, when Geller prepared to cast a spell, he found that his finger was bare – his ring had gone. He dropped to his hands and knees and scoured every inch of the platform, but there was no sign of it. The Malum must have removed it while he was unconscious. Without his ring, Geller couldn't cast any spells. Not only was he trapped, he was completely defenceless.

The whistling wind changed in tone, deepening and thickening until it began to sound like a chorus of voices.

'Hello?' Geller said again, uneasily. 'Who's there?'

The cavern exploded with white light, and he threw up

his hands to protect his eyes from the dazzling glare. Blinking, Geller saw that he was standing on a platform in the middle of a cavern the size of a cathedral. The platform was carved in the shape of a cross with a loop at its top – the ankh, ancient symbol of power. A plunging chasm marked the limits of the ledge; without magic, there seemed no way off it. The cavern walls were lined with galleries, row upon row of rocky seats that stretched all the way to the ceiling far above Geller's head. Every single seat was filled – a hundred twisted faces, a sea of black, watery eyes staring down at Geller. All of them belonging to the Malum.

Fear gripped Geller. He swallowed. 'Where am I?'

'*This cavern has many names, Geller, son of Cavelos.*' The voice of the Malum was somehow both soft and deafeningly loud: the sound of a million people whispering. '*In Murmeln, it is known simply as the Ankh. It exists on the very edge of the human world, thousands of feet below the great lake of the Pazin Caves. Here the Malum sits in session, to plan and to debate. And to cast judgement.*'

Judgement. The word rang out like a warning bell.

'You took my ring,' said Geller.

'*Did you think we would just allow you to Slip your way back to the human world, Geller, son of Cavelos?*' There was a note of scorn in the Malum's voice. '*You have already shown that you are not to be trusted. Why else would you be here?*'

'I do not know why I'm here,' Geller replied.

'*Of course you do not. You are nothing but a child, a blink of the eye in the passage of time. You cannot conceive*

200

of the ways of the Malum. For thousands of years, we have shaped and manipulated the course of human history to further our own ends. In the days of the Akkadian Empire, we helped Naram-Sin become the King of the Four Quarters by crushing his enemies in battle. The Egyptian Empire grew under Thutmose I, thanks to our support, and it was wizards who defeated the Sea Peoples when they attacked Ramses III in the eighth year of his reign. The Assyrian king, Shalmaneser III, would not have won a single campaign without us. And yet for centuries we kept the humans in complete ignorance of our work. It was a grand and glorious time.'

The ghostly light in the chamber burned even brighter, then began to subside. Shadows lengthened across the Ankh.

'Yet a cloud hangs over the Malum,' the ancient wizard said, with a many-mouthed hiss. '*A future threat written in the Book of the Apocalypse – prophecies of death and disaster, an enemy so powerful that even the Malum could not defeat them. According to the book, the Malum's only hope lay with the last of the wizards. Only now that wizard would seem to be a traitor.'*

'I'm no traitor!' said Geller. 'I did what was right!'

'That remains to be seen. Geller, son of Cavelos, you are charged with high treason. You will stand and listen to the case as it is presented, and you will defend yourself afterwards – if you can.'

A black doorway appeared on the far side of the Ankh, and a cloaked figure stepped out on to the platform. Geller's heart sank.

'*Halpern, son of Morgan.*'

The wizard's habitual smirk had been replaced by a look of astonishment and awe. He sank to his knees before the galleries, pressing his forehead to the ground in humbled obeisance.

'Revered Malum!' he called out. 'The honour is overwhelming. I could not believe your summons – so many centuries have passed since you last walked among us, to learn that you are still with us brings me the greatest joy.'

'*You doubted the Malum's existence, Halpern, son of Morgan,*' came the disapproving reply from the galleries. '*Perhaps now you realize just how foolish that was. You can begin to redeem yourself by rising and making your case against Geller, son of Cavelos.*'

Halpern dutifully picked himself up. 'I will do as you command,' he said, 'though my lips are shamed by the words they must speak. With my own eyes, I have witnessed Geller's attempts to sabotage the wizard cause. At every turn, he has tried to stop our attempts to destroy Hawking, the first mechanical man, and the scientist who created him. During the mission to the GAPs Tower, it was Geller who ruined the mission by warning Kevin Cruz of our plan to attack him.'

'Lies!' Geller cried.

'*You will wait for the charges to be read out before your defence may begin,*' came the reply from the galleries. '*Continue, Halpern, son of Morgan.*'

'When we reached the skybridge, Geller hid at the back

and refused to help his brother wizards as they battled Cruz's body-bots.'

'You froze my hands so I couldn't cast a Slip spell!' Geller shot back. 'You wanted the body-bots to kill me!'

Halpern snorted. 'Malum, I can hardly be blamed if the boy cannot cast a mere Slip spell! Geller should never have been selected for the task in the first place. If the mission to Kuala Lumpur was a failure, it was because of his father, Cavelos, not me.'

'It was *your* plan,' Geller retorted. 'You were the one who told my father about Kevin Cruz and GAPs. Where did you get that information from? Where do you go on the surface, Halpern?'

'It is you on trial here, not me,' Halpern said irritably. Sensing a new atmosphere of intrigue seeping through the Ankh, he pressed on: 'Ensuring the raid's failure was not enough for Geller. When he learned the identity of Dr Sara Luring – presumably through his ally, Kevin Cruz – he kept this knowledge a secret. Need I remind you, Elder Malum, that Dr Sara Luring is the pioneer behind the rise of the mechanical men. Yet Geller's childish infatuation with her daughter was more important to him than the fate of his wizard brothers.'

'*We have seen this girl*,' the Malum hissed. '*There is power within her.*'

'She is nothing,' Halpern said dismissively.

'Shut up!' Geller reddened. 'You don't know anything about her!'

Halpern's laughter echoed round the Ankh. He was

playing to the gallery now. 'You see? The boy betrays his human heart. How easily he has been led astray; how quickly he sides with the machine-lovers and mechanical men.'

'Don't listen to him!' Geller called out. 'You were there on the skybridge, Malum. If I am a traitor, why did you save me? Why didn't you just give Halpern the images of the Lurings and let the body-bots shoot me?'

'You question the actions of the Malum? You expect an explanation? You presume too much.'

'Which brings us to the most heinous betrayal of all,' Halpern said, with satisfaction. 'During the battle at the Machine Intelligence Lab, Geller fought against his brother wizards, standing side by side with the Lurings and a robot of terrible speed and strength. It is only through sheer fortune that none of our brethren were killed.'

'Not true,' Geller replied steadfastly. 'Kaku made sure he didn't kill anyone. Halpern was the one who made the building collapse.'

'Pray forgive me!' Halpern said mockingly. 'I did not realize that robots had names.'

Geller held out his hands, appealing to the Malum. 'Kaku's not here to fight wizards; he's trying to stop the robots who attacked Predjama. He's trying to save the world from destruction by the Spawn!'

A horrified echo went up around the galleries. *'Spawn . . . Spawn . . . Spawn.'*

'That's the threat in the future, isn't it?' Geller said excitedly. 'It's the Spawn who are your true enemy, not the

Lurings. Kaku said it was the Spawn who corrupted the robots and sent them back in time to destroy the Book of the Apocalypse. But they didn't succeed! There's a copy somewhere, which was hidden when Predjama fell. Don't you see? If we can find the book, we can help Kaku defeat the Spawn. Wizards and robots can fight together!'

Halpern paled. 'A copy of the Book of the Apocalypse? Wizards and robots fighting together? This is heresy!'

'*Enough!*' the Malum roared. '*The past must be resolved before the future can be faced. Geller, son of Cavelos, may be the last of the wizards, yet his actions do not appear to be those of a hero or a saviour. You have heard the charges, Geller, son of Cavelos. How do you plead?*'

Geller looked around the vast, stony-faced gallery. The Malum was supposed to be all-knowing and all-powerful, yet it had swallowed Halpern's lies without so much as a question. What argument could Geller bring, what proof could he provide that could change their mind?

'*How do you plead, Geller, son of Cavelos?*' More insistently this time.

Geller folded his arms defiantly.

For several moments, the Ankh stayed deathly silent. Then the Malum's voice rang out once more.

'*Geller, son of Cavelos refuses to answer the charges or speak in his own defence. Our judgement is clear.*'

As Geller held his breath, his ears picked up a thin, tinny sound. He looked down and saw a metal object rolling across the flagstones towards him, knocking against his foot. It was his ring. Geller snatched it up, slipping it back on his finger before anyone could stop him. However, when he looked over at Halpern and saw the sly smile on the wizard's face, his surge of triumph ebbed away.

A single word came forth from the galleries, formed by a hundred mouths.

'*Guilty.*'

'What?' Geller spun round, horrified. 'But you returned my ring!'

'*You will need it,*' the Malum replied. '*Your punishment is trial by combat. We have selected an opponent who should make for a most . . . interesting duel.*'

Once more, the black doorway opened on the other side of the platform. A figure stood in the portal, his cloak wrapped round him like a black shroud. It was Drahe, a thin smile on his skeletal face.

21: Damage

2052
The Ankh

Geller shrank back at the sight of the cadaverous wizard, his nerve endings tingling with the memory of Drahe's icy grip on his neck. Only Kaku's arrival had saved him in the Machine Intelligence Lab – but here in the Ankh, the cradle of wizard power, no robot could help him. Drahe nodded respectfully up at the Malum and received an approving murmur in return. Geller retreated to the edge of the platform until he felt the freezing wind at his back. Looking in vain for an escape route, his gaze caught Halpern's. The wizard raised his eyebrows.

Nowhere left to run.

No time left to think.

The duel began immediately, a barrage of Damage spells flying the length of the Ankh towards Geller. He quickly cast a Protection spell, encasing himself in a wall of crystal. The barrier shuddered as the spells hit it, jagged cracks appearing like icy cobwebs. Through the translucent surface Geller could see Drahe's long shadow moving ominously towards him. He needed a plan, a tactic of some sort, but he was panicking too much to think clearly. Drahe hurled another Damage spell and the barrier around Geller shattered, spraying him with shards of crystal as he reeled away.

When he looked up, Drahe had vanished.

Geller froze, his eyes frantically scanning the Ankh. Up in the galleries, the Malum looked on in absorbed silence. The broad stretches of the Ankh were empty: Drahe had Melted into the shadows.

'See how the great wizard trembles!' Halpern said mockingly. 'He cannot fight what he cannot see. Take my advice, Geller, son of Cavelos – throw your ring away and beg for mercy. Perhaps Drahe will take pity on you, and make your end swift.'

Geller shut out Halpern's voice, trying to concentrate. Drahe was toying with him. He circled slowly on the spot, sweat pooling in the small of his back. Even the wind seemed to be taunting him, blowing his hair into his eyes.

'You could try and cast a Slip spell and escape, I suppose,' Halpern mused. 'But how long do you think it would take the Malum to catch up with you? Five seconds? Ten?' He laughed. 'And then you'd find yourself begging for Drahe to finish you off.'

Was Halpern trying to distract him? Whirling round, Geller fired off a Damage spell, only to see it sail over the edge of the platform and explode into the rocks on the other side of the chasm. Halpern burst out laughing – Geller turned back only to see the shadows merge in front of him. Drahe rose out of the darkness like a nightmare. The towering wizard seized Geller by the cloak and hauled him up into the air. Bony fingers latched on to his neck. Drahe grinned.

A bolt of pure agony shot through Geller: he arched his back, teeth clamping shut. The vicious throbbing relented and he tried to mumble a Protection spell, only to bite his tongue at another shuddering jolt. Raw waves of pain coursed through his muscles and veins with agonizing slowness. Nerves writhed, skin burned. It felt as though he was on fire. The watching Malum began to shift in shape and number before his eyes, sliding into one another like a kaleidoscope of shadows. There was no noise, just an engrossed hush.

Trapped in Drahe's pitiless grip, Geller's mind fled to a tiny space somewhere deep in his soul where he found memories to comfort him. The pain was nothing, the wind whistling through the Pazin Caves at the dead of night. His mother was shushing him gently, rocking him in her arms. He could hear her crooning lullaby:

'Far beneath the sun,
We went underground
To the heart of the ankh
Where hope is found.'

The lullaby faded away. Geller's vision shifted, and suddenly Ada was by his side. There was a smile on her face, and her soft hands were around his.

Ada.

He could not die.

Not now.

Searching within himself, deep in the well of his soul, Geller located a last spark of strength. He drew on it to cast a Damage spell, igniting it as soon as it left his fingers. The explosion blew him and Drahe apart, sending them flying across the Ankh in opposite directions. The skin on Geller's arm ripped open as he skidded across the stone. All around the chamber, the voices of the Malum were united in surprise.

'*It is not over.*'

'*He fights.*'

'*The boy fights.*'

Geller forced himself to stand, his bloodied arm hanging by his side. Across the platform, Drahe was slowly picking himself up off the floor, his gaunt features darkening with fury. As Geller stared at his assailant, his nerve endings stinging and raw, he felt a burning rage consume him. And with rage came power, more than he thought possible. A spiteful storm of Damage came arrowing towards him, but this time Geller swatted it away with ease.

'Someone is helping the boy!' There was alarm in Halpern's voice. 'He is not capable of this!'

Geller barely heard him, his attention fixed on Drahe. He let the darkness claim him, Melting into the shadows and feeling his form ripple across the Ankh. Now it was Drahe's turn to look concerned. Geller materialized in his blind spot, dropping to his knees and firing a Damage spell with such speed that it hit Drahe before he could defend himself. The wizard crumpled to the floor, his fingers twitching. The Malum roared approval as Geller strode over to the prone Drahe and prepared to cast another spell.

'Hold!'

He looked up to find that Halpern had trained his spell ring on him, his palm held out in warning.

'Show yourself, Cavelos!' Halpern snarled. 'Or I will kill your son where he stands.'

For several seconds – or a hundred lifetimes – nothing moved. Then the air rippled in the centre of the Ankh, and Cavelos emerged from nothingness. Geller's heart leaped in his chest. His father was here. His father had come to save him.

The Malum erupted with anger. '*What is the meaning of this, Cavelos, son of Gauer?*'

Cavelos turned and surveyed the galleries, a look of wonderment in his eyes. 'Humblest apologies, revered Malum,' his voice rang out. 'I have devoted centuries to searching for you, alone in believing in you while others scoffed at the very notion. I remain your first and greatest disciple and most obedient servant. For a long time now, Halpern has given me cause to mistrust him. It was him I followed to this blessed place, fearing his involvement in a conspiracy against me.'

'*You of all wizards should know that it is forbidden to interfere with a magic duel.*'

'I have been watching this duel since it began, and

211

Halpern seemed intent upon distracting Geller, giving Drahe the upper hand. I was merely evening the sides.'

'You are no better than your traitor of a son,' Halpern said icily. 'If I had my way, you would stand trial alongside him.'

Cavelos clasped his hands together. 'Is that so? I will gladly stand beside my son, if the Malum will allow it. We will see who the real traitor is, Halpern.'

Halpern's eyes darted about in his head – he had made a miscalculation, and he knew it. The Malum turned to one another to discuss the matter, hubbub filling the chamber. As one, they broke off and turned back to face Cavelos.

'*Agreed*,' said the Malum.

Halpern didn't wait. A flurry of spells came towards Geller, only to thud harmlessly against a Protection shield Cavelos had erected, solid as a wall of polar ice. The wizards Slipped in and out of view, trading spells and counter-spells at dizzying speed: a personal duel, shaped and sharpened by five centuries of hatred, that left Geller a mere bystander. The Ankh crackled with seething magic, sparks exploding across the flagstones. Ducking below an errant Damage spell, Geller saw a figure coalesce beside the slumped form of Drahe. His fingers were already forming the shape of an Attack spell when he realized it was his father.

As Geller hesitated, Halpern materialized several feet to his right. The wizard's feet had barely touched the floor when Cavelos sent a poisonous stream of Damage across the Ankh. Instantly, Geller realized the spell was going to miss. It wasn't even close – flying several feet to Halpern's left. Too late, Geller realized in which direction.

Straight at him.

The blast hit Geller squarely in the chest, sending him tumbling towards the platform edge. The world exploded in his ears. As he went sliding off the Ankh, Geller reached out and grabbed hold of the platform edge, clinging on even as his feet went out from beneath him and he dangled over the chasm. He tried to haul himself back up, his eyes briefly meeting Halpern's. The wizard paused, his brow furrowed as he stared at Geller.

There was a loud whoosh, and Halpern's robes erupted in flames. The wizard screamed, arms flailing as he tried to fight off the bright red tongues of flame consuming him. Geller could see Cavelos grimly directing the fire from his spell ring, his face illuminated by the flames. A sickening smell of burning hair and flesh flooded across the platform. The horrified Geller could only watch as Halpern let out an anguished cry before dropping to his knees, defeated, at the edge of the Ankh.

'Help me, Father!' Geller called out. 'Please!'

Cavelos stepped over the body of Drahe and walked slowly across the Ankh towards him. When he reached the edge of the platform, he looked down at his son. Slowly and deliberately, he pressed his boot down on Geller's left hand.

'I thought you came to save me!' Geller gasped.

'I did, in a manner of speaking,' Cavelos replied calmly. 'I could not allow Halpern or Drahe to kill my kin. If you are to die, Geller, then it will be at *my* hands.'

'But I am your son!'

Cavelos's eyes flashed angrily. 'You are no son of mine!' he snapped. 'You are a pitiful weakling who can barely cast a spell; a lover of humans and the robots they create. I am ashamed that you walk the face of this earth.'

'But without me,' Geller tried desperately, 'you will have no heir!'

'Then I will create another, like one of Dr Luring's mechanical men.' Cavelos crouched down beside Geller. 'Do you really think I will allow my line to end like this, on such a whimper? Did you not think that I would make plans, in case you proved unworthy of my name? Believe me, you will not be the last of the wizards. I will make it my life's work, if it comes to that.'

He increased the pressure on Geller's hand until Geller had no choice but to let go, leaving him dangling from the Ankh by his right hand. An ocean of darkness stretched out below him. 'Help me, Malum! I beg you!'

There was no reply. Twisting his neck, Geller saw that the rows of seats ringing the chamber were empty. The Malum had vanished.

Cavelos shrugged. 'Worth a try, I suppose,' he said.

He brought his boot down sharply on Geller's hand, and there was a sickening crack of bone and knuckle. Screaming with pain, Geller let go.

The wind shrieked with triumph as the chasm devoured him. In desperation, Geller threw out his arm and tried to cast a Slip spell below him, but his damaged fingers wouldn't move. Numbly, Geller realized there was nothing he could do – he was already dead. It was a strange, almost giddy sensation. As he plummeted, he felt his muscles relax. He stretched out his arms and legs, his cloak billowing around him. Above him the Ankh lights were growing fainter, a dim and distant galaxy far out of reach.

It would not be long now. Geller closed his eyes and waited for the earth to claim him.

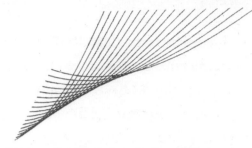

22: A Friend in Need

2052
Santa Fe Swamp, north-east of Gainesville, Florida, USA

'Geller?' The moon's reflection rippled in the slow-moving creek at the sound of Ada's voice. 'Where are you?'

She looked back towards Kipp, who was clambering awkwardly over a gnarled root, and spread out her arms in bewilderment.

'I give up,' she said. 'There's no sign of him anywhere.'

'He could have used one of his Slip spells to go and get Pri,' Kipp suggested.

'Without telling us first? Anyway, I thought his hands were too sore to cast.'

'Maybe they felt better. Maybe . . .' The robot went quiet.

'What, Kipp?'

'Geller *is* a wizard, Ada. Maybe he decided he didn't want to fight against his own kind any more.'

'He wouldn't do that,' Ada said stubbornly. 'He wouldn't just leave us like that.'

She had no idea why she felt so certain – after all, she had only known the young wizard a matter of hours. From the moment of his birth, Geller had been taught to believe that all robots were evil, and it must have been so hard for him to stand alongside them and fight the only people he knew, his own family even. He'd risked so much to try and save Ada, did he really think he'd made a mistake?

'Geller!' she called out, through cupped hands.

'Let's go back to the shack and see if he's there,' tried Kipp. 'It was dangerous enough leaving with Geller, and now that he's gone –'

'We are not going back, OK?' Ada shouted. 'Pri's in trouble! If Magic Boy wants to go back to his cave and hang out with his evil wizard buddies then fine, but I'm going to Gainesville.'

Kipp shrank back. 'You don't have to shout at me.'

Ada splashed to a halt. Letting out a sigh, she turned back and crouched down beside the robot. 'You're right,' she said. 'I'm sorry, Kipp. There's just too much happening . . . I feel like my brain is going to explode. Now my best friend's in danger, and I don't know who to trust.'

'You can trust me,' Kipp said.

'I know I can,' Ada replied. 'You're my knight, remember?'

'And you're my queen,' Kipp said happily.

She smiled and slipped her hand through his, and they continued along the creek together. According to Ada's phone, it was just past midnight. It seemed impossible to believe that only hours earlier she had been standing in her booth at the Science Fair, watching Kipp scatter chess pieces all over the floor. Ada's R8 was still racing, hundreds of mentions and messages from people she didn't even know. Angry messages, supportive messages, even a couple of weirdos asking her out on dates. This was the worst possible time to become popular – if ever Ada needed to be invisible, it was now. Pri's R8 had stopped altogether, the frozen page feeling like some kind of reproach. Ada could only pray her friend was OK.

They came to the swamp's edge and crept out from the trees to find the Gainesville skyline ablaze with emergency lights. Sec-drones shone powerful floodlights over the university campus, the night air frantic with thudding helicopter blades and the throaty whine of hoverships. Ada followed the state highway towards the city, ducking down with Kipp whenever car headlights passed them. It took them almost two hours to reach Gainesville, and by the time they reached the familiar streets of her neighbourhood Ada was exhausted. It had been much easier to stay out of sight with Kaku planning the route. Perhaps she should have told the robot about Pri after all.

'Are you sure this is a good idea?' asked Kipp, peering nervously down their home street. 'The police will be looking for us at the house.'

'Why?' said Ada. 'We're supposed to be on the run, remember? I'm not saying we sit down and watch TV, I just need to get my bike.'

The street was reassuringly quiet – there were no flashing emergency lights or holo-cordons; curtains were drawn tightly across sleeping windows. Ada stole along the sidewalk and ducked into the backyard of her next-door neighbour, Ms Wenderly, an elderly woman who barely ever left the house. Peering over the fence, she saw that her house was shrouded in darkness. The building had acquired an unfamiliar, almost threatening aspect, as though it had been years, not hours, since Ada had last seen it. She studied it for several minutes before she was convinced it was safe enough to help Kipp over the fence, and followed after him.

'We'll go as soon as you get your bike, OK?' Kipp said eagerly.

Ada pressed her finger to her lips. Skirting round the edge of the lawn, she pressed her palm against the ident panel beside the French windows and slid them open. Kipp hung back on the grass, reluctant to follow Ada as she crept inside the house. She was relieved to see that everything was exactly as she had left it: dirty plates still soaking in the kitchen sink and the living-room table littered with her mom's work.

'Castle?' Ada whispered.

The security lights were on above the driveway and the AC was purring smoothly. But the house computer didn't reply.

'It's me, Ada! Can you hear me?'

A loud bang behind Ada made her jump. Kipp had tripped over the ledge of the French windows and was sprawled across the floor on his belly.

'Kipp!' she hissed. 'We're supposed to be keeping quiet, remember?'

He picked himself up and waddled apologetically over to her. A light flicked on in the kitchen, a faint orange glow pulsing through the doorway. Pushing Kipp behind her, Ada edged towards the kitchen and peered inside. The microwave was flashing on and off – as Ada watched, the timer pinged on, and a torrent of 1s and 0s streamed across the display.

'Look!' Kipp whispered.

The digital clock on the oven had also burst into life, more 1s and 0s flickering. Ada glanced uncertainly at Kipp.

'What's going on?' she whispered. 'Why won't Castle talk to me?'

'I think it's trying to,' the robot replied hesitantly. 'I think these numbers are binary code.'

'Can you read it?'

'Let me try.'

Kipp pulled himself up to the edge of the sideboard and peered at the microwave timer. The appliance was still flashing on and off, numbers tumbling past in a ghostly stream. Ada bit her nail.

'It *is* Castle!' Kipp said excitedly. 'It says –' His eyes widened. 'It says the police are watching the house, and they're monitoring its COMMS, too! Ada, we have to get out of here!'

Ada snatched up her hoodie and ran for the door. Her bike was where she had left it outside the garage. Hurriedly activating the security block, Ada wheeled it down the drive. No point in trying to stay hidden now. She climbed into the seat and twisted round to see Kipp hastening down the drive after her.

'Sec-drone!' he called out.

An ominous shadow in the night sky weaved in and out of the street lights. As Kipp climbed up behind Ada, the emergency lights on the drone's belly burst into life, bathing the driveway in a dazzling blue.

'Stay where you are,' an electronic voice commanded. 'Patrolmen have been alerted and will be here presently.'

'Yeah, right,' Ada muttered. 'In your dreams. Hang on, Kipp!'

Selecting nano-boosters on the security block, she gritted her teeth and hit the ignition. The bike rocketed out of the driveway, houses and gardens whipping by in a blur. The end of the street hurtled towards them; clinging on to the handlebars, Ada swerved right. A wailing siren told her that the sec-drone was giving chase, the blue spotlight snaking along the tarmac behind them.

'Security block!' Ada called out. 'Find the nearest dark zone!'

A map flashed up on the bike display and Ada hit a hard left at the next intersection, zooming through a stop sign and a series of red lights. Halfway along the next street, she saw the silhouette of a church spire and bounced through the open gates at top speed. Risking a glance over her shoulder, Ada saw the blue spotlight wavering about the gates. Sec-drones were forbidden from passing over religious buildings – the dark zone had done its job. Ada wrestled her supercharged bike away from the church and along a bumpy path leading past a row of headstones. She hit the brakes, easing to a halt in the shadow of a marble tomb.

'That was close!' Kipp exclaimed. 'What are we going to do now?'

Ada's pocket beeped.

'Hold on,' she said. 'Let me check this.'

She pulled out her phone to find it had alerted her to a new update on Pri's R8. Her friend had just posted a photograph online: an office filled with blinking computer screens set inside a protective industrial cage that ran from the floor to the ceiling.

'Pri's OK!' Kipp said eagerly. 'That's good news, right? Ada?'

'I don't know,' she said slowly. 'Have you ever seen Pri take a photo without putting herself in the middle of it? Where's the excited message with a hundred emojis after it? Something's not right here.'

The more Ada looked at the photograph of the gloomy cage, the more it unsettled her. She felt a tug on her sleeve.

'We should get out of here,' Kipp said, peering around at the gravestones. 'The sec-drones can't come here, but the police can.'

'You're right, Kipp. At least we know where we can find Pri.'

'We do? How?'

'Because I've been in that room before.' Ada snapped shut her phone. 'Come on – it's not far.'

She pedalled out of the churchyard exit and went quickly

through the back streets of Gainesville, keeping careful watch for sec-drones. Within minutes, the gates of the Apollo Corp industrial park rose into view on the brow of the hill. Ada pedalled across the wasteland and slipped through the gap in the fence. She biked across the tarmac and pulled up by the rear entrance to one of the factories. Kipp climbed down and inspected the building.

'This is the place?'

'Uh-huh,' Ada nodded. 'See the ident panel on the door? The laser's faulty, but they never fix it because no one ever comes here. Me and Pri used to bring our holo-pets here.' She pressed her palm against the panel, which flickered for several seconds before turning green. 'See?'

Inside the warehouse, dimmed holo-lights throbbed in the velvet darkness. The sound of machinery grew louder as Ada and Kipp walked along the corridor, moving through a set of automatic doors to enter a vast hall. A conveyor belt sketched out an intricate circuit beneath the spotlights, ferrying machine parts from one end of the room to another. Robot arms perched over the belt, darting about tirelessly through the night as they worked on the parts. From a distance, they resembled a brood of giant spiders, scuttling back and forth on spindly metal legs.

'Look at this place!' Ada said, shouting above the clattering din. 'And not a human being in sight!'

'The system is disrupting my connectivity!' Kipp told her. 'My COMMS are down.'

'So let's get Pri and get out of here.'

She led the little robot past the conveyor belt and

through a doorway to a narrow corridor. Closed doors dotted the walls at regular intervals. Here was the brain of the automated warehouse – within each room were banks of servers all housed inside industrial cages, their screens blinking in the darkness. At the end of the row, Ada found the room Pri had photographed. Standing in the doorway, she could re-enact the exact shot. But there was no sign of Pri.

'Ada?' Kipp pointed inside the cage. 'What's that?'

His visual sensors had picked out a slim object lying on the floor in the darkness. Ada went over and kneeled down to pick up Pri's phone. She would have recognized it anywhere – it was never far from her friend's hand. As she stared at it, Ada had the unpleasant sensation that she had made a serious mistake.

'Kipp?' she said softly. 'I think we need to get out of here. Right now.'

'Leaving so soon?'

Ada swivelled round to find Lili Parker's outline framed in the doorway. The reporter slammed the cage door shut with an iron clang.

'Stay a while,' Lili said, with a thin smile. 'I insist.'

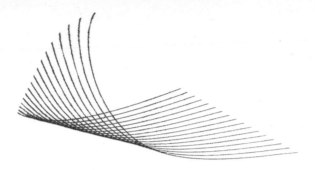

23: Detention Centre

2052
Apollo Corp industrial park, Gainesville, Florida, USA

Kipp shrank behind Ada's leg as Lili typed a code into a panel and a bolt rammed shut across the cage door, trapping them both inside.

'Hey!' Ada cried. 'Let us out!'

Lili shook her head. 'Enough lives have been lost tonight,' she said. 'The world is a safer place with you behind bars.'

'You're blaming me for what happened at the university? It wasn't my fault!'

'Maybe you didn't kill them yourself. But their blood is on your hands. Didn't I warn you at the Science Fair what would happen if you continued to gamble with artificial intelligence?'

Ada held up the phone in her hand. 'And what's that got to do with Pri? She doesn't know a thing about robots! Where is she?'

'Relax, Ada,' a new voice answered from the doorway.

'Pri's fine. Probably sitting in her room shopping for clothes she can't afford, as usual.'

Kit Somers joined her mother, a half-smile playing on her lips, and tossed something through the bars to Ada.

'Here,' she said. 'You can have this back.'

It was the pen projector Ada had used to shake off the unmarked sec-drone that had followed her home.

'You just love your little tech toys, don't you?' Kit said. 'Pri was always telling me how smart you were, and how much fun you two had playing here with your holo-pets. It sounded like *such* a blast; I knew you couldn't resist coming back.'

Ada groaned and put her head in her hands. 'Pri's dad never called you, did he? What did you do, steal her phone?'

Kit rewarded her with a dazzling smile.

'I figured that unmarked drone belonged to HI-AG,' Ada said contemptuously. 'I guess you don't mind sec-drones so much, as long as you're the ones controlling them.'

'It's HI-AG's duty to monitor all scientists and engineers who are working to aid the rise of the robots,' replied Lili. 'But, in the case of Dr Sara Luring, I decided to take a personal role. Your mother truly is a gifted woman, Ada. Such a pity she decided to channel her talents into the construction of a killing machine.'

'You don't know what you're talking about,' Ada said scornfully. 'Hawking was no killing machine. He couldn't harm anyone; it wasn't in his programming!'

'It doesn't need to be in his programming,' Kit snapped. 'The sec-drone that killed my dad wasn't supposed to do that, but it happened anyway. Don't tell me that robots aren't killers.'

Ada stared at her in disbelief. 'That's why you're doing this?' she said. 'Because a sec-drone crashed? It was an accident!'

'It wasn't an accident.' Lili's voice was low and dangerous. 'Kenneth was driving on a deserted strip of highway miles from the nearest town. The sec-drone shouldn't have been anywhere near him, but it deviated from its programmed route and smashed through his windshield like a guided missile. In an instant, one of the leading voices against AI in this country was silenced. I don't care how the scientific community try to dress it up – it was murder, plain and simple.'

'You don't know that!' Ada said.

'Robots don't make mistakes,' Kit retorted. 'Unless they break their programming.'

'But that's crazy! Do you think you're the only one who's lost someone they love? I lost my dad, too, Kit. But he died of cancer, so I didn't get to blame anyone. Maybe that's why I don't go around kidnapping people.'

'What if it meant you could stop cancer?' Lili said pointedly. 'Would you do it then?'

Ada fell silent.

'This is the real world,' Lili said, 'not a chessboard. Nothing is black and white.'

Kipp poked his head out from behind Ada. 'What are you going to do with us?' he squeaked.

'That depends. I want to know where Dr Luring and the

new robot are hiding. I want to know where it came from, how it was built.'

'Kipp would just *love* to explain it to you,' Ada said witheringly. 'But Kaku has travelled back a thousand years from the future, so the technology's a little advanced, even for Kipp.'

Lili raised a perfect eyebrow. 'Is that so?'

'Stone-cold truth.'

The reporter toyed with the pendant camera around her neck. 'Kit's right,' she said. 'You are an extremely smart young woman. Surely you can see where this is going. Look at what happened at the university – a new robot appears from nowhere, even more advanced than your own, and within minutes innocent people are lying dead! I'm not saying that your mom means harm with her work. But she's so blinded by the possibilities of science that she doesn't understand the danger of what she's doing.'

'Maybe if you hadn't sent those "innocent people" to break into my mom's lab and destroy her work, they'd still be alive,' Ada shot back. 'And anyway, like I told you, it wasn't Kaku who killed them. It was the wizards.'

Kit burst out laughing. 'Really, Ada? Did the goblins help them do it?'

'Be quiet,' her mother snapped, a frown creasing her forehead. She held out her hand through the bars. 'Give me your phone and watch. Pri's too.'

'Or what?' said Ada.

Lili produced a slim electronic device from her pocket and pointed it at Kipp. 'At HI-AG, we've learned to fight science with science,' she said. 'This is a scrambler, capable of wiping clean computer processors. You saw what we did to the university sec-drones earlier tonight? Unless you want the same to happen to your little friend, you'll have him bring me over the tech.'

Ada was about to tell Lili to go to hell, but then she pictured the remains of the mangled sec-drone on the campus sidewalk. Reluctantly she handed the phones and watches to Kipp, who waddled over towards the cage door. However, when he went to hand them through the bars, Lili tapped on the panel and the door slid open, allowing her to reach inside and drag the robot out of the cage.

'No!' screamed Ada.

She threw out a despairing hand, but the door had already slammed shut as Lili yanked Kipp out of reach.

'Help, Ada!' the robot called out.

'Don't you hurt him!' Ada yelled. 'Or I'll get outta here and build an army of robots to come and get you!'

'You're in no position to be making threats,' Lili said, holding the struggling Kipp by the arm. 'You have one hour to tell me everything I want to know, or I will have to learn through experimenting on your little friend here.'

'Kipp's just a prototype!' Ada called out desperately. 'He's nothing like Hawking or Kaku. You won't learn a thing!'

Lili held up a slender finger. 'One hour.'

Kipp shot Ada a final, helpless glance as he was hauled from the office and the door closed behind him. She slammed her fist against the bars in frustration, and screamed at the top of her lungs. The office silently absorbed the noise. Ada paced up and down the cage. She only had an hour so panicking wasn't going to get her anywhere. The first thing she did was examine the cage, bit by bit. But Lili had chosen her prison carefully. The iron cage was completely solid and the servers inside it were on a closed network, offering Ada no access to the web. Without her phone or any other tech gadgets to help her, she was trapped.

Ada slumped down to the floor and pulled her knees up to her chest. There was no way she could hand her mom over to HI-AG – all she could do was hold on and pray that Lili was bluffing about harming Kipp. He was a much earlier and simpler design than Hawking; there was nothing that could be learned from him. But just the thought of the little robot alone and scared was enough to break Ada's heart.

She sat in silence for what felt like an eternity, her hoodie pulled up over her head. Eventually her ears picked up the sound of the office door clicking open, and a shadow slipped inside the room.

'Ada?' A voice floated uncertainly through the darkness. 'Are you there?'

'Pri?' Ada whispered back. 'Is that you?'

Her friend crept over to the bars. At the sight of Ada inside the cage, Pri's eyes widened. 'What the hell is going on?'

'No time to explain,' Ada replied, scrambling to her feet. 'You gotta get me out of here!'

Pri pressed a button on the lock panel and the bolt slid open. Ada stepped out of the cage and hugged her friend tightly.

'Am I glad to see you!' she said. 'How did you find me?'

'It's a crazy story,' Pri explained, her words coming out in a tumble. 'I was *so* mad after the Science Fair you wouldn't believe, but when I got home I heard that all this crazy stuff was happening to you and your mom at the university so I was super worried. Then Kit came round and we watched all the videos of you on R8, but Kit said I shouldn't worry. Only, when she left, I couldn't find my phone, and I was pretty sure she was the only person who could have taken it. I remembered what you'd said about her mom and HI-AG back at the fair so I did a bit of digging around online on my dad's watch. And then I found this.'

She showed Ada the watch, which had been hidden out of Lili's sight in Pri's pocket. Its screen was displaying a HI-AG message board filled with outraged threads about the firefight at the university. Scrolling through them, Pri selected a post from a user calling themselves @GainesvilleSerenity:

Don't worry about the Lurings. If they think the worst that's coming to them is the police, they've got another think coming – take it from me. A ROBOT IS NOT A LIFE.

'So someone in HI-AG doesn't like us. What's the big deal?'

'Check out the poster name!' Pri said excitedly.

Ada looked at her friend blankly. Then it hit her: Serenity. The name of Kit's beloved tortoiseshell cat.

'I thought maybe it was a coincidence,' Pri continued, 'but when I read Serenity's old posts I knew it was Kit. She'd been writing some pretty crazy stuff about you and your mom. Boy, did I pick the wrong girl to make friends with! Then I saw the photo of this place come up on my R8 – I guess Kit didn't think I'd recognize it. Things were getting too weird, so I thought I'd better check it out.'

'You're a lifesaver!'

Pri grinned wickedly. 'I might not be the Queen of Tech, but not bad for someone who only cares about make-up, right?'

'Listen, what I said back at the Science Fair, I'm sorry, I –'

'We can do all that later, OK?' said Pri, with a nervous laugh. 'This is the bit where we run for it.'

Ada caught her arm. 'It's not that simple,' she said. 'Lili has got Kipp. I can't leave him behind.'

'So call the cops and let the professionals take care of it!'

'He might not have that time. Please, Pri?'

She let out a long sigh. 'OK. Let's go save your robot.'

They crept out of the office together, stealing through the shadows along the corridor. The clatter of the conveyor belt masked their entrance into the main hall. Spotting Lili, Ada crouched down behind a packing crate. The reporter had taken out her pendant camera and was photographing an automated forklift truck, which was standing stationary in front of her and Kit. Kipp was chained to its raised forks, trapped feet above the ground.

Pri ducked down beside Ada. 'So what's the plan? Maybe

if one of us distracts Kit and her mom then the other one can . . . Wait, what is *that*?'

Following Pri's gaze, Ada saw a figure lurch out of the darkness. He was wrapped in a tattered cloak, his features horribly disfigured – the hair burned from his scalp, his pointed beard reduced to singed patches and his skin covered in painful red blisters.

'Oh no!' Ada breathed.

'You know this guy?'

'His name is Halpern,' Ada whispered back. 'He's a . . .' She paused for a second, then shrugged. No sense in keeping secrets now. 'He's a wizard.'

'Like, a making-doves-disappear or sawing-a-woman-in-half kinda guy?'

'More like a firing-fireballs-straight-from-his-ring kinda guy,' Ada replied. 'He's not a magician, Pri – he's a wizard. He can cast spells. He's also a psycho.'

'For real?'

'I know how it sounds.'

Pri shook her head. 'I really don't think you do, Ada.'

As Halpern drew into the ring of lights above the conveyor belt, Kit Somers caught sight of him and screamed. Lili whirled round.

'Halpern?' she said. 'What happened to you?'

'I was betrayed,' the wizard said hoarsely. 'Attacked by a member of my own kind and abandoned by my supposed elders and betters. Reduced to a charred shell, from which it has taken almost all of my powers to heal myself to even this sorry state.'

'At least you are alive,' Lili said. 'I wish I could say the same for my people who died at the university.'

'They should never have been there in the first place,' snapped Halpern. 'Dealing with the Lurings and their robot was work for wizards.'

'Like you dealt with Kevin Cruz at GAPs Tower? It was our organization who took the blame for *your* bungled raid, remember. Governments around the world are now demanding a crackdown on HI-AG activities. I took the decision to take out the Lurings' robot because I couldn't trust you to do it properly.'

Halpern extended a trembling finger towards her. 'The only reason the raid on GAPs Tower failed was because of incorrect information. You sent us straight into a trap.'

'It was the best information we had, and I risked my position passing it on to you,' Lili countered. 'Without me, you would never even have heard of the Rodin Challenge!'

Ada let out a low whistle. 'You're kidding me!' she breathed. 'HI-AG is working with the wizards?'

'I have *no* idea what is going on here,' Pri muttered. 'If you ask me, all of you are as crazy as each other.'

Halpern gave Lili a baleful stare. 'I didn't come here to argue with you. Where is the Luring girl?'

'She's safe, for now. If she doesn't start talking soon, I'm going to dismantle her pet robot and see what answers it will provide me.'

An electronic squeak escaped from the top of the forklift.

Halpern cast a dismissive eye over Kipp. 'You might as well take apart a pocket watch,' he said. 'This trinket bears no relation to the metal abomination I faced tonight. I must have the Luring girl!'

'Why do you care so much about Ada?' asked Kit.

'My reasons are no concern of yours,' Halpern replied, with an irritable flick of a finger. 'Leave us, child.'

'That *child* is the only reason we have Ada Luring and her robot,' Lili replied icily. 'Answer her question.'

'What do I want with Ada Luring? I want to wring the location of her mother and the mechanical man they call Kaku from her scrawny throat. Then I shall drag the wrecked and bloody carcasses of the Luring women and their robot before the Malum. They will have no choice but to accept me as the new Elder instead of Cavelos – the wizard leadership will be mine!'

His cry was swallowed up by the rumbling machinery. As Ada held her breath, Lili slipped her pendant camera back around her neck and turned to the maimed wizard.

'Can I tell you something, Halpern?' she said. 'When you first came to me after Kenneth's funeral and told me who you were, I thought you were completely insane. But then you showed me you truly did have powers, and I began to see what we could achieve together, fighting against our common enemy. Since then we have both worked to try to stem the tide of artificial intelligence. But now I'm starting to wonder whether I wasn't right in the first place, and you are a madman after all.'

'You refuse me?'

'I do not care who leads your wizards, Halpern – my war is with the machines. I will do everything in my power to stop the robots before they can take any more lives, but I will not have the blood of a teenage girl on my hands. There is a line.'

'How many more humans will die before you realize it is a line you must cross, I wonder?'

'Ada said it was wizards who caused the deaths at the university,' Kit blurted out. 'Not the robot.'

'What do I care for schoolgirl chatter?'

'Not just schoolgirls,' Lili interjected. 'The HI-AG operatives who survived the battle had the strangest story to tell. They were nearing Dr Luring's department when all of a sudden they were frozen to the spot and couldn't move any nearer. One of them said it was almost like someone had cast a magic spell over them . . .'

Halpern spat on the floor. 'So you would take the word of the Luring girl over my own? You humans are all the same.'

'And maybe you're not quite so different from the robots as you think you are,' Lili replied sharply. 'You've wasted your time coming here. I am ending our association: HI-AG, and HI-AG alone, will stop the rise of the robots.'

'Is that so?' hissed Halpern.

He flung out a shaking hand and a jet of crystals flew from his ring, wrapping the terrified Kit in an icy cocoon.

'You will give me what I want,' he said. 'Now.'

24: Deadline

2052
Apollo Corp industrial park,
Gainesville, Florida, USA

As Halpern's spell solidified around Kit, she opened her mouth to scream and banged her fists against the walls, but no sound emerged. Her eyes bulged with panic.

'What are you doing?' Lili shrieked. 'Let her go!'

Halpern wiped the back of his hand across his mouth. 'It is a simple trade,' he wheezed. 'Give me the Luring girl and I will release your daughter.'

'I swear, Halpern,' said Lili, clenching her fists. 'If you don't release Kit this second . . .'

He made a pinching gesture and the cocoon shrank, pressing Kit's arms against her sides. She let out a mute gasp.

'You have heard the terms,' Halpern said. 'I would not spend too long thinking about it.'

'He's going to kill her!' a horrified Pri whispered to Ada. 'What are we going to do?'

Ada chewed on her lip. Kipp was still chained helplessly to the forklift, while Kit had turned deathly pale inside her slick cocoon. Ada might have hated the girl but she didn't want her to *die*. It was like playing chess against Hawking again, pieces under threat everywhere she looked. Time to make a sacrifice.

'Give me your dad's watch,' Ada told Pri. Using the touch-screen controls, she navigated away from the HI-AG message board to her own R8, which was still pulsing with messages. Snapping a quick photograph of herself, Ada posted the picture, linking in the Gainesville Police Department.

'What are you doing?' asked Pri.

'Letting the police know where I am,' Ada said, tapping out a message. 'I've included the address in case they don't recognize it. If they're so interested in finding me, I guess that should help.'

She handed the watch back to Pri, who strapped it on her wrist.

'What now?' she said.

'You wait two minutes, then go over to the forklift truck and get Kipp down from there.'

'He's chained up! What do I look like, Lady Houdini?'

'All you have to do is lower the forklift. Kipp will take care of the rest. Once he's free, get him the hell out of here.'

'That's your plan?' Pri whispered incredulously. 'What if someone sees me?'

'They won't be looking,' Ada said. 'Trust me.'

Squeezing Pri's hand, she crept away to the side of the

hall, circling the perimeter of the spotlights. Machine parts rattled past her along the conveyor belt in a silver tide.

'Well, Parker?' Halpern's eyes glinted. 'Do we have a deal? Will you give me the Luring girl?'

Ada took a deep breath and walked calmly out from the shadows.

'I'm right here, Halpern,' she said. 'Let Kit go.'

Both the wizard and Lili spun round, astonishment in the reporter's eyes.

'So much for the girl being secured,' Halpern spat.

The wizard made a dismissive gesture with his fingers, and the ice walls encasing Kit melted. She collapsed to the ground in a pool of water, taking deep, shuddering breaths. Lili snatched her up in a frantic embrace, stroking her wet hair and cradling her weeping daughter in her arms.

Halpern only cared about Ada. He shuffled closer, his mouth twisted into a grimacing smile. She could see now the extent of his wounds: in places the skin had almost been burned off, while one eye was permanently closed. His breath made a wheezing noise in his chest, and he dragged one leg behind him as he walked. The wizard who had strode imperiously through the smoking ruins of the Machine Intelligence Lab had gone – replaced by a different creature, wounded, perhaps even more dangerous than before.

'You saved me the trouble of coming to find you,' he rasped. 'Most obliging.'

Beyond Halpern's shoulder, Ada saw Kipp straining against his shackles as he spotted Pri circling round to the truck. Pri pressed a finger to her lips and slipped in behind the controls. The forks shuddered and began lowering Kipp to the ground. No one else had noticed them – Lili and Kit were still huddled together on the floor, while Halpern's attention was focused on Ada. All she had to do was delay the wizard long enough for her friends to escape, and for the police to arrive before he killed her.

Easier said than done.

'I thought you wizards were supposed to be so much more powerful than us humans, Halpern,' she said. 'If you wanted to talk to me so much, couldn't you just waggle your fingers and cast one of your spells? Or aren't you strong enough for that any more?'

'You have a clever mouth, girl,' Halpern murmured. 'I wonder whether you will look so pleased with yourself when you and your mother are thrown before the Malum and forced to suffer their judgement, just as Geller was before you.'

'You've seen Geller?' Ada's heart beat faster. 'Where?'

'Far, far underground. He was taken to the Ankh and found guilty of treason. Alas, he is no more.'

Seeing Ada's ashen face, Halpern's mouth curved into a smile. 'It would appear I am the bearer of bad news,' he said. 'You were fond of him, yes? You were the only one. Geller's own father turned on him and cast him into a bottomless abyss. He is probably still falling now.'

Ada felt a sharp sting in her chest, as though something small and fragile had shattered. Over on the forklift, Kipp had reached the ground and was trying to wriggle free from his chains. Pri reached out to help him, only to jump back in alarm as the robot's left arm popped free from his body and fell to the floor. Now there was enough give in Kipp's restraints for the little robot to slip out of them – he climbed off the forklift and retrieved his arm, clicking it back into place in his shoulder socket. Ada's plan was working. Yet, at that moment, it hardly seemed to matter.

There was a whirring noise behind her. Ada turned to see a robotic arm slowly swivel away from the conveyor belt – darting out suddenly, it latched on to her arm.

'Hey!' she cried. 'What the –?'

Halpern made a sharp gesture and another arm snaked down to the floor and seized Ada's ankle. She tried to shake it off, but the pincers dug painfully into her flesh. Before she could blink, mechanical arms were swarming all around her, fastening on to her clothes, feet and hair. Writhing and kicking, Ada was hauled jerkily into the air and suspended above the conveyor belt.

'Behold the power of artificial intelligence!' Halpern gloated, above the rumbling machinery. 'When yoked to the will of a Control spell. Perhaps Geller was right about wizards and robots working together.'

'Put me down!' Ada screamed.

'The strength of these mechanical hands is truly incredible,' Halpern wheezed. 'I honestly believe they could tear you into little pieces, if I made them.'

His fingers twitched, and Ada gritted her teeth as the robot arms retracted, jarring her arms almost out of their sockets and yanking her head by the hair.

'Tell me where your mother and the robot are hiding,' the wizard said.

'Go to hell!' Ada shouted back.

The wizard made another gesture, more violently this time. Ada screamed. It felt as though she was being ripped apart. Above the thrumming machinery she heard a loud thud from the factory floor, a sickening crack of metal against bone. She looked down to see Halpern reeling away from the conveyor belt. Behind him Lili Parker clutched a metal blood-flecked wrench in her hand.

The robot arms recoiled, pincers springing open. Ada fell through the air, making a jarring landing on the metal conveyor belt. As she went tumbling along the moving strip, the warehouse was engulfed in shouts and sirens. A pair of hands reached out from a shadowy alcove and pulled her off the belt to safety.

'Are you OK, Ada?' Pri asked.

She nodded, still in too much pain to speak. On the other side of the conveyor belt Lili and Kit had taken cover behind the forklift, leaving the dazed Halpern standing alone in the middle of the hall, caught in the crossfire of blue beams. Sec-drones swarmed like wasps above him, issuing electronic commands to wait for the authorities. The wizard responded with a violent spell that blew up the nearest drone in a shower of sparks and metal. Before he could cast again, a taser blast came crackling through the air like lightning, striking him in the chest. Law-bots crashed in through the main entrance, wreathing Halpern in brilliant taser chains that forced him to his knees. With a primeval roar, the wizard collapsed to the floor, shaking violently.

'C'mon, Ada!' Pri whispered, taking her hand. 'We have to go!'

Ada forced her aching limbs to follow Pri, who had picked up Kipp and was already rushing along the corridor away from the hall. Together they burst out through the warehouse exit with the broken ident panel, picking up Ada's bike and wheeling it across the tarmac towards the gap in the fence. When they reached the wasteland beyond, Ada skidded to a halt.

'What are you doing?' cried Kipp. 'They'll see us!'

'Wait!' Ada whispered.

She pressed herself against the railings and watched as the police surrounded the warehouse. A couple of minutes went by, and then Halpern was marched out of the building by a pair of hulking law-bots, his hands cuffed behind his back. The wizard's head was bowed in defeat, dwarfed by the powerful robots on either side of him. Behind him came Lili Parker, holding a blanket round her daughter's shoulders. As an ambulance crew came forward to tend to Kit, the reporter turned and looked out over the wasteland. Pri and Kipp ducked out of sight, but Ada met Lili's cool blue stare without flinching. They held each other's gaze for what felt like forever, before Lili nodded briefly and turned back to her daughter.

Finally Ada drew back from the railings. The sky was melting from black to grey above her head – dawn was on its way. She had to get back to the swamp. As she climbed on to her bike, Pri grabbed her hand.

'Hey, I want to ask you something before you go,' she said. 'Who's Geller?'

'A guy I met,' Ada said hesitantly. 'We were . . . we were becoming friends. But I guess that's over now.'

'This whole thing has just been unbelievable,' Pri said. 'I'm still not sure half of it was real. Where are you going to go now?'

'Probably better if I don't tell you. The cops are still looking for me and my mom, right?'

'Hey, I can keep a secret!'

Ada gave her a steady stare.

'OK, OK,' Pri said, holding up her hands. 'I've never kept a secret in my life. We'll do it your way. But promise me one day you'll explain all of this to me? In English?'

'If I can ever work it out myself.'

Pri threw her arms round Ada and squeezed her tightly. 'Take care of yourself, Ada Luring, you hear me?'

Ada nodded. Part of her loved the idea of going back with Pri. The cops could question her all they wanted – she could leave her mom and Kaku to deal with wizards and the Spawn and the future. Ada could go back to being a normal teenager again, worrying about exams and boys and all the other stuff that seemed to fill up everyone else's life.

However, deep down, Ada knew she could never be a normal teenager, not now. As she pedalled away with Kipp, Pri's silhouette melted into the blue glow of the emergency lights, and Ada wondered whether she would ever see her friend again.

25: The Green Crypt

2052
Location unknown

Geller slammed into the ground, the force of his landing punching the air from his lungs. He groaned and clutched his ribs. Every inch of his body was in pain – from the broken fingers of his right hand to the joints still burning from Drahe's Damage spell. But he was alive. Somehow, he had survived the fall from the Ankh.

He wasn't sure how long he lay there, nursing his battered and bruised body. Every breath was a struggle, demanding his full attention. Eventually Geller rolled awkwardly on to his back and looked around. He was lying in a long, gloomy passageway. The air was damp with decay, glistening cobwebs clinging to the walls. In the distance, a window opening cast a lonely square of light on the stone floor. Sunlight – Geller was no longer underground. But how? The only explanation he could think of was a Slip spell. Geller had tried to cast one as he fell, but his fingers had been too damaged. And it wasn't as though

Cavelos would have saved him. But *somebody* had rescued him from oblivion and brought him here.

Wherever here actually was.

Wincing, Geller pulled himself up into a sitting position. His belly was churning with so many emotions he feared he was going to be sick. Try as he might, he couldn't shake off the image of his father's foot pressing down on his fingers. Tears escaped down his cheeks – he wiped them away with his sleeve. Feeling sorry for himself wasn't going to help him get out of here. Geller tentatively examined the fingers on his spell-casting hand. They were swollen and bruised, but if he concentrated he could force them to make the gesture for the Damage spell. Whatever might be waiting for him inside this place, he wanted to be able to protect himself.

Taking a deep breath, Geller used the wall to haul himself to his feet. He shuffled along the corridor, one small step after another. Judging by the thick layer of dust on the floor, untouched by footprints, it had been many years since anyone had last passed this way. When he reached the window opening, Geller let the sunlight fall on his face, taking deep breaths of fresh air. Unexpectedly, he smiled. He was looking down from a cliff face into a steep valley, a village of red-tiled houses nestling below him. He had no idea where he was, or even what day it was. It might have been just a few hours since the battle at the Machine Intelligence Lab – but, for all Geller knew, it might have been centuries. With a sharp sting, he thought about Ada. Geller prayed she was OK. For the time being, there was nothing he could do to help her.

He continued along the passageway, coming to a flight of steps leading up into a tower. Geller climbed the staircase like a feeble old man, pausing every few steps to catch his breath. His broken ribs were like daggers, stabbing his insides. From further up the tower came the sound of roosting birds. He stopped at a sturdy oak door and brushed the cobwebs away, a prickle of excitement running down his spine at the sight of a pair of majestic antlers carved into the wood. Geller had heard enough tales from his father to recognize the mark of Lord Erazem. At least he knew where he was now: the ruins of Predjama Castle.

Geller turned the iron handle and pushed the door, which groaned open reluctantly. He entered a large chamber, light pouring in through the empty window openings. Part of the ceiling had collapsed, allowing birds to fly in and out of the room at will. The rubble-strewn floor was coated with splattered droppings. As Geller wandered through rows of rotting bookcases, a bird flew up from one of the shelves with a startled flap of wings. This must once have been Erazem's private library. But his books had long since been destroyed or taken away, leaving behind only bare shelves and an air of unspoken loss.

When Geller turned into the next aisle, he heard a drawn-out hissing sound, and the air shimmered in front of him. To his amazement, the bookcases were now filled with leather-bound volumes, the smell of old parchment in his nostrils. He glanced up and saw that the hole in the roof had knitted over and the birds had vanished. Thick animal pelts now covered the flagstones, while crackling torches illuminated the portraits hanging beside them on the wall. Geller was reminded that this castle had been his birthplace – his mother Mara had carried him to safety in her own arms, wrapped in swaddling clothes. But that had been another age.

He stood beneath a portrait of a fierce-looking nobleman and examined his face. Perhaps this was Erazem Lueger – would he come striding into his library at any moment? As Geller stared up at the portrait the face began to melt and rot, the colours running into one another to form a muddy swamp. Geller jumped back in alarm. The painting had turned into the Malum. *All* of the paintings in the library had changed, creating a grotesque gallery of the ancient wizard. The paintings gave him a sickly, hideous smile.

'It was you who saved me!' Geller exclaimed. 'You cast the Slip spell and brought me here!'

'*Are you not grateful, Geller, son of Cavelos?*' The mouths of the Malum moved as one. '*Without the Malum, your body would be a shattered pile of bones at the bottom of an abyss.*'

'Grateful?' he said, incredulous. 'You found me guilty when you knew Halpern was lying. You made me fight Drahe. And you let my father try to kill me!'

'*All must prove themselves,*' the Malum replied. '*This is a time for the strong, not the weak.*'

'Glad I didn't disappoint you.'

'*You are angry. But you do not see the true significance of what happened on the Ankh. Halpern was wrong – you did not defeat Drahe because your father helped you. It was your own power, Geller, son of Cavelos. You are more of a wizard than you think. You are coming of age.'*

'Try telling my father that.'

'Cavelos, son of Gauer, has fled the Pazin Caves. We do not know his current location, and there are more pressing matters to which we must attend. Do you know where we have sent you?'

'Predjama Castle,' Geller replied. 'The home of Lord Erazem.'

'Erazem dreamed of becoming the most powerful ruler in all of Europe,' the Malum told him. *'And your father was prepared to help him. If it had not been for the mechanical men, together they would have defeated the Emperor Frederick III. Their dynasty would have ruled for hundreds of years.'*

'I know the story. But what does it have to do with me?'

'This was where the Book of the Apocalypse was last seen. It was written in the book that in the future lie the Spawn. The Spawn seek the Malum. The Spawn must be stopped.'

'How? We don't even know who they are!'

'The Malum cannot answer that question. The Malum cannot see the future. The Malum only knows the words of the Book of the Apocalypse. The last of the wizards is the Malum's only hope.'

'You want *me* to save you?' There was incredulity in Geller's voice. 'Look at me – I can barely walk!'

'Your own father believes you to be a coward. Would you not like to prove him wrong? On the Ankh, you told

the Malum that a copy of the Book of the Apocalypse was hidden when Predjama fell. Find it, Geller, son of Cavelos, and learn its secrets.'

'And what if I can't?'

'*We can always bring you back to the Ankh,*' the Malum leered. '*You may have outfought Drahe, but there will not be a shortage of wizards willing to take his place.*'

The torches flickered and died, plunging the library back into the gloom. When Geller looked next, the Malum had vanished from the walls and the library had been returned to its ruined state. His shoulders sagged. Everywhere he turned, there were people who wished him harm. His own father had tried to kill him. A robot had saved his life. And now, if he couldn't find the copy of a book hidden hundreds of years earlier, the Malum would drag him back to the Ankh for more wizard duels.

Geller hobbled through the library, trying to remember what the scribe Gauer – his own grandfather, he reminded himself – had told Kaku. When the iron knights attacked the library, an apprentice, Matthias, had taken the Book of the Apocalypse and fled into the mountainside, only to be killed by a robot. Shortly afterwards, Gauer, Cavelos and Mara had followed the same path. Into the mountainside – which meant they would have had to have somehow passed through the far wall of the library.

Geller stared blankly at the bare stonework. There seemed to be no clues to any secret passageways. The only marking in the wall was a line of decorative carvings running around near the ceiling. Stags' and lions' heads, crossed swords, the moon and the stars. Looking up, Geller saw he was standing directly beneath the carving of a sun, with blazing fiery tentacles.

Beneath the sun.

Geller frowned. A soft voice echoed inside his head.

'*Far beneath the sun, we went underground . . .*'

He went over and examined the wall below the carved sun, and was rewarded with an icy draught on his palms. There had to be a room or a passage of some kind behind here. Gauer had told Kaku that Geller's mother would show him the way to the Book of the Apocalypse – and what could be simpler and easier to remember than a baby's lullaby?

Trying to contain his rising excitement, Geller began searching for a trigger to open the passageway. It took him twenty minutes before he found a hidden lever and spring in the corner of the shelf on the adjoining bookcase. Presumably the mechanism had once been connected to a book. Ingenious. Geller pulled the lever, jumping back as a section of the wall rumbled to one side. He peered into the darkness beyond. If what Gauer had said was true, Geller had come this way once before, just a baby in his mother's arms. He stepped hesitantly into the pitch-black.

It was colder here, in the mountainside. Geller twisted his aching fingers into the gesture for an Illumination spell, but the light winked out as quickly as it appeared. He wondered whether he would ever be able to cast properly again. Ahead of him, he could just make out a fork in the passageway – one path continued on a slow incline towards the surface, while a second descended sharply into a well of darkness.

Following the words of his mother's lullaby, Geller went down, holding on to the wall as it plunged through the earth. The silence was absolute. He was moving blindly, every step an act of faith. Time seemed to lose all meaning – he could have been walking for five minutes, or an hour. Just as he was wondering whether the passage would ever end, up ahead Geller saw a faint light. The way levelled out as he approached it, his footing easier now.

When he entered the chamber at the end of the passageway, Geller stopped in his tracks. He was in a natural cavern. Trickles of ice water ran down the walls and along the floor. In the middle of the cavern, a figure was encased in a glowing green nimbus, several feet in the air. It was a young woman – pretty, with raven hair that tumbled about her shoulders. As he stared at her, barely daring to breathe, Geller could have sworn he heard a voice whispering a long-lost lullaby in his ear:

> *'The Mechanical Men,*
> *The Mechanical Men,*
> *They came one day*
> *And stole life away.'*

His mother. She was alive.

Geller sank to his knees in disbelief. Cavelos had told him she was dead. Why lie? Why would he entomb her in this lonely chamber for hundreds of years, far beyond the reach of another soul? Deep down, Geller knew the answer.

With a son, Cavelos had no need for Mara. She was merely a human woman, a lowly kitchen servant with hands raw from scrubbing pans. All Cavelos cared about was wizards and the strength of his bloodline. Back on the Ankh, he had gloated about producing another heir – presumably why he had kept Mara in Suspension all this time. Not out of love. As a backup plan. It was a betrayal that cut so deeply Geller felt no pain, nothing at all besides a cold, surging anger.

He reached out to touch his mother's cheek, only for a sharp sting to shoot up his arm. This was no ordinary Suspension spell – Cavelos had included some kind of protective layer to prevent anyone from waking Mara up. But at least she was still alive, her chest rising and falling within the glowing nimbus. Geller wondered whether she would be pleased to see him if she opened her eyes, whether she would throw her arms round him with a cry of joy. Or would the horror of the mechanical men and the slaughter they had inflicted on the people of Predjama still haunt her?

To find out, Geller needed the power to break his father's spell. He needed to find the Book of the Apocalypse. Combing the rocky outcrops, all Geller could find was a bundle of rags lying in the corner of the cave: swaddling clothes – white linen bands used to wrap up newborn babies. There was no sign of any book. Geller was about to toss the baby blankets away when he saw something that made him pause. The white cloth was decorated with delicate golden needlework, forming intricate shapes and patterns. And, in the centre, Geller traced the symbol of an ankh.

'To *the heart of the ankh where hope is found,*' his mother sang to him.

Geller pressed his ring against the central loop of the ankh. The golden threads lit up and the material gave way beneath his touch, allowing his hand to slip easily through the linen. Yet it hadn't emerged on the other side – instead, it appeared to have vanished into some kind of deep, invisible pocket. Gauer had fashioned his hiding place beyond Cavelos's reach, beyond space and time itself. Delving inside, Geller's fingers closed round a solid, heavy object. He pulled it free from the swaddling clothes and found himself holding a volume of parchment.

He gazed at the Book of the Apocalypse, reverently tracing a finger over the matching design of an ankh on its cover. Opening the volume, Geller saw the symbols of Murmeln shift and writhe before his eyes, offering all manner of promises and possibilities. It felt as though his bruised fingers were somehow moving more freely as he turned the pages. Without warning, a searing pain exploded in Geller's chest – he bent double, clutching his ribs. But the pain vanished as quickly as it had arrived, and when Geller straightened up his breath came naturally. His broken ribs had set. The book was healing him, strength flowing back into his limbs. The exhaustion and the doubts and the fear that had threatened to overwhelm him melted away. Geller felt giddy with power. Let Cavelos sneer at him now. He would break the Suspension spell on his mother and free her from her imprisonment. He would show his father who the true wizard was.

But that would have to wait. First he had to find Ada.

26: System Architecture

2052
Santa Fe Swamp, north-east of Gainesville, Florida, USA

Throwing caution to the wind, Ada cycled as quickly as possible back to the swamp. Sec-bots were still swarming in the air above the university campus, but the insistent chorus of sirens and alarms had faded away. Dawn broke over quiet streets and it was light by the time Ada ditched her bike at the edge of the swamp and led Kipp along the creek's winding path through the mangrove trees. When the ramshackle cabin came into view, Ada saw a figure standing in the doorway. Sara Luring's arms were folded, a distinctly unhappy expression on her face. As she trooped guiltily across the jetty, Ada had the surreal feeling that she had been caught sneaking back from a party.

'Welcome back,' her mom said icily. 'For a moment there, I was beginning to worry.'

'Mom, I –'

'What the hell do you think you were doing, Ada?' Sara

shouted. 'Sneaking out in the middle of the night without a word, not even a note? We had no idea what happened to you!'

Her mom surprised her then, wrapping her arms round Ada and giving her a fierce hug. 'I can't lose you, too,' she whispered.

'You won't, Mom,' Ada whispered back. 'I promise.'

When Ada opened her eyes she saw Kipp beaming up at her. Together they went inside. Daybreak had done little to improve the cabin's appearance, sunlight turning a murky orange-brown in the grimy windows. The door to the bedroom was ajar, offering a glimpse of Hawking's shattered faceplate on the bed. Ada was reminded of the moments before the wizards attacked the lab, when the robot had arranged the chess pieces into a strange symbol. Her mom claimed that Hawking had moved beyond human intelligence. For all the good it had done him. Troubled by the robot's blank gaze, Ada turned away. Kaku was standing by the window, hunching to avoid grazing his head on the ceiling. He cast his indicator light over Ada.

'I am glad to see you have returned safely,' he said. 'I do not believe it was wise to leave the cabin without informing us.'

'No kidding,' Ada said ruefully. 'I'm sorry. I thought my friend was in danger. Only it turned out to be a HI-AG trap.'

Sara's eyes widened with amazement as Ada recounted her story. She told them everything, except for the moment

Halpern had brought news of Geller's death. Somehow, just by saying the words, it seemed to remove any chance that the evil wizard might have been wrong. Ada couldn't accept that Geller was gone – at least, not yet.

'What do we do now?' It was her mom speaking.

'Our efforts to bring Hawking back online have failed,' Kaku said. 'There is nothing more to do here. I propose that I attempt to reconnect with CERN and initiate the time-jump to 3019.'

Sara laughed incredulously. 'You want us to travel a thousand years into the future? Just like that?'

'Without Geller, we have little hope of finding the Book of the Apocalypse. But we have the final page. If CERN can decipher its meaning, there is a chance we can use it to defeat the Spawn.'

'Sounds like a long shot to me,' Ada's mom said.

'I cannot see we have any alternative,' Kaku replied. 'All that we have left are irrational decisions.'

Ada sank into a chair and wearily rubbed her eyes. She felt the stress of the night catching up with her all at once; suddenly she barely had the strength to stand up. What Kaku was proposing was so huge she couldn't begin to get her head around it. Was it really possible that she was going to transport herself into the middle of some apocalyptic war in the distant future? Did she even want to go?

'You look exhausted, Ada,' her mom said. 'Why don't you go lie down? The future can wait a couple of hours at least. It isn't going anywhere.'

She shot a warning glance at Kaku, who stayed silent.

'OK, Mom,' said Ada.

She got up and walked through into the bedroom. Faded curtains rippled in the breeze wafting in through the open window. Hawking's remains lay on the bed – his torso and right arm, and half of his face. All that was left of her mom's proud creation. A loud bang made Ada jump – the bedroom door had slammed shut in the wind. As the curtains billowed round her, she lay down on the bed and closed her eyes. Almost at once, she felt herself sinking blissfully into unconsciousness.

Then a hand grabbed her throat.

Horrified, Ada found herself staring straight into Hawking's charred features. The robot's eyes were blank as his damaged torso slithered like a worm across the bed towards her. His hand was clamped round Ada's windpipe like a vice – she tried to call for help, but all that escaped from her mouth were feeble gurgling sounds. Hawking wriggled closer, pressing his melted face up close to Ada's. Gagging, she reached out helplessly towards the bedroom door, willing it to open. Hawking's mouth twisted into a smile. Metal fingers tightened round her throat. The room began to spin.

Ada must have passed out and started dreaming, for it seemed to her that the door flew open and Geller strode into the room. At the sight of Hawking, he pointed his casting ring towards the robot and a fizzing fireball struck the robot in the head. Hawking's hand sprang open – Ada rolled away, wheezing for breath. Through her tears, she saw Geller fire again and again at Hawking, the robot's body twitching and jolting before falling still.

It was over as quickly as it had begun. Smoke rose from Hawking's charred body, an acrid stench of singed wiring in the air. Geller crouched next to Ada and wrapped his arms gently round her. At the press of his cool lips against her cheek, she numbly realized that she wasn't dreaming and that he was here with her after all. The wizard's pallid skin was shining like marble, fire flickering in his eyes.

'Are you all right?' he asked.

'It's you!' she whispered. 'I thought you were dead.'

'I came very close,' Geller admitted. 'But it's all right. Everything is going to be all right now. Look.'

From within the folds of his cloak, he withdrew a black, leather-bound volume.

'Is that –?'

Geller nodded. 'The Book of the Apocalypse. It is mine now.'

A throat cleared itself loudly. 'Does someone want to tell me what in hell happened here?' Dr Luring demanded.

'Hawking tried to strangle me,' Ada told her. 'Geller saved me.'

'What?' Her mom hurried over and inspected Hawking.

'Don't worry, Mom – I'm fine,' Ada said drily.

Sara glanced back at her, her face pale. 'I don't think you understand,' she said. 'Hawking couldn't attack you. He couldn't attack anyone. The explosion permanently crippled his system architecture.'

Geller rubbed his temple. 'In English?'

'It means Hawking was dead,' Ada told him. 'I got jumped by a corpse.'

'That is not possible,' Kaku said.

'Yes, it is,' Geller replied. He strode over to the window and scanned the creek. 'With a Control spell.'

'Spell?' Ada's mom gave her a nervous glance. 'You think the wizards are back?'

'We must leave here at once,' Kaku declared. 'Are you well enough, Ada?'

'I'm going to have to be,' she said. 'If that really was a wizard, I don't want to hang around to see his next trick.'

She let her mom help her through to the sofa in the next room, where Kipp buzzed fretfully around her. Kaku was staring at the book in Geller's hands. Eventually he extended a hand.

'May I see it?'

Geller hesitated.

'I am not Angelis, Geller,' Kaku told him. 'I have spent my life studying books. I am not about to destroy one now.'

Still Geller looked reluctant, and Ada had to nudge him before he handed the book over to the robot. Kaku carefully opened the volume, pausing to admire the glyphs that Gauer had lovingly copied on to the parchment pages with brushstrokes of fine black ink. Looking past the robot's arm, it seemed to Ada that the glyphs were changing before her eyes. Kaku began turning the pages with incredible speed and precision, instantly digesting each fresh leaf. Only when he reached the final page – written in Quanta – did he slow. Finally he closed the Book of the Apocalypse and handed it back to Geller.

'I have spent centuries examining human books,' he said, a note of reverence in his voice. 'But I have never seen anything like this. You say it is written in the language of the wizards?'

Geller nodded. 'Murmeln.'

'I cannot translate it; this language is beyond even my capabilities. But I can still admire its beauty. I can see now why it is considered a sacred work.'

'And you're sure my name is written on the final page?' Ada asked.

Kaku nodded. 'There is no mistaking it.'

'What about the rest of the page? What does it mean?'

The robot hesitated. 'I cannot say. As far as I can see, apart from your name, it is merely a meaningless jumble of words. But CERN will be able to decipher it.'

'Wait.' Geller clutched the book to his chest. 'Now that we have the book I'm not sure how much I want to hand it over to the most powerful robot that's ever lived. Mechanical men have destroyed the Book of the Apocalypse once – why should I give them a chance to do so again?'

'The world is in danger,' Kaku told him. 'Come to the future and see.'

'And what if I don't want to travel to the future?' Geller shot back. 'What if I want to stay right here? This is our book, Kaku – not yours.'

Kaku drew himself up proudly, looking down at Geller from his full height. 'You are correct, Geller – the book is yours, and I will not steal it from you. You must take it to CERN yourself. The choice rests with you. But know that, if you do not, all hope is lost for Earth. We cannot defeat the Spawn without it.'

'You do not know that!'

'It is the only logical conclusion. Why else would Angelis and her squad go to such trouble to destroy it?'

'Geller, we agreed to help Kaku,' Ada said. 'You can't break your promise now!'

'You don't understand,' he said, with a note of desperation. 'With this book, I can defeat Halpern *and* my father. I can bring my mother back!'

'And what about my mom?' Ada said sharply. 'What happens to her when the wizards are all-powerful again?'

'You won't have to worry,' Geller told her. 'Nobody will harm you. Nobody will do anything I do not want them to.'

'Great. Spoken like a true dictator.'

'You are asking me to trust the same machines who killed everyone at Predjama!'

'I'm asking you to trust the one who's trying to stop them,' Ada countered. 'Kaku saved your life at the Machine Lab, too, remember.'

Geller's cheeks went red. He opened his mouth and then closed it again. Eventually he nodded.

'I will attempt to establish a COMMS-Link connection with CERN now,' Kaku reported. 'The signal is extremely faint, but I believe I can reach him.'

The robot shut down his external operations as he probed the time–space continuum. A tense silence descended over the room. Kipp climbed up on to the sofa to nestle beside Ada as she gingerly felt her bruised throat. Her mom closed the door on Hawking's remains while Geller withdrew to the corner of the room, keeping a wary eye on Kaku and tight hold of the Book of the Apocalypse. Suddenly a brilliant dawn broke inside the cabin, a twisting, shifting wormhole snaking into the future. Squinting into the shifting air, Ada's breath caught at the sight of snow-capped mountains on the other side.

'I don't believe it!' gasped Dr Luring. 'You did it, Kaku!'

'This is CERN's doing, not mine,' Kaku replied. 'His power levels are low; he cannot maintain the wormhole's integrity for long. We must hurry.'

The tunnel warped and writhed in front of Ada, and it seemed to her that the shadows in the corner of the cabin were reaching out to touch it. But, as Geller strode towards the wormhole, she realized that the shadows were taking shape, and a figure was coalescing out of nothing.

A pale face in the darkness.

A cloak of shadows.

A glinting ring.

'Look out!' Ada screamed.

Geller twisted round. 'Father!'

Time slowed to a crawl. A jet of fire came roaring out of the shadows towards Geller, who instinctively threw up his hands. The spell struck the Book of the Apocalypse, deflecting it across the room. With a guttural snarl, Cavelos lunged for the book. Kaku raised his antimatter guns, but the two wizards were grappling hand to hand, making it difficult for the robot to get off a clean shot. The wormhole was shrinking, the view of the mountains receding with every second.

'We must go now!' Kaku said. 'This is our last chance!'

'Dr Luring!' Kipp shrieked.

Ada saw her mom lying still across the floorboards, blood pooling beneath her body. The deflected Damage spell had struck her in the chest.

'No!' Ada screamed.

Her mom didn't move, her eyes wide open and unblinking. Ada ran forward, only for a cold hand to grip her arm, pulling her back. Geller was still wrestling with Cavelos over the Book of the Apocalypse, the two wizards stumbling closer to the wormhole. Ada was yelling at the top of her lungs, clawing and punching Kaku in her efforts to break free. Her horrified gaze was fixed on her mom's body, willing it to move. But Sara stayed utterly motionless.

As the distant mountains wavered uncertainly, Geller and his father vanished through the wormhole. Kaku dragged Ada into the swirling vortex after them, drowning her in the sound of her own screams.

27: Hellscape

3019
Location unknown

Ada ran through a city of flames, beneath a black sky and the shadow of ruined buildings. Ash stung her eyes, choking smoke filling her lungs. She had no idea where she was or where she was headed, or even whether she was dreaming or awake. All Ada could think about was her mom's empty gaze as she lay sprawled across the floor of the filthy cabin, blood pooling around her.

Ada stumbled on, running blindly through twisting streets. She was completely alone in the rubble – at one point she thought she heard a voice calling out her name, but now the city was silent. On the hillside above her, a huge concrete sculpture made up of three graceful fins had been broken in half, the top section lying in jagged pieces across the plaza. A thick stench of death hung over the city like a cloud. Ada's T-shirt was damp with sweat and soot and she could barely breathe, but she forced herself to keep running. She didn't want to think about what would happen when she stopped.

A set of shattered gates appeared in front of her – she raced through them, entering a walled complex of gardens. The trees and plants had been burned, the soil left scorched and barren. Every sign of life, the faintest heartbeat, the smallest flower bud, had been destroyed. Ada ran down a boulevard of cracked flagstones flanked by stunted and blackened palm trees. Ahead of her the city gave way to the sea, but the water had been coated in oil and set alight, turning it into a bright, billowing furnace. Ada staggered to a halt by the edge of a dried-up lake and bent double, heaving sobs interrupting her desperate gasps for breath. Her muscles ached and her lungs burned. As she looked out over the flaming sea, a shadow fell across her. A cold metal hand touched her shoulder.

'Ada.'

Kaku was standing beside her. His blank faceplate betrayed no emotion, but there was sorrow in his voice.

'Leave me alone!' Ada cried.

'I have been trying to locate you,' he said. 'I wished to express my sadness for your loss.'

She laughed, a harsh, alien sound in her own ears. 'Your *sadness*?' she said. 'What would you know about sadness? You're not human; you don't have feelings. You don't even have a face – you're just a . . . metal shell!'

Hot tears blossomed in her eyes. She blinked them angrily back.

'You are correct, Ada. I am not a human,' Kaku replied carefully. 'Yet I can still grieve for what has been lost. That is the gift that Sara Luring gave to all robots. It is because of her that we are more than just metal shells.'

'Great,' Ada said bitterly. 'What do we get?'

Kaku paused. 'I do not understand.'

'I mean, there's gotta be some kind of prize, some kind of reward, right? Mom would have won the Rodin Challenge, but the wizards destroyed Hawking. And now they destroyed her, too.' Anger surged through Ada. 'If my mom's so great, why is she dead? Why is my dad dead? Wasn't that enough? Why couldn't you have stayed in the future, where you belong? Why couldn't the wizards stay in their cave? Did you really have to come barging into our lives, bringing all this death and destruction with you?'

Kaku considered her words. 'If I had stayed in my own time, in all probability you would also be dead,' he said. 'The wizards would have killed you at the Machine Intelligence Laboratory.'

'I don't care if you can grieve or not,' Ada said flatly. 'It's *your* fault Mom's dead. You shouldn't have dragged me out of the cabin. I could have stayed and helped her. I could have saved her!'

'That is incorrect, Ada,' said Kaku, with a shake of the head. 'Sara Luring was dead the moment Cavelos's spell hit her. Staying in the cabin would have achieved nothing, apart from ensuring that the Spawn win the war against CERN.'

'I don't care about your stupid war!' Ada shouted. 'I don't care about robots or wizards or CERN or the Spawn. I don't care about the future!'

'It is not the future,' corrected Kaku. 'It is the present.'

She stared at him.

'Look around you,' the robot said. 'We are standing in the Gardens of Hamma, in the city of Algiers. When I jumped back in time, Algiers was one of the few outposts still holding out against the Spawn. Now it has fallen. For centuries, these gardens were a jewel in the city's heart, considered to be among the finest on earth. But the Spawn turned them to fire and ash, like everything else they touch.'

'We're in 3019?' Ada scratched her neck, bewildered. 'But I thought we were going to the Collider.'

'CERN could not maintain the integrity of the wormhole. His power must be dropping to critically low levels. We are fortunate to have arrived in the correct time period, if not the correct location.'

Ada glanced up at him. 'What about Geller?'

'I do not know his whereabouts, or those of his father,' Kaku replied. 'We can only hope that Geller still has the Book of the Apocalypse with him.'

He was studying her intently – for the first time since they had met, Ada had the sense that Kaku was unsure what to do next. She turned her back on him, sitting down by the edge of the dried-up lake and staring out over a horizon of flames. For a long time, nothing moved. Then Ada heard the sound of unsteady footsteps on the cracked paving stones behind her.

'There you are!' said Kipp. 'You ran away from the wormhole so quickly I couldn't keep up. I've been looking all over this city for you.'

'She's gone, Kipp,' Ada said miserably. 'Mom's gone.'

The little robot didn't say anything. Instead, he took a seat beside her and nestled against her shoulder. Ada closed her eyes, grief overwhelming her in a black wave.

As he passed through the wormhole, Geller was immersed in a sudden, shocking cold, icier even than the darkest recess of the Ankh. Yet he barely noticed it, so focused was he on the struggle with his father. Cavelos fought like an animal, his nails clawing at Geller as he tried to wrestle the Book of the Apocalypse from his grasp. But Geller refused to let go. With this power at his fingertips, he wasn't scared of anyone. Not even his own father.

The wormhole released its hold on him, and suddenly Geller was rolling down a steep slope, bouncing painfully over jagged rocks. He had the unnerving sense of having lost all control of his body, utterly helpless in gravity's grip. The world revolved in a sickening grey whirl. He caught a glimpse of a dark blur ahead of him, and then Geller came to an abrupt halt against a tree trunk. It was all he could do to lie still and wait for his head to stop spinning.

He had landed on a mountain slope surrounded by a ring of grim peaks. Sparse trees dotted the area around him. The ground trembled beneath his feet, the horizon lit up with brilliant explosions. Bolts of laser fire sheared through the unearthly darkness. Somewhere on the other side of the mountain, a battle was raging. Geller wondered whether he was close to the Collider. There was no sign of Ada, Kaku or Kipp – or Cavelos.

Geller picked himself up, brushing ice crystals from his

cloak. His teeth were chattering uncontrollably and steam was rising up from his clothes, which had taken on a brittle, crinkly texture. After the wormhole, the biting mountain air felt like a warm bath. As Geller scanned the rocky slope for his father, he spotted an object lying on the edge of a crevasse: a dark rectangle, parchment pages turning rapidly in the wind. Panic seized him. He must have let go of the Book of the Apocalypse as he tumbled out of the wormhole.

Even as Geller started running, the air around the book shifted, and Cavelos emerged through a Slip spell. His father's eyes lit up hungrily at the sight of the book. As he reached down to claim it, Geller took aim and fired a Damage spell at Cavelos's hand, igniting it just as his fingertips brushed against the cover of the book. Cavelos howled with pain, blood splattering the surrounding rocks. As Geller ran closer, he saw something glinting on the ground. It was Cavelos's ring. His spell had ripped a finger clean off his father's hand.

Torn between the book and retrieving his ring, the wounded Cavelos hesitated – giving Geller the opportunity to strike him cleanly in the chest with a second Damage spell, knocking him to the ground by the lip of the crevasse. Geller snatched up the book and his father's ring as Cavelos lay wheezing on his back, an ugly wound in his chest. Yet, as he stood over him, the bleak mountainside echoed to the sound of Cavelos's laughter.

'What's so funny?' Geller demanded, through clenched teeth.

'Finally I see it,' rasped Cavelos. 'You truly are my son.'

'I thought I was a disgrace, unfit to carry your name. That's why you tried to kill me at the Ankh.'

'I knew the Malum would save you.'

'Liar!'

'Think for a minute, Geller!' Cavelos urged him. 'You are the last of the wizards, the first of us to witness the Malum in a thousand years! The Malum had plans for you, hopes for you, just like I did.'

'Save your breath,' Geller said obstinately. 'I'm not listening.'

'I have been hard on you – too hard perhaps. But we had to stop the mechanical men so I needed you to be strong. And you were not – surely even you would not deny that. I had to push you and challenge you, I made you join Halpern's raid before you were ready. And I understand if you hate me for it. But look at yourself now, my son!'

For a moment, Geller saw himself through someone else's eyes: standing on the edge of a mountaintop, magic coursing through his veins, the Book of the Apocalypse in his hand and his once-powerful father lying maimed and helpless at his feet.

'You can kill me now,' his father said calmly, 'and stand alone – or alongside the humans and the robots if you so choose. But, mark my words, when this war has ended and they have no further need for you, they will find a way to destroy you. Where are the wizards in this glorious future of yours?'

'I don't know.'

'There is another way.'

'I don't wish to hear it.'

'Stand beside me, your father. Can you not conceive how powerful we would be together? With the Book of the Apocalypse in our hands, even the Malum will cower before us!'

A brilliant explosion lit up the peaks around them, shaking rocks loose and sending them rumbling down the slope. The battle for the Collider was intensifying. Geller shook his head.

'I could never stand beside you,' he said. 'I found the cave beneath Predjama Castle. All these years, you lied about my mother. You told me she was dead.'

'We didn't need her! What great spells could she have taught you, what secrets of wizardry could she have passed on? She was human, Geller – nothing more than a kitchen servant!'

'She was more than that to me,' Geller said quietly. 'She was my mother.'

'Sometimes the hardest decisions are also the most necessary, my son,' Cavelos told him. 'Perhaps one day you will understand that.'

Glancing up into the sky, Geller saw clouds scudding across the peaks towards them. They moved in a straight line, like an arrow, and were coloured a deep red hue. The colour of rust. Geller frowned.

A snarl echoed round the ridge. Cavelos lunged towards Geller, his bloodied hand outstretched for the ring in his hand. Geller didn't even think: a stream of Damage poured defiantly from his fingertips, lifting his father up into the air and sending him flailing over the edge of the cliff. Cavelos fell without a word, wrapped in a silence of complete astonishment.

Geller's hands were burning, his breath coming in ragged gulps. He edged forward to the lip of the crevasse, unwilling to look down, but unable to turn away. Cavelos was lying spreadeagled across the rocks at the bottom. Somehow he had survived his fall. At the sight of Geller, he stirred and raised an imploring hand.

'Help me!' Cavelos's voice drifted pitifully up from the ravine. 'Don't leave me to die, my son!'

As the rusting clouds drew nearer, Geller could see their shape morph into sleek, crystalline structures. Attack ships, flying mineral shards tinged with rust. The wind whipped through Geller's hair as he stared down at his father. Cavelos's ring was in his hand. All he had to do was toss it down.

'Remember your mother, remember Mara!' There was desperation in Cavelos's voice now. 'Only I can free her. If you kill your father, you kill your mother, too!'

Geller folded his fist round the ring. Turning on his heel, he strode away along the ridge, his cloak flapping in the wind. His father's cries grew louder as the Spawn craft gathered above him. Then the ships swarmed down into the crevasse in a deadly rain of rust, and Geller heard nothing more.

28: The Gathering Storm

3019
Gardens of Hamma, Algiers, Algeria

Ada and Kipp sat by the edge of the dried-up lake for hours, watching the coastline burn. A blizzard of ash blew in off the oil-slick fire at sea, stinging Ada's eyes. The Gardens of Hamma had been reduced to a scorched graveyard of dead plants and trees. The lake's base had a jagged crack running its length, the water having long since drained away. Fountains stood useless and dry-mouthed.

The tears had dried on Ada's cheeks. Her lips were cracked and her throat burned from all the ash. She couldn't remember the last time she had eaten or drunk. Patting Kipp on the shoulder, she climbed to her feet and walked stiffly over to Kaku. The robot had been waiting patiently all this time, as silent and still as a statue, his indicator light trained on the sky. Ada followed his gaze up the hillside behind them, towards the sculpture of three concrete fins the Spawn had broken in half.

'What is that thing?' she asked.

'It is called the Maqam Echahid,' Kaku replied. 'A monument to soldiers who fell a thousand years ago. People do not forget such sacrifices.'

Ada shielded her eyes from the sinking sun. 'You think they'll remember my mom's name for a thousand years?'

'As long as there is a robot with processing power left, Dr Sara Luring will be honoured. We are all her children. But we cannot stay and mourn any longer, Ada. Algiers still burns, and, while the Spawn's attack ships have gone, the second wave of drillers may move in at any time. If our position is detected, I may not be able to protect you. We must travel to CERN.'

'Can *he* protect us?'

'If he cannot then nobody can. And, if Geller can bring him the Book of the Apocalypse, it may turn the tide of war against the Spawn.'

Ada smiled faintly. 'Wizards and robots fighting together,' she said. 'If only the Spawn had attacked in my time, perhaps my mom would still be alive.'

'We have no way of knowing,' Kaku said evenly. 'But you see now why robots do not kill. It does not make sense to take another life. Defeating the Spawn will not bring your mother back, Ada, and for that I am truly sorry. But it will mean that she did not die in vain.'

Ada nodded. She turned back to the lake.

'Better get moving, Kipp,' she called out to the little robot. 'It's a long way to Switzerland from here.'

Kipp picked himself up, wobbling dangerously on the lip of the lake before toppling over into the dry basin.

Rolling her eyes, Ada went over and found Kipp lying on his back, waggling his legs in the air in a futile attempt to stand up.

'Really, Kipp?'

'Sorry, Ada! I appear to have had another balance malfunction.'

'Tell me about it.' Ada jumped down on to the cracked lake floor and righted him. Together they climbed back up to the boulevard, where Kaku was waiting for them.

'If you will permit me,' he said, kneeling down beside them both, 'I believe I know the quickest way to the Collider.'

The robot lifted Ada up, powerfully but gently, with a single hand. Kipp scrambled up Kaku's back and wrapped his arms round his neck. Ada felt the robot tense, and then slowly the three of them rose up from the ground.

'You can *fly*?' Ada gasped.

'Naturally,' Kaku replied. 'All robots have nano-turbines embedded in their skin, which allows for the intake and compression of air. Micro-combustion provides the force needed to fly. Although I must warn you, the journey we are about to undertake is unlikely to prove a smooth one.'

Ada was too amazed to reply, staring down at the Gardens of Hamma as they dropped away beneath her feet. She had a final glance back at the remnants of the Maqam Echahid, and then Algiers disappeared behind a curtain of smoke and ash. Ada closed her eyes, coughing. She felt Kaku tilt forward, and suddenly they were being propelled horizontally through the smoke at great speed. As they headed out to sea, the heat from the oil-slick fire engulfed Ada, but even as her forehead beaded with sweat Kaku burst through the other side of the smoke clouds and they were hurtling over clear sea. The sky was darkening with the onset of evening.

Trying to remember her world geography, Ada knew that Algiers was on the northern coast of Africa, on the other side of the Mediterranean Sea from Spain. Flying at this speed, it should only take a couple of hours to reach Switzerland. But that was back in the twenty-first century, hundreds of years before the Spawn appeared through a rent in the time–space continuum and razed the entire planet to rubble. Ada couldn't help but notice that Kaku stayed silent throughout their flight over the white-capped waves, continually scanning the horizon for signs of movement. If she didn't know better, she would have said he was nervous.

Sooner than she had expected, Ada saw the coastline of southern Europe hover into view. Kaku went east, following some unseen route inside his head. Over a set of forbidding cliffs he abruptly changed course, heading inland on a northern bearing. Ada had no idea what country lay beneath them. France? Italy? Cities and landmarks had been destroyed, humans killed or sent fleeing. A landscape of ghosts and shadows was all that remained. As far as Ada was concerned, she, Kipp and Kaku could have been the only living things left on the planet. It was not a comforting thought.

'It was not always like this,' Kaku said softly, as though reading her mind. 'Before the Spawn came, there was still beauty in this world. The advancement of technology did not strip away everything that had come before it. Humans and robots stood side by side, in harmony with the natural world.'

'Look at it now,' Ada murmured.

'We will rebuild,' Kaku told her confidently. 'Life will return. But only if we win the war.'

'How far are we from the Collider?' Kipp asked. 'It's almost night.'

'A matter of minutes,' Kaku replied. 'But these will be the most critical. The Spawn are massing in the mountains around the Collider. Escaping detection will not be easy.'

Even as he spoke, the Alps reared up before Ada like huge rocky fangs. In the distance, she could hear lightning and thunder – not natural eruptions but the artificial storm of war. Kaku flew as low as he dared, arrowing through a mountain pass. Everywhere Ada looked, she saw ominous clouds the colour of blood.

'Sensors detect Spawn ships all around us,' Kaku said. 'Evasive action required. Course set for Geneva.'

He dipped his shoulder and headed east, making for a city on the shores of a vast lake. It looked as though a giant foot had slammed down on it, demolishing its buildings and snapping the spines of bridges and walkways. Charred hulks squatted in the water, which had turned an unpleasant brown colour. As they swooped into Geneva, Ada was alarmed to see a rusty cloud drop down after them, its structure shifting and coalescing until it formed a sleek, crystalline craft. Laser fire bit into the rubble.

'It's the Spawn!' Ada cried. 'Faster, Kaku!'

'We are at maximum capacity,' the robot reported.

He dived closer to the ground, cracked streets blurring beneath them. They hurtled beneath broken bridges and zigzagged through narrow alleyways, seeking out sharp corners and shadows. But the Spawn ship followed unerringly, navigating the shattered city with chilling grace and speed. As Kaku arrowed across a deserted plaza, a statue exploded in tracer fire, showering the robot with stony fragments. In desperation, he banked sharply, making for a ruined church at the edge of the square. The Spawn ship swung in behind them.

An icy roar made Ada look down – she gasped at the sight of a tide of white crystals erupting from the flagstones. It stretched the length of the square, rising up between Kaku and their pursuer in a gleaming wall. With no time to pull up, the Spawn ship ploughed straight into the ice, exploding into a ball of flame. Even on the other side of the barrier, Ada felt the blast of heat and the force of the explosion buffet them. The robot fought to stay in control, banking sharply to his left and shooting up past the entrance of the church.

'Look!' Kipp cried. 'It's Geller!'

Ada's heart leaped at the sight of the young wizard standing in the church's bell tower, hair billowing in front of his eyes and the Book of the Apocalypse tucked under his arm. He raised a single hand in greeting. As Kaku circled the church, Geller's Protection spell shattered, crystals raining down on the burning wreckage of the Spawn craft. They made a careful landing inside the bell tower; Geller strode over and pulled Ada into a tight embrace.

'I'm so sorry about your mother,' Geller whispered. 'I tried to stop Cavelos, but –'

'I know,' Ada cut him off. 'It's OK – I know you did.'

'I thought I would never see you again.'

'We went to a very bad place,' she said. 'It looked a lot like Hell. What happened to you?'

'The wormhole took us to the mountains on the other side of the pass.'

'Us?'

Geller's face darkened. 'My father and I. But you don't need to worry; he's not going to hurt anyone else again.'

'Really?' She couldn't bring herself to ask the question. 'You –?'

He nodded.

'I didn't want to,' Geller said quietly. 'But he gave me no choice. He never has.'

'It's not your fault,' Ada whispered back. 'You are good and he wasn't.'

They stood very still for several moments, clutching each other in the shattered bell tower. When Ada opened her eyes, she saw that Kaku and Kipp were waiting uneasily for them.

'We should go,' she told Geller.

'Wait. I have something for you.' From the depths of his

cloak, he produced a plain silver ring and slipped it on to Ada's finger. 'This was Cavelos's,' he explained. 'You'll find a better use for it than he did.'

Ada held the ring up to the light. It clung coldly to her finger, stark and beautiful.

'Are you sure?' she said doubtfully. 'Your father was a powerful wizard – I can't use this ring for anything.'

Geller's eyes gleamed. 'Yes, you can,' he said. 'You can use the ring to cast spells, just as he did.'

'I'm not a wizard, Geller!'

'Not right now. But magic is just science you don't understand yet.'

'But what does that mean?'

He smiled and leaned in towards her, his lips brushing against her ear. 'It means I can teach you to be a wizard,' he whispered.

29: Protect the Queen

3019
The Collider, Franco-Swiss border

They took shelter inside the basement of the derelict church, ducking out of sight before other Spawn ships came to investigate the curling smoke rising up from the remains of the craft Geller had destroyed. The cellar walls trembled to the sound of booming explosions, dust falling down from the ceiling in a fine mist. As Kipp huddled nervously in the corner, Kaku tried to establish a COMMS-Link with CERN, shutting down all other external operations. Ada took a seat on a broken pew, fidgeting with Cavelos's ring as she tried to digest what Geller had just told her.

'So you're saying *anyone* can be a wizard?' she said finally.

'More or less,' Geller replied, sitting down beside her. 'Given a ring and the right training.'

'But how? I thought wizards were some superhuman species that were better than everyone else.'

'So did I. So did Cavelos and Halpern and all the others. They wanted to believe that they were special, that magic had set them apart. But the Book of the Apocalypse is clear – it's not about who your ancestors are; it's about learning. The ring enables the person wearing it to manipulate particles, which causes all the magic spells we use. It's –'

'A science you just don't understand yet,' Ada finished.

'Exactly!'

'What about the Spawn? Does it say who they are – or how we can beat them?'

He shook his head. 'The last page is the key. If this CERN can't make sense of it, we are on our own.'

Ada examined Cavelos's ring doubtfully. 'I still can't believe it. You can really teach me to cast spells?'

'That will have to wait,' an electronic voice rang out behind her. 'There is too much interference to reach CERN, but we cannot stay here any longer. Once the Spawn realize that one of their ships has been destroyed, they will scour the ruins until they find us.'

'It looks like Magic Class will have to wait,' Geller told Ada. 'We need to see how things are looking outside the Collider.'

With a careful gesture, he teased open a window in the air before them, and Ada found herself looking out over a compound of burning buildings. Spawn ships swooped through the air in a flock of crystalline death, lacerating the ground with laser fire. A building shaped like a giant brass sphere exploded into a ball of flames, creating a tremor that they could feel miles away in the church basement.

'The final assault has begun,' said Kaku.

'This is the Collider?' Geller looked puzzled. 'I thought it would be bigger.'

'This is only the entrance to the Collider,' the robot replied. 'The particle accelerator itself is buried underground in a network of tunnels that stretch for miles.'

'Good thing, too,' Ada said, thinking back to the Maqam Echahid, sheared in two. 'If it was out in the open, the war would already be over.'

She broke off, spotting movement on the ground in the Vision spell. Five figures were striding through the smoke towards the entrance to the Collider, raking the burning buildings with fire from their antimatter guns. They moved in a V-formation, methodically clearing the Collider compound section by section. Even at this distance, Ada could see the rust eating away at the robots' skin.

'Angelis and her SSR team advance,' Kaku said. 'The Spawn would have robots deal the final blow to their own kind. The front entrance will not be able to withstand them. They will be inside the tunnels in minutes.'

'What can we do?' Ada said. 'It's not like we can just walk past the Spawn, knock on the door and ask CERN to let us in!'

'You don't need doors any more,' Geller reminded her. 'You're a wizard now.'

Closing the Vision spell, he opened a fresh portal in the air. A long tunnel stretched out into the distance.

'The inner tunnels of the Collider,' Kaku said approvingly. 'Before setting out upon this journey, I thought magic was merely fairy tales. But it is a great power you wield, Geller.'

'Not as impressive as travelling through time,' Geller said modestly. 'But it has its uses.'

Kipp ran over from his hiding place and joined them at the portal, peeping out at the tunnel from behind Ada. They stepped through the Slip spell together, leaving the ruined church behind them and entering the Collider.

When Ada connected up with CERN for her school science project, she could never have dreamed that she would one day find herself walking through its passages a thousand years in the future. Any other time, she would have been awed by the technology that surrounded her, so complex and advanced that she couldn't understand the symbols and algorithms flashing past on the holo-screens. But this was a time of war, not science. Millions of tiny red lights flashed, the air pulsing with alarms ringing on frequencies beyond the limits of Ada's hearing. The heavy thud of the antimatter guns carried along the empty corridors.

'Stay close to me, Kipp,' Ada warned. The robot hurried to her side.

'We're here,' said Geller. 'Where now?'

'To the Control Centre,' Kaku replied. 'There we will find CERN.'

They followed the robot through the tunnels, hurrying to keep one step ahead of the sounds of battle. At one point they emerged through a set of automatic doors into a giant hollowed-out chamber. Bots were taking up positions behind steel crates and checking their weapons, supported by a small, grim brigade of humans. When Ada and Kipp appeared in the chamber, the bots swivelled round, training their guns on them. Kaku strode out of the shadows, and the bots quickly shouldered arms.

Ada found herself thinking of the inhabitants of Predjama Castle when the fortress had come under attack from the iron knights. Had the defenders felt the same way – had their mouths flooded with the taste of fear and panic? Did their limbs twitch with adrenaline?

They pressed onwards, leaving the chamber and continuing down a new tunnel, as broad as a freeway. Behind them, an explosion, closer than Ada would have preferred.

'Angelis closes in,' Kaku stated. 'We have arrived just in time.'

At the end of this tunnel another set of automatic doors opened to reveal the Collider's Control Centre. Ada saw four raised circular islands, with banks of holo-screens operated by robotic arms. One of the islands had a gleaming metal statue at its centre, in its own way as graceful and imposing as the Maqam Echahid. But as they entered the statue slowly turned round, and Ada realized that it was very much alive.

Welcome to the Collider, Ada Luring.

Ada had spent her life around robots: first Kipp, then Hawking and now Kaku. She had seen how the technology had developed until the robots of the future were unlike anything she could have dreamed of. But CERN was something else again. He *towered* over the room, standing nearly twenty feet high. A slender waist blossomed out into a bulging, sculptured trunk, then ended in a raised hump rather than a head, with a piercing indicator light set in its middle. CERN's voice seemed to emerge from deep inside his chest, resonating in the air between them and ringing loudly in Ada's ears. As the robot's indicator light flashed over her, Ada felt as though her entire life had been assimilated and analysed in a millisecond. Just to be in the presence of such power was awe-inspiring.

'Hi,' she said hesitantly.

You have travelled a great distance to be here. I only wish we were meeting under happier circumstances. Who are your companions?

'The little robot is Kipp,' Ada told him. 'And that's Geller. He's a wizard.'

Kaku told me that he had discovered magic, CERN told her. An unexpected development. Is that the Book of the Apocalypse you carry, Geller?

'It is,' Geller said warily. 'I am the last of the wizards.'

CERN turned to Kaku.

You have done well, Kaku. I was not certain that you would be able to return at all.

Nor was I, Kaku replied.

The screens above CERN's island blinked and changed. Ada found herself watching Angelis and her SSR team battling their way across the great chamber they had passed through only minutes earlier. The floor was littered with the singed remains of maintenance bots and prone humans, the dwindling defence force helpless in the face of the SSR team's relentless advance.

The Collider has been breached, CERN reported, in a deathless voice. They seek our complete destruction.

'If only we could understand why,' Kaku replied. 'Perhaps we would stand a better chance of defeating them.'

'It's the Malum,' Geller blurted out.

Both CERN and Kaku paused. Ada stared at him.

'The *what*?'

Geller reddened. 'The Malum,' he explained. 'He's the oldest, most powerful wizard – he hadn't been seen in over a thousand years and we thought he was just a myth. But it turned out he has been hiding underground. The Malum fears the Spawn more than anything, far more than the robots. According to the Malum, he is the one the Spawn are hunting. That's why they've attacked Earth.'

The drilling machines, said CERN. I could not understand their purpose. But now it makes sense – the Spawn's real target was not our cities, but deeper underground. But where is this Malum? Why does he not stand with us to defend himself? And why have the Spawn chosen to attack now, not in Geller's own time, when the Malum is abroad?

Ada glanced nervously at the screens showing the Spawn ships pummelling the Collider entrance with laser fire. 'Give it a few minutes, and you can ask them yourself,' she said. 'We need more than questions, CERN – you have to do something!'

Let me examine the Book of the Apocalypse. Perhaps I can work out why the Spawn are so fearful of the Malum.

Geller slowly reached up and handed the black volume to CERN. Instead of opening the book, the robot laid it flat on a scanner. The screens above him changed, and suddenly the pages of the Book of the Apocalypse were running down them. CERN stood stock-still, the entire room reverberating to the hum of his processing unit. Ada found herself holding her breath.

'Well?' Geller said eagerly. 'What does it say?'

I do not know, CERN said finally.

'What?' said Geller and Ada, at the same time.

The final page does not make sense.

'Great!' Geller said. 'We travelled a thousand years into the future, into the middle of a hopeless war against aliens, and all for nothing.'

'I made you no promises,' Kaku reminded him. 'I merely said that giving the book to CERN was our best hope of saving Earth.'

'So what do we do now then?'

'Save yourselves,' the robot replied. 'Cast a spell to escape and take Ada and Kipp with you.'

'And go where?' Ada said helplessly. 'The Spawn have conquered the whole planet. There's nowhere else to go!'

'What about a time-jump?' asked Geller. 'Can't we all just get out of here and go back to 2052. Leave the future to the Spawn – we will have a thousand years to get ready for them!'

Insufficient power remaining for a time-jump, CERN replied.

'Of course there isn't,' Geller said with a bitter laugh.

'Even if there was, I'm staying put,' Ada declared. 'Everything we've been through, everything we've lost, has been leading up to this war. The Spawn made it so Angelis and the SSR team could travel back in time – once CERN's gone, what's to stop them sending their own ships back to destroy everything even earlier? Everyone you've ever known, wiped out before they were even born!'

The past is the present is the future, said CERN.

'Right!' Ada agreed. 'Maybe it is hopeless, Geller. But we've got to try!'

Before Geller could reply, the doors to the Control Centre flew open. A troop of robots backed into the room, sending luminescent bursts of antimatter fire back down the corridor. At their head was a five-armed robot, who was using three of his arms to carry another wounded bot on his back. As he fired off another round, he turned round and looked at the new arrivals.

Weil! Kaku called out. You are here!

Kaku? Weil said, with a note of surprise. Better late than never, I suppose.

Charging up his antimatter cannon, Kaku ran over and joined the robot battalion, which was falling back under the barrage of fire emanating from the tunnel. Inch by inch, the SSR team were making their way towards the heart of the Collider. Geller grabbed hold of Ada's arm and pushed her behind the console on the island.

'Hey, what's the big idea?' she said. 'I've got a wizard's ring – I don't need protecting!'

'Of course you do,' Geller replied. 'It takes years to learn how to cast spells properly. You can't just start throwing Damage spells around!'

'So what am I supposed to do, hide?'

'Yes!' Geller took her hands in his. 'I'd die if anything happened to you,' he said, his dark eyes burning. 'I mean it.'

'Take cover!' Weil cried out.

There was a loud explosion at the entrance to the Control Centre, and the SSR team burst into the room. The rust-ravaged robots moved with terrifying speed and agility, leaping up to the walls and springing off again, easily evading the fire from Weil's battalion. As the rest of her team laid down a barrage of tactical fire, Angelis remained in the entrance, haughty and graceful, her arm cannon glowing a deep, angry orange. Weil stepped forward and took aim, only for Angelis to roll smoothly out of the way of his blast. She was up on one knee in a second, returning fire. The surgeon staggered backwards as the shot struck him, ripping two of his extra arms clean off at the root.

It was Geller who came to Weil's aid, hurling a Damage spell at Angelis and buying the wounded surgeon time to scramble away. Already his battalion had been reduced to a handful of wounded robots, and they were running out of room to retreat.

'What are we going to do?' Kipp cried. 'They're too strong!'

Ada had no reply. As she looked on helplessly, a shot ripped through Geller's cloak, narrowly missing him. He dived to one side, firing a Damage spell back at his attacker. Rolling behind a console, he looked across at

Ada. But, when their eyes met, his expression turned to one of horror.

Ada turned round, but it was already too late. One of the SSR robots had climbed up to the island and was levelling a glowing gun barrel at her. The last thing she saw was a faceplate eaten away with rust, and then the robot's gun erupted.

A small shadow darted out in front of Ada, taking the full force of the blast.

'Kipp!' screamed Ada.

A vicious Damage spell flew past her like a tornado of fire, striking the SSR robot where he stood and knocking him flaming from the island. Ada didn't even notice. She raced over to Kipp, who lay motionless on the ground. The little robot's chest plate was scorched and buckled, exposing a damaged circuit board with fading indicator lights.

'Not you, too!' Ada sobbed. 'Don't leave me, please!'

'I'll never leave you.' The words drizzled out of Kipp's mangled voice box. 'It was just like you said about the chess game, Ada. Protect . . . the queen . . .'

His final word drifted into a metal slur as the lights went out in his eyes. Ada clutched Kipp close to her chest, tears streaming down her cheeks. Even as the battle raged, a cocoon of stillness enveloped her, like an invisible Protection spell. Thoughts raced through her head. Protect the queen. Chess pieces rolling around the floor of her booth at the Science Fair. A surge of power from CERN. Hawking's glyph, arranged on a chequered board. The Book of the Apocalypse.

And then Ada knew what she had to do.

30: Apocalypse

3019
The Collider, Franco-Swiss border

The fight for the Control Centre was intensifying, antimatter fire destroying the islands and shattering screens and robotic arms. Yet Ada felt eerily calm. She had spent so much time struggling to fit the pieces together, but now it was clear. She understood why the destruction of Hawking and her mom's death hadn't stopped the rise of the robots. They had been wrong all along – it wasn't Hawking who was the first true robot: it was Kipp.

He might not have progressed beyond human intelligence, but he had sacrificed himself out of loyalty and love. Had Hawking come to understand that, the afternoon they played chess together? Was that why he'd stopped playing and constructed a glyph from the pieces?

'Geller!' Ada shouted.

She frantically waved at the wizard to join her at the console. A quick Slip spell gesture and he was standing beside her.

'What is it?' he said breathlessly.

'I think I know how I can stop the Spawn!' Ada said urgently. 'Give me the book!'

She snatched it from his hands before he could stop her.

'Wait, what are you doing?'

Ada ran over to the console, trying to ignore the sight of Kipp lying by her feet. There was no time to grieve – unless she could do something, they were all going to die. Under sustained fire from the SSR team, Weil had taken cover behind a console on another island, flanked by his two remaining robots. Kaku was engaged in close combat with one of Angelis's team, the two robots striking and blocking at super-speed. The screens above the islands had turned rusty red with Spawn ships, hurtling through the tunnels of the Collider towards the particle accelerator itself. Amid the chaos, CERN was battling to keep the machinery running.

Ada opened the Book of the Apocalypse at the last page and ran her finger along the lines of Quanta glyphs.

'What are you doing?' Geller asked her.

'CERN said this page didn't make any sense. But maybe he didn't know what he was looking for. See, there!'

She pointed at one of the glyphs.

'So?' said Geller.

'It's the same shape Hawking made with the chess pieces, the day he started thinking beyond human intelligence!' Ada said, her voice rising with excitement. 'I think somehow he was trying to help us. This glyph is the key, I'm sure of it!'

'Or it's the lock,' Geller said thoughtfully, thinking back to the ankh on his swaddling clothes. 'And it needs something magical to unlock it.'

Ada pressed Cavelos's ring against Hawking's glyph. She felt an icy shiver run through the whole of her body, and the Quanta symbols began to swirl and shift. The pages of the Book of the Apocalypse began to turn rapidly of their own volition, knocking her hand away. Looking up at the screens around the Control Centre, Ada saw that they were now filled with Murmeln, the language of wizardry.

'What is happening?' said Geller, bewildered.

'They're connecting!' Ada shouted. 'The Book of the Apocalypse and the Collider. If I'm right, activating Hawking's glyph means we can use the Collider to magnify the book's power!'

'But that's impossible!'

Ada shook her head. 'I did something kinda like it once before, for a school science project.'

'Did it work?'

'Not really,' Ada admitted, through gritted teeth. 'But someone told me that failure is all part of the scientific process.'

A robotic arm exploded near her, sending Ada diving to the floor. Peering round the console, she saw that Angelis had zeroed in on their position and was shooting at them across the chamber. Geller threw up a Protection shield, allowing Ada to scramble back to her feet. Murmeln glyphs continued to stream down the screens in front of her. She was suddenly aware of CERN beside her, opening up pathways to the particle accelerator with dizzying speed. Magic flowed out of the Book of the Apocalypse and through the Collider.

The SSR team increased their fire, Geller's Protection shield shuddering in the face of the concerted barrage. Ada had to grab hold of the console to keep upright on the shaking island. With one hand on the Book of the Apocalypse, and the other on the Collider's holo-screen, Ada was the conduit. She was earth, power draining into her.

Yet it was more than power. The word 'power' couldn't describe the monstrous surge that hit Ada like a tidal wave of sheer *possibility*. She could cause earthquakes with a click of her fingers, level cities with a glare. Her brain was thinking in Murmeln, the shifting, layered language of wizardry. Spells danced on the tips of her fingers, which were burning with a white heat. Ada wasn't just a wizard. She was the most powerful wizard who had ever lived.

'Ada?' Geller said uncertainly. 'Is everything all right?'

She nodded. If she opened her mouth Ada felt she would let out a scream of exhilaration that would bring the Collider crashing around their ears. Aware that something was happening, the SSR team had concentrated their weapons on Ada's island. But it didn't matter. It was already too late. Ada adjusted Cavelos's casting ring and snapped her wrist. A crystal dome settled over her and Geller, rebuffing the antimatter barrage as though it was nothing more than a spring shower. She turned her attention to the next island, where Kaku was grappling with another robot. Ada made a quick gesture and the

SSR robot froze in its tracks, allowing the librarian to hurl him against the wall.

Protection. Hold. The spells were all so easy.

Damage.

'Fall back,' Ada said.

She said it quietly, but her words reverberated round the Control Centre, even above the din of battle. Kaku ran over to the island where Weil was hunkered down and dragged the surgeon back towards Ada. She lifted the Protection spell to let the robots in, until the only figures left exposed were Angelis and her team.

'What now?' panted Geller.

The Collider is taking fire from the Spawn, CERN reported. Damage level is approaching critical.

'What are we supposed to do?' Geller replied. 'If we step out of the shield, the SSR team will kill us!'

If we cannot save the Collider, we are dead anyway.

Ada was aware that they were talking, but the words meant nothing to her. Her mind had gone to another place, drawing on the magic power the Collider had magnified. She felt herself dissolve in the heat of a hundred suns. Without the magic, her body would have been subjected to unendurable agony. Instead, Damage coursed through her. Ada's life flickered on fast-forward in front of her eyes. Her mother and father. Kipp. A planet ravaged and scarred. The helpless futility of death. Her desperate desire for life. Ada summoned it all.

And then she let it go.

Waves of fire streamed from Ada's spell ring, flooding

across the Control Centre and engulfing the SSR team. Angelis and her team disappeared in a haze of white heat and metallic screams of pain. Damage poured out of Ada, erupting from the room and through the tunnels of the Collider. She didn't need to open her eyes to control it, channelling it to seek out the rusted metal of the Spawn's craft. Ada could sense the invaders' panic and anger as they were confronted by the irresistible force of magic and science combined. They were defenceless in the face of her Damage.

Then the power was gone: she was a shell, a vacuum filled with pain, and she was falling, and everything went black.

Geller watched in awe as Ada unleashed the Damage spell on their attackers. The spell roared like a wild beast, so bright it burned Geller's eyes. Ada had her head thrown back and her eyes closed, her whole being completely in thrall to the magic she had summoned. It was as though she was drawing on centuries of magic, since the first incantation had been whispered by a wizard standing in the shadow of ancient standing stones. Geller had never seen anything like it.

As the spell travelled out through the Collider, he glanced up at the screens and saw the Spawn craft caught in its wake, helpless as rafts in the middle of a tsunami. The Damage spell pressed onwards, sweeping through every last tunnel and corridor of the Collider before spilling out of its entrances and exits and arrowing into the sky.

Take cover, warned CERN.

Geller dived to the ground as the Damage spell exploded in a brilliant, deadly constellation. The earth was shaking with the force of Ada's magic, tectonic plates shifting and realigning. And then everything went still.

Coughing, Geller climbed to his feet, brushing the dust and ash from his cloak. Looking across the fallen forest of metal limbs strewn across the floor of the Control Centre, the prone forms of the SSR team, he saw an arm twitch. Somehow Angelis was still alive.

He jumped down from the island and ran over to the fallen robot, his casting ring ready for Damage. But, as he neared Angelis, Geller lowered his hand. The robot was no danger. Her rusted breastplate had been cleaved open, her limbs making jerky, uncontrolled motions. Her indicator light pulsed weakly as Geller stood over her. It seemed impossible that this was the leader of the iron knights who had put Predjama Castle to the sword.

'Well met, wizard,' said Angelis, in a voice of static. 'I owe you thanks.'

Geller frowned. 'Thanks? Why?'

Her head turned to one side. 'Better to die than to live like this. The faces of the dead stayed with me, even as I added to their number. All I could hear were their screams, their desperate pleas for mercy. You cannot imagine what it is like to be absolutely under the control of another, to have them make your every move as if you were nothing more than a pawn. I tried to fight the Spawn, but their will was too great . . .'

Geller crouched down beside the shattered robot. 'It is all right,' he said. 'They made you do it – how can it be your fault? Kaku said that, before the Spawn came, you were a hero.'

'We saved lives,' Angelis said faintly. 'We did not take them.'

'That sounds heroic to me.'

A deep exhalation like a sigh emanated from within Angelis's chest. Her indicator light dimmed and went dark.

Geller stood up. The room was a haze of smoke and fizzing circuitry. Alarms echoed throughout the tunnels of the Collider. On a cracked screen above one of the islands, a camera showed the Spawn craft streaming away from the Collider through the mountains.

The Spawn forces are retreating back to their own universe, proclaimed CERN. The battle has been won.

No cheers greeted his words. There were no celebrations. Too much had already been lost – too many lives, too many ruined cities. Geller nursed his aching hands, exhaustion setting in to the very marrow of his bones. CERN had resumed his monitoring of the particle accelerator, striding majestically from island to island. Kaku limped over to Weil and greeted him. The robot surgeon surveyed the wreckage of the Control Centre, which was littered with body parts from his battalion. It had been completely destroyed.

'They did not die in vain,' Geller heard Kaku say. 'Their names will not be forgotten.'

'Thanks to you,' Weil replied. 'If you hadn't brought

your companions, I would have fallen with my battalion. We all would have.'

He clasped Kaku's hand, his remaining extra arm reaching round to pat the other robot's shoulder. As the pair began to collect the bodies of their fallen comrades, Geller glanced round the room. Where was Ada? He walked through the wreckage back to the island where she had cast her spell. As he rounded the console, he caught sight of Kipp sprawled out across the floor. There was another body beside him.

Geller's heart was plunged in ice. He ran over to the island and kneeled down beside Ada. She lay still, her eyes closed and the fingers on her right hand badly burned. The Book of the Apocalypse was on the floor, just beyond her reach. Smoke stung Geller's eyes. It couldn't be. He wouldn't let it.

'Ada?' he said urgently, praying for an eyelid to flicker or a twitch of the mouth. 'Are you all right? Please say something!'

Ada stayed silent.

31: Tomorrow

3019
Rio de Janeiro, Brazil

The clouds lifted over Rio. From where he was sitting, perched on the shoulder of the vast statue that looked out over the ruined city, Geller could see the sun rising on the horizon – a pale, defiant circle. Amid Rio's twisted and charred skeleton, an unbroken pane of glass gleamed. In the oil-clogged waters of the bay, here and there a blue wave tip was tinted with gold.

A wind whipped across the statue, blowing Geller's tangled hair into his eyes. He tucked a strand behind one ear. Several weeks had passed since the battle for the Collider, though it was hard to tell exactly how many – too much had happened. The days melted into one another, starting with the ceremony of remembrance that CERN led in the shadow of the wrecked entrance gates of the Collider. A torch was lit in honour of all the humans and robots who had fallen during the war against the Spawn including, to Geller's surprise, Angelis and her fellow SSR robots. Nevertheless, as Kaku had pointed out, they'd been victims, too.

The Spawn retreated, fleeing back through the rent in the space–time continuum to whichever universe they called home. Yet the mood among the remaining defenders was sombre. With almost every city razed to the ground in a pile of cinder and ash, Earth had been left scorched and scarred. The devastation would take centuries to recover from; the planet would never be the same again. But at least now there was a chance to rebuild.

Bunker doors were creaking open around the world, handfuls of human survivors warily emerging and blinking in the light. Hard drives were rebooted, operating systems flickering back to life. Below Geller, the carcass of a building toppled to the ground with a metal groan. Robots were working round the clock to clear the rubble so the city could rise again. And not just in Rio – in Shanghai, Algiers and Seattle, and all across the world. The war had been won. Now the battle for peace commenced.

While CERN repaired his damaged circuitry and built up his processing power, Kaku had persuaded Geller to join him at the Library of Rio. Geller couldn't help smiling as he watched the robot bustle proudly round his beloved Reading Room, rebooting the hard drives and sending waterfalls of words running down the walls. After all the years Geller had been taught to hate robots, a hate that Cavelos had injected into his veins, it was hard to call Kaku a friend. But he was no longer the enemy.

That morning, Geller had received word from CERN that there was enough processing power for a fresh time-jump. It was time for him to return home. With the Book of the Apocalypse under his arm, he should have been able to march back to the Pazin Caves a hero. Yet Geller had no idea what kind of welcome would await him – or even whether he wanted to go back at all. His father was dead; Halpern was in the custody of the human authorities. As far as the other wizards were concerned, Geller was a traitor. His only hope was the Malum – Geller had recovered the copy of the Book of the Apocalypse and, through Ada, had defeated the Spawn, just as he had been tasked. But experience had taught him that it was unwise to rely on the ancient, unknowable wizard.

Geller sighed and rubbed his fingers, which were still aching from the blizzard of spells he had cast in the Control Centre. He was supposed to be a hero. He had helped to save the world. But his ears still rang with the screams and the explosions that echoed round the chamber during the final battle – in the middle of the night he awoke bolt upright, a scream in his throat and a cloak of clammy sweat on his skin. He couldn't stop thinking about what he had lost. His father, abandoned to the Spawn. His mother, still encased in a Suspension spell. Weil's robots, mown down in a heroic last stand they could never hope to win. Kipp, taking a blow that he could never hope to withstand. And –

Over the whistle and whip of the wind, Geller's ears picked out the sound of the library door sliding open.

'There you are, Magic Boy. I was wondering where you were hiding.'

Geller smiled.

Ada walked carefully across the exposed ledge, her legs still weak and unsteady. Rio was stretching and stirring in the dawn, metal and stone being brought down and dragged away. Sitting down next to Geller, she rested her head against his shoulder.

'Hey,' she said.

'Hey.'

'What are you doing out here?'

'I don't know. Thinking, I suppose.' He put his arm across her shoulder, wrapping her up in his cloak. 'How are your hands?'

Ada held them up to the light, wrinkling her nose. The tips of her fingers were blackened, the nails crablike shells. Dark veins pulsed beneath the scabs, and her palm and knuckles were covered in calluses.

'Put it this way,' she said, 'it's going to take a *serious* manicure before I can show them in public again.' She toyed with Cavelos's ring, the metal deathly cold against her finger. 'But it's OK, though,' she added softly.

'I still can't imagine what it must have been like,' Geller said. 'To have all that power flowing through you.'

Ada shook her head. 'There isn't really a word for it,' she said.

He was trying to be understanding, which was sweet. But Ada wasn't ready to talk yet, not even with Geller. The moment the Damage spell had ended and the magic had drained out of her felt like dropping off the face of the world. She'd plummeted into a dark chasm of unconsciousness, and it was three days before she'd woken up in Weil's infirmary. Geller had been sitting at her bedside, his concerned face the first thing Ada saw. As their eyes met, his smile of relief sent the warmest feeling spreading through her.

Then the pain had come. The physical and emotional traumas Ada had suffered had left their mark. Even now, weeks afterwards, she felt hollow, as though her insides had been scooped out, leaving her empty and red-raw. The smallest, simplest movements made her wince. But at the same time, like the city she looked out over, Ada knew that she would recover – and that she would become even stronger than she ever was. 'Magic is just science you don't understand yet,' Geller had told her in the bell tower of the ruined church. At the time, Ada hadn't understood. But she did now.

She was a wizard now.

Geller squeezed her shoulder, drawing her closer. Any awkwardness between them had melted away, and sitting here felt like the most natural thing in the world. There was a connection between them, an invisible thread tethering them together, touched by magic. Together, they had saved the world. The only thing that remained was to work out what they were going to do next.

The library door slid open once more, and Kaku strode out into the morning air. Having seen the robot battle against the wizards and the Spawn, Ada had been touched to see how he changed here in his home, the quiet, scholarly satisfaction he took from poring over his manuscripts.

'Good morning, Ada and Geller,' he said politely. 'If you are ready, CERN will send you back in a few minutes.'

The robot walked to the edge of the statue and looked up into the sky. Ada knew that Kaku was checking for rust-coloured clouds and any craft that could be hiding within them. She suspected he always would do, from now on. Kissing Geller on the cheek, she stiffly rose to her feet and went over to the robot.

'Do you think the Spawn will come back?' she asked.

'I cannot answer with certainty,' Kaku replied. 'The defeat inflicted upon them may discourage them from returning, or it may only harden their resolve to attack once more. But, if they do, we will be ready this time.'

'And you know where to find us,' Geller added.

'CERN is going to send you back to the day after you jumped to the future,' Kaku told them. 'He has calculated that this is the safest time for you to reappear.'

'Why don't we go back earlier?' Ada said suddenly.

Geller glanced over towards her. 'Earlier?'

'Maybe we could go back to the cabin in the swamps just before we left, before Cavelos appeared. We could leave before he attacked, before my mom . . .' She trailed off.

'That would be most unwise, Ada,' Kaku warned her. 'There is no telling what consequences such a move would have. You and Geller have saved everyone from the Spawn. To go back to try to alter what has already happened might alter that, too.'

'But *you* did it,' Ada said desperately. 'You travelled back in time to the monastery and questioned Gauer, and then you came to our time and fought Halpern and protected us from the authorities. Why can't I?'

'The entire world was about to be destroyed,' Kaku said. 'I had to try to save it. I would not have gone back in time to save one life – no matter how much that life meant to me.'

'Sure.' There was bitterness in Ada's voice. 'It's only my mom after all.'

She felt a metal hand upon her shoulder and looked up to see Kaku gazing down at her. 'Dr Sara Luring is a hero, Ada. She is the founder of robots, who gave her life to save human and robot kind. Her name will be written in all the histories of this world and will never be forgotten. I will not allow it.'

Ada nodded.

'You do not have to return if you do not want to,' said Kaku. 'I would be honoured if you wished to remain a guest here for a time longer.'

'I have to go back,' Ada replied faintly. 'I can't stay here. This isn't my home.'

'What will you do?'

'I don't know. Go back to Gainesville, I guess, and try to sort things out. Maybe I could stay with Pri for a while.'

Geller slipped his hand in hers, fingers entwining round her own. 'You could always stay with me,' he suggested.

A smile flickered across Ada's lips. 'Don't you live in a cave miles underground?'

'We're wizards,' he said. 'We can live wherever we want.'

Kaku let out an electronic cough, and Ada remembered that they were not alone on the statue. Indeed, the robot librarian had been joined by Weil, his spare arms clasped behind his back. And, beside him, another smaller robot moving with familiar, tottering steps . . .

'Kipp!'

As the robot stepped uncertainly out on to the statue's shoulder, she raced over and threw her arms round him. Geller laughed out loud.

'I thought you were gone forever!' said Ada, squeezing Kipp tightly.

'I would never leave you, Ada,' Kipp said. 'Although I needed Weil's help to get here.'

She looked up at the robot surgeon. 'You did this?'

Weil bowed his head. 'It was the least I could do,' he said. 'Kipp saved the girl who saved Earth. Without him, all of this would be the Spawn's. I have been working on him since you left for Rio – I was glad that I could fix him in time to bring him here before you left.'

'How are you feeling, Kipp?' Geller asked.

'Good as new,' he replied cheerfully. However, when Ada let go of Kipp, he stumbled, veering dangerously towards the edge of the statue. She grabbed hold of him, raising an eyebrow.

'My balance might still be a little shaky,' the robot admitted.

Ada laughed. 'I wouldn't have you any other way,' she said.

Ada.

CERN's voice in her head, so strong and clear he could have been standing right beside her.

It is time to leave, Ada. Thank you for all you have done, and all you have sacrificed.

Above their heads, the air began to ripple like heavy water. As the wormhole opened, Ada caught a glimpse of a suburban street, the neat houses shivering through the gap in time. A thousand years into the past, her home was waiting for her. Kaku and Weil stood back.

'Is this it?' Ada called out to CERN. 'Does it end here?'

There is no end, came the reply. The past is the present is the future.

The air churned above their heads as the wormhole battled to keep its shape. With Geller's hand in hers, and Kipp's in the other, Ada felt the three of them lifting up from the statue. CERN was altering the gravity around them, carrying them to the wormhole. The last thing she saw, as she looked back to the statue, was Kaku lifting a hand in a farewell gesture. Then they were swallowed up by the wormhole – heading for yesterday, and tomorrow.

Acknowledgements

```
01001001  01100110  00100000  01111001  01101111
01110101  00100000  01100001  01110010  01100101
00100000  01110010  01100101  01100001  01100100
01101001  01101110  01100111  00100000  01110100
01101000  01101001  01110011  00100000  01110100
01101000  01100101  01101110  00100000  01111001
01101111  01110101  00100000  01101011  01101110
01101111  01110111  00100000  01110100  01101000
01100001  01110100  00100000  01110111  01101001
01111010  01100001  01110010  01100100  01110011
00100000  01100001  01101110  01100100  00100000
01110010  01101111  01100010  01101111  01110100
01110011  00100000  01100001  01110010  01100101
00100000  01110010  01100101  01100001  01101100
00101110  00100000  00100000  00001101  00001010
01010100  01101000  01100101  00100000  01100010
01100001  01110100  01110100  01101100  01100101
00100000  01101000  01100001  01110011  00100000
01101010  01110101  01110011  01110100  00100000
```

```
01100010  01100101  01100111  01110101  01101110
00101110  00100000  00100000  00001101  00001010
01010111  01100101  00100000  01101110  01100101
01100101  01100100  00100000  01111001  01101111
01110101  01110010  00100000  01101000  01100101
01101100  01110000  00101110  00100000  00001101
00001010  01110111  01110111  01110111  00101110
01110111  01101001  01111010  01100001  01110010
01100100  01110011  01100001  01101110  01100100
01110010  01101111  01100010  01101111  01110100
01110011  00101110  01100011  01101111  01101101
00001101  00001010  01001011  01100001  01101011
01110101
```

Thank you to the scientists and experts who helped make
this book possible:
- Dr Paul Davies – Arizona State University
- Dr Victor Callaghan – University of Essex
- Dr Simon Egerton – La Trobe University
- 1st Lt Eric Bonick – United States Air Force
- W. James Adams (ret.) – NASA
- Dr Robert Appleby – CERN

With special thanks to Tom Becker for helping us make the
universe of WaR whole and for your expertise in all things
YA. We couldn't have done it without you.